THE REDWOOD CON

REAGAN KEETER

Irresistible Publishing
Marietta, Georgia

This book is a work of fiction. Names, characters, places, and incidents are either the product of the author's imagination or are use fictitiously. Any resemblance to actual persons living or dead, events, or locales is entirely coincidental.

FIRST EDITION

Printed in the United States of America

LCCN 2020900507

ISBN 978-1-7343945-0-4
ISBN 978-1-7343945-1-1 (ebook)

GET AN EXCLUSIVE COPY OF
THE LAYOVER

Connor Callahan has been through a lot. More than anyone should. It has left him with an overdeveloped sense of justice. Perhaps that is why when he sees a man discreetly tag a stranger's suitcase with a black magic marker, he sets out to discover what is going on. It's a decision that will thrust Connor into a conflict far more dangerous than he could have imagined, and when it's over he will know one thing for sure: You're not always safer on the ground.

Details can be found at the end of this book.

Elise Whitman

ELISE CHARGED INTO HER apartment, trying not to think about what she had done tonight. Her Pomeranian followed her to the window, jumping on her leg, yapping to get her attention. She patted the dog on the head. "Not now, Chloe." Then she pulled her phone out of her purse to see if she had a message from Liam. She didn't. She cursed herself for not waiting to hear from him before calling the others and sent a text.

I need to see you.

Gripping her phone in one hand, she crossed her arms over her chest and waited.

Elise had only lived in this apartment for three months. It was small, hastily decorated. The quasi-retro furniture from Value Interiors wasn't her. Still, she'd come to like the place a lot. Part of it was because, at twenty-eight, it was the first apartment she'd ever had in her name. The other part was the location.

From the window, Elise could see the quiet, tree-lined street that ran in front of her building. The old three and four-story condominium buildings lining most of it were charming. The neighbors were friendly, and she could walk to a grocery store and a coffee shop.

She hoped that after tonight she wouldn't have to leave. She hoped that by being honest with Liam her life would become something new and better than it was now. But if he didn't take the news well, she knew she'd have no choice. She'd pack up the things she could as soon as everyone was gone and disappear.

She looked at her phone again. Still no response. It had only been a minute, but she didn't have time to wait, so she sent two more messages, back to back.

I'm serious.

I need you to come over right now.

Then Elise got a bottle of Smirnoff from the kitchen to calm her nerves. She didn't have any glasses, so she filled a mug to the brim, took one big gulp. She placed the mug on the coffee table and paced the room, rehearsing what she was going to say. She'd only get one shot at this. She'd better make it count.

And, of course, she looked at her phone again.

Come on, seriously?

What was taking so long?

She sent another text to Liam: *Why don't you answer me?*

Finally, she got a response: *I'm on my way. We need to talk.*

Although Elise could tell she'd gotten under his skin, she didn't care. What mattered was he was coming over. After tonight, the last thing he'd be thinking about was those messages.

She returned to the window. If she craned her neck, she could almost see the entrance to her building. She thought it would be a good idea to keep a lookout, know who showed up first. But her mind wandered, back to what she would say and how she would say it— "Liam, you're in danger"—and when someone knocked on the door, sending Chloe into a tizzy, she had no idea who it was. Since she was expecting company, she didn't bother to check the peephole. She just tossed her phone onto the coffee table and turned the deadbolt.

Liam Parker

LIAM SAT AT THE lone poker table in Midwest Design's private room. The space was small but elegant, with polished hardwood floors and walls made of smooth brown tile. A combination of inset lighting and modern, ornate sconces cast the space in a warm glow. The only way in or out was through a door that opened onto the company's darkened public spaces.

At this hour, there were very few people in the building. The doors to the street were locked. A lone security guard manned the lobby nine floors below.

The night had started with six players. The two who remained at the table with Liam were Emily Stewart, a regular, and a new guy he had taken to calling "the Grunter." Their dealer, according to the nametag pinned to his tuxedo vest, was Jacob.

Emily had stately features and short, black hair plastered to her head with large quantities of gel. Having already folded, she could do nothing with the jack that appeared on the river but scowl at it. Liam wasn't sure if that look meant the card would've helped her or hurt her—his guess was the former—although it didn't matter either way. Once you're out, you're out.

Now he had to convince the Grunter to do the same. With a pair of twos, bluffing his way through this hand was about the only way to win it.

Liam doubled down on his bet.

The Grunter rolled his shoulders around in his tailored sports coat. He looked from his cards to those on the table and back. He shifted a toothpick from one side of his mouth to the other. Then, as Liam had come to expect, he grunted.

"All right," Jacob said, "play it or fold it. Make a move." Jacob was smiling and Liam could hear it in his voice. He didn't intend to aggravate the Grunter, he was just gregarious. He'd introduce himself to every new player, welcome back every old one, ask about their work, their family, and their pets.

Still, aggravate the Grunter he did.

"Shut up." The Grunter looked at Liam and Liam winked, trying to unnerve him. It almost worked too. The Grunter closed his cards into one hand, tapped them on the table like he did when he was about to fold, and hesitated. The corners of his lips curled down and his nose wrinkled up as if he smelled something rotten. "No," the Grunter mumbled. He scooped up a stack of chips and threw them into the pile. "You got shit."

Liam didn't know what to say. The Grunter was right. Still, he felt like he needed to say something. But his phone vibrated in his pocket, distracting him. He pulled it out, saw a text from Elise: *I need to see you.*

Before he could settle on his next move, two more texts came in rapid succession.

I'm serious.

I need you to come over right now.

He ground his teeth together. *Fine.* Elise wasn't going to give up until she got what she wanted, and the Grunter wasn't going to fold. Sometimes the closest you can get to a win is to quit. He placed his cards face down on the table and got to his feet.

"You're out?" the Grunter asked.

"I am."

The Grunter threw one fist into the air and laughing with a sort of hee-haw chuckle. "Boom!" He tossed his cards onto the pile of chips— a four of hearts and an eight of spades. "I don't know what you had, but it couldn't have been worse than that."

He was right. It wasn't. A pair of twos would've beaten him. *But,* Liam thought again, *once you're out, you're out.* So, as Emily groaned and the Grunter gleefully stacked up his chips, he did his best to smile and walked away from the table.

He cashed out and said goodbye to Ava Perez, the owner of Midwest Design. She nodded to one of the two men standing guard by the door and the man opened it. Liam navigated his way around the tables where designers and clients would huddle during the day, looking at photos, fabrics swatches, and sketches, and took the elevator to the underground garage.

He trekked the thirty feet through the cold to his Tesla, got in, and started the engine. Before he could put the car into drive, his phone vibrated again. Elise, no doubt. He took the phone out of his pocket and read the message.

Why don't you answer me?

He typed: *I'm on my way. This isn't working. We need to talk.*

Before hitting SEND, though, he thought about the morning they'd spent down at the lake, sitting on the beach and watching a sailboat ease its way across the dark horizon. They were on the tail end of their first date. Dinner at Alinea had turned into drinks at Eno, which had, through a series of events long since lost to the bottle, turned into quiet conversation near the water.

They'd learned a lot about each other that night; they'd both grown up in Oak Park and in households they would be hard-pressed to call middle class, their moms went to church and their dads liked fishing, they both worked in advertising, both liked '70s rock, and neither one of them cared that discussing politics was taboo.

He deleted the line "This isn't working." Elise might interpret that to mean he planned on breaking up with her, which wasn't the case. Elise was something special. But they did need to talk. She had to start giving him some space.

Liam traded his parking spot in the garage for one on the street near Elise's building. The midrise had a fob-activated security door but, unlike his building, no concierge, and most people paid the security protocol little mind. So it was no surprise when a young woman on her way out held the door for him.

The elevator rose to the fourth floor in fits and starts, then opened onto a long, narrow hallway that forked at each end. The paint was fresh, but the lights along the ceiling bathed the walls in a grayish-yellow that could make you think otherwise. From the look of it, the carpet hadn't received the same care. Worn thin, Liam suspected it had seen a decade's worth of traffic since it had last been replaced.

He headed down the hall to Elise's apartment, Unit 423, and knocked. Per usual, Chloe started to bark. The Pomeranian wouldn't quiet down until Elise opened the door and the dog got to sniff his shoes. Only thing was, she didn't open the door.

After thirty seconds or so, Liam knocked again. "Elise! Open up. It's Liam."

When that didn't work, he tried to call, waited an impossibly long time for her voicemail to answer, and didn't bother to leave a message.

Something was wrong. Even if Elise was mad, she'd at least open the door to tell him.

He turned the doorknob, not expecting much, and the door glided away from the frame. Chloe trotted into the hall, gave his loafers a sniff, then started panting.

Stepping deeper into the apartment, the Pomeranian at his side, Liam grew increasingly uneasy. "Elise?"

The apartment wasn't much bigger than the one he'd been in when he'd married his ex-wife. Liam could see most of it by merely rotating his head ninety degrees. The floors were an oak-strip laminate and the walls were the same color as those in the hall.

Elise was good about keeping things where they belonged and refrained from cluttering the space with things she didn't need. Liam would have been able to tell right away if anything were amiss.

The bathroom door was closed and, less than a minute later, it was the last room to check. Liam knocked, listened, heard only the sound of running water. As he stood there, he remembered Elise telling him once she didn't leave her front door unlocked. There were bad people out there, she'd said. "You never know what could happen."

Screw this. Liam flung the bathroom door open. He thought he was ready for whatever he might find on the other side.

He wasn't.

Liam Parker

ELISE WAS LYING IN the bathtub. Her thin face was slack, eyes closed, mouth open. Her head hung to one side, resting against the tiles running from tub to ceiling. The mascara around her left eye was smeared down to her cheek. The faucets were on, the water spilling onto the floor and red from her blood.

It took only two steps for Liam to cross from the door to the tub. He was muttering, asking for help, from God, from anyone. He reached into the water, scooping his hands under her armpits so he could drag her out. Liam didn't care that her blood was soaking into his clothes. He didn't even notice. He shouted her name, hoping she'd react, maybe say something or open her eyes or give him some sign she was still alive. Because she could be. The water was warm. She was warm. Maybe it wasn't too late.

He lifted, twisted, fought against her weight and the water. Her clothes, black slacks and blouse, clung to her body. She slipped out of his grip and back into the tub with a splash.

That was when he saw the cuts to her wrists. Telltale signs of a suicide.

It didn't make sense. Elise wasn't suicidal. But there was no time to think about that now. He needed to call 911. He should have called them as soon as he'd found the body, but he wasn't thinking clearly.

Liam went for the cell in his pocket, only to realize he'd left it in the car. He looked around, trying to figure out what to do. He remembered seeing Elise's iPhone sitting on the coffee table. He grabbed it, pressed the home button. It asked for a passcode.

Liam didn't have time to start guessing combinations. He dropped the phone and ran back into the hall, pounded on the nearest door. No one answered. He tried another. When no one answered that one either, he ran for the stairs. They were cement and narrower than they should be. Keeping one hand above the chipped rail so he could grab it if he fell, Liam took them fast. Starting at the top of each flight, he went two or three steps and jumped to the next landing.

He bolted out of the door leading into to the lobby and nearly ran into an old woman. She was hunched over and wearing something blue with white flowers on it. Her eyes popped open and she screamed. Liam suspected it was the sight of all the blood. As he'd hauled Elise out of the water, it had gotten onto everything, but was most visible across the front of his chest where it had stained his white dress shirt.

He didn't stop to explain or ask for help. He simply weaved around the stranger and kept going. He could hear her screaming until he exited the building and he wasn't even sure she'd stopped then.

His car was close. As he ran toward it, he fished the keys out of his pocket, pressed the unlock button. The lights flashed. His breath swirled in front of him. The cold seeped through his wet clothes and into his skin.

Liam reached in through the passenger door and grabbed his cell from the center console. Standing in the road, hands shaking, he unlocked the device and saw a small red dot on the corner of the phone icon with the number twelve in it. When he'd pulled it out of his pocket to read the first text from Elise, he'd seen a notification announcing he'd missed a call from her, but hadn't given it any thought. Ava had a strict "no calls" policy. His ringer had been on silent, and one missed call was no more significant than the message that had followed it. He cursed himself for not noticing the actual number of calls at the time, wondered if it would have made any difference, and dialed 911.

"Nine-one-one. How can I help?" the operator asked.

"My girlfriend needs assistance." Liam gave her the address, and told her about the blood.

He was barely off the phone when a police car, lights flashing, rounded the corner at the end of the block.

Thank God.

He flagged down the black-and-white and the cop rolled down his window. The driver had a meaty face that crowded in on his small eyes. His partner was lean and cloaked in shadow. Before either of them could speak, Liam said, "You're here for Elise, right? Elise Whitman? Where's the ambulance? She needs an ambulance right away."

"Relax. It's coming."

The paramedics did what they could, but Elise was gone, and the apartment immediately transformed into a crime scene. Liam hadn't been allowed back into the unit since the first officers arrived. With the apartment's new status, he wasn't even allowed to wait outside her door.

"We need to make some room," the meaty officer said, ushering Liam down the hall, past those ugly yellow walls that now looked even uglier.

Liam didn't respond. He felt numb. He couldn't understand why Elise would kill herself. Maybe they'd find a note.

On the elevator, the officer added, "I'm sorry for your loss" and, once they reached the lobby, "Have a seat on the bench over there. A detective will be along soon. They'll want to talk to you."

"Sure." Liam didn't see the point; the cops already knew everything he did. But he didn't see much reason to do anything else either.

He sat down on a metal bench that had been designed more for form than function. Directly in front of him, a flat screen TV mounted to the wall flipped between an ad for rooftop yoga and the status of the morning trains. Right now, all the lines had green dots beside them to indicate the trains would be running on time. Liam doubted that would last much past eight.

He called his receptionist's office line. Even if he didn't end up staying here all night, he'd be in no shape to go to work tomorrow. Her voicemail answered on the third ring and the message he left was brief. "Hey. I'm not feeling great. I'm going to be out Friday. Please reschedule any meetings." (While she would get the time with the message and might think he'd been out late drinking, the nice thing about being the boss was it didn't matter.) Then he called his business partner, David Hayes, and left a similar message.

After he watched the screen rotate a dozen or so times, Liam turned his attention to the bank of mailboxes beside the TV. 101. 102. 103. He read every apartment number up through the third floor and started again. Anything to keep from thinking about Elise's body.

The few tenants who came in or out were rerouted through the garage, so at least Liam didn't have to deal with them glancing suspiciously in his direction.

When the detective finally arrived, he stopped outside the building and spoke briefly with the cop by the door. He was wearing a charcoal suit and had a thick mane of gray hair brushed away from his face. The cop pointed to Liam. The detective entered the lobby and said on his way to the elevator, "I'll be right back. Stay put, okay?"

Liam nodded and started reading the mailboxes again.

The detective sat down next to Liam. For several seconds, he said nothing. Then he leaned forward, placing his elbows on his knees, and sighed. "That's a real shame." The detective waited another beat, perhaps giving Liam a chance to respond, before adding, "One of the officers upstairs tells me her name was Elise Whitman."

It wasn't a question, but since Liam could tell the detective was trying to engage with him, he said, "Yeah. It is," then silently corrected himself. *Was.* It *was* Elise Whitman. Because that was what happened when you died. You were no longer anything. And you certainly never *would* be anything. Like Elise Parker.

Liam had never thought seriously about them getting married. They had only been dating for two months; it was too soon for those kinds of thoughts. But the fact that the possibility had been ripped away seemed unfair.

The detective nodded thoughtfully, perhaps even sympathetically, and tilted his head toward Liam. "Sebastian Wyatt," he said. "Call me Bash."

"Liam Parker."

"How did you two meet?" the detective asked.

They had met at Ava's. In fact, Elise had even been one of tonight's six players, but had bowed out early, claiming a headache. Liam, of course, couldn't tell Bash any of that. The games were illegal. Still, he had to say something. "A bar," he replied. "Downtown."

"Which one?"

More specificity. Think. "The Tap."

"Nice place. A little out of my budget, but . . ." Bash shrugged. "So, tell me what happened."

"Well, I knocked on her door and when she didn't answer, I tried the handle to see if it was unlocked." Liam shifted in his seat a little in an attempt to make the metal bench more comfortable.

"Was it?"

"Yes, it was, which surprised me."

"Why is that?"

"Elise kept her door locked all the time."

The detective looked past Liam at the computerized directory on the wall. "How did you get into the building?"

"There was a girl going out. She held the door for me."

"Do you know who she was?"

"I've never seen her before."

"After you got inside the apartment, what happened next?"

"I found Elise in the tub," Liam said, uselessly trying to recount the actions without visualizing them. "I tried to pull her out. When I couldn't, I called 911."

"That's how you got the blood on you?"

"Yeah."

Liam remembered Chloe greeting him when he opened the door to the apartment. Where was she? He thought he'd seen one of the paramedics lock her in the bedroom, but he couldn't be certain. He wondered what would happen to her. With no owner to take care of her, Chloe would probably get put in a shelter. If she didn't get adopted, the shelter would most likely put her to sleep. Liam couldn't let that happen. Elise wouldn't like it.

"The dog," he said, shifting his gaze away from the mailboxes to meet Bash's, "can I take her with me?"

13

The detective frowned. "I guess so." Then he asked Liam more questions. No, Liam didn't know of anybody who was angry with Elise. He didn't know if she kept a spare key with the neighbors. He was at home before he came here.

Bash ended the conversation by asking Liam if he knew how to get in touch with Elise's family.

"I'm sorry," Liam said, "I don't."

"That's fine. I'm sure we can figure out how to reach them." The detective gave Liam his card. "Call me if you remember anything important."

Liam slid the card into his jacket pocket. "Detective Wyatt, you don't think somebody . . . ?" He could barely get the words out. When the apartment had been designated a crime scene, he had figured it was standard operating procedure, even for suicides. Now he wasn't so sure, and he didn't want to leave wondering if his imagination was running away with him. "You don't think somebody killed her, do you?"

"We don't know," the officer replied, which Liam figured was cop-speak for yes.

Fuck, Liam thought while he waited for Bash to return with Chloe. *Fuck, fuck, fuck.* Suicide was bad, but murder would be so much worse.

Jacob Reed

JACOB WAS, IN ALL manner of ways, forgettable. Some of that was by birth. (He was five-ten and of average weight. His oval face was neither particularly handsome nor ugly. His nose was straight and without defect. His eyes were a murky blue bordering on brown.)

But most of it was by design. He kept his blond hair short, had no piercings or tattoos, even though he wanted them, and shopped at stores like The Gap, buying their most nondescript items.

Jacob liked being forgettable.

People who were forgettable were hard to find. Even if anybody did remember what he looked like, a description to the police would be so generic as to be useless.

The tuxedo vest and bowtie he wore when dealing cards at Ava's were too distinct to meet his standards. Before heading home, he changed into an olive sweater, a wool coat with no distinguishing characteristics, and a pair of blue jeans. He packed his work clothes into a backpack, then took a bus north and made his way down West Bourbon, hands in his pockets and dodging pedestrians.

This was a popular area with college students and young professionals. Both sides of the street were lined with greasy restaurants, cheap bars, and hip boutiques like Wag-A-Lot and Berg's Apothecary.

Jacob had started his career in crime as a pickpocket. It was something he still did occasionally, mostly as a way of staying sharp.

Over time, he'd worked his way up through a series of increasingly complex cons and from there into the world of cybercrime. These days, he did a little of both.

He watched how the men and women around him moved, whether they staggered along in a zigzag or walked steadily forward. He noticed what they were wearing, if their coats were open or closed, if their hands were in their pockets, if the women wore their purses across their chests or over their shoulders.

Jacob didn't plan on stealing from anyone tonight. He was working something big, something involving Liam, and didn't see any good reason to take the risk. Still, he couldn't help looking for opportunities. It had become second nature.

He stepped to the right to avoid a couple holding hands, to the left to avoid a pack of college kids. Then Jacob saw a man exit a bar at the corner of Belmont and West Bourbon. He was built like a boxer and "dressed for show," as Jacob's mom used to say. His tailored suit was probably Armani, his patent-leather shoes most likely Corthay.

Jacob recognized him immediately. This man had been one of the first marks he and his partner had targeted. They'd worked a scam on him called The Ring. He'd caught on to it, though, and instead of simply taking off like so many others would, he'd beaten Jacob until he was just this side of unconscious and punched Jacob's partner hard, leaning into the swing and connecting with her right eye before pushing her to the ground. That had pissed Jacob off, but there wasn't much he could do about it at the time.

The man turned in Jacob's direction. The distance between them began evaporating quickly. Jacob's fingers flexed the way they did sometimes when he was getting ready to slip his hand into a stranger's pocket. He thought of himself as a man in control. He reminded himself that this chance encounter changed nothing. This probably wasn't the first time he'd passed a mark on the street. The smart thing to do was leave him alone. Still, his fingers flexed.

Jacob imagined waving the wallet in his partner's face and saying, "Look what I got," certain she would take as much joy from the theft as he would. He imagined this man going home, finding his wallet gone, and having nobody to punch but himself.

Jacob looked to his right, pretending to be distracted. He had to do it, he decided. It would be justice—or, at least, justice of a sort. He stepped into the stranger's path and they collided. "Oh, Christ, man. I'm sorry," Jacob said, putting one hand on the man's chest in a way that looked like he was trying to stabilize himself while at the same time reaching around to the man's back pocket.

The man pushed him away. "Idiot. Watch where you're going."

"Sorry," Jacob said again. He had his head down to make sure the man couldn't get a good look at him. His hands were now in the pockets of his wool coat.

Grumbling, the man went on his way. Jacob watched him as he charged into the distance, putting five feet between them, then ten. He felt a rush of adrenaline as he fingered the wallet. He wondered what he'd find inside. Cash, hopefully. Credit cards, for sure. Probably a license and an insurance card. But sometimes there were other things too. Once he'd found a punch-out card for Al's Beef that got him a free sandwich and another time he found a twenty-dollar gift card for Starbucks. He'd also found bus passes, dry cleaning tickets, and family photos.

Jacob thought of those photos as little treasures, glimpses into a life that could have been his if he'd gone a different way. He'd keep them for a while, carrying them around in the pocket of his jeans until they were worn out and cracked, pulling them out every so often to wonder what might have been and, perhaps one day, what might be.

The man was twenty feet away when he stopped, felt for his wallet, and spun around. "You little shit!" His square face was screwed up tight and his hands were curled into fists. He pointed at Jacob. "You think you can steal from me?"

Everyone within earshot turned to look. Upon seeing the man, some checked the traffic and scurried across the street.

Jacob broke into a sprint and the man came after him, moving just as fast. Jacob was slight and agile. He gracefully dodged pedestrians like a running back headed for the end zone. The mark, who might be able to stare down a bear if he had to, simply shouldered people out of his way.

Jacob turned onto Belmont. There was less foot traffic here. He could go faster. He passed a church and thought about trying the doors, but if they were locked, the narrow lead he had would be lost. He passed an alley and thought about running down that too, but what if it led to a dead end?

Beyond the Lincoln Belmont library, the street became residential, with old brick houses and small fenced yards. There was no one in front of him now but a homeless man pushing a shopping cart.

Jacob was getting tired. He could feel the mark gaining on him. Eventually he crossed underneath the Belmont station. Not sure where to go but unable to run much farther, he heard a train rattling to a stop on the tracks overhead.

That was his ticket out of this mess. His only chance. He broke to his left and ran across the street. A series of faces, cartoonish in proportion and color, had been painted onto the cement pillars supporting the tracks. He fished his metro card out of his pocket and fed it into the turnstile's reader.

If Jacob could have jumped over the turnstile, he would have. But Chicago turnstiles worked like revolving doors, with over eight vertical feet of rotating bars. The city had made sure that if you wanted to get through, you were going to pay.

The reader rejected his card. He could feel the painted faces staring down at him, telling him he wouldn't escape, not this time. He shook away the doubt and inserted the card again.

His pursuer's footsteps were getting louder, his winded voice shouting obscenities, telling Jacob to stay where he was, threating to kill him.

As tempting as it was to look back, Jacob kept his eyes on the reader. A wasted second might be all it would take to lose his lead.

This time the reader processed the metro card without issue. Jacob snatched it up and pushed into the turnstile. A hand grabbed his jacket and tugged, but his momentum kept him moving forward. As the turnstile rotated and the metal bars closed in behind him, the hand released.

"You son of a bitch!" the man shouted.

Jacob bolted up the stairs to the platform, taking them two at a time. The red, purple, and brown lines all came through this stop. He didn't care which train was up there. He just wanted to make sure he was on it when it pulled away.

The train's doors were still open when he reached the top of the stairs. Jacob slipped through them right before they closed. The car wasn't crowded—no surprise, considering the hour—and he took a seat by the window.

He watched the stairs until they were out of sight. That was close. Was he getting sloppy? He replayed the theft in his mind. Hand to the chest, hand to the back pocket. An apology. No, he wasn't. That was as good a lift as he had ever done. But this man had figured it out.

He pulled the mark's wallet out of his jacket. Inside, he found a stack of cash and counted it. Two hundred and thirty-two dollars. He slipped the money into his coat. Then he pulled out the only photo and pocketed it too. It was of the man and a much younger woman. She was draped over him in a loving way that, like so many wallet photos, reminded him of the relationship he wished to have.

Jacob was about to close the wallet, ready to dump it in the trashcan at the next station, when he felt something on an inside pocket that caught his attention. He looked, slid out a key. It was for a safety deposit box, that much he could say for sure. His curiosity was piqued. People kept valuable things in safety deposit boxes. What bank did this key go to? Jacob could find that out as long as he had a name. He checked the man's license. Christopher Bell. It sounded vaguely familiar. Perhaps it was just that the name was so ordinary.

Well, he decided, even if he was going to forgo further pickpocketing for a while (and, after what had happened tonight, he meant it), there was no reason not to see what was in this man's safety deposit box. Wouldn't that, too, be justice?

Liam Parker

THE NEXT COUPLE OF days were a blur of comfort food and crap TV. Liam slept when he could, which wasn't much, and cried when he needed to, which was often. He only left the condo for brief trips outside to walk Chloe and a stop at Petco for dog food. On the first of those walks, the concierge told Liam she was a nice-looking dog on the way out and said the kids are going to like her on the way back in.

Liam figured the concierge was probably right and, with a weak smile, managed to say, "Thanks."

By Sunday morning, he was starting to feel a little better. He was still a long way from being okay, but he was finally ready for some company. He called David Hayes to see if they could meet for lunch.

David said he could and suggested a restaurant called The Crown.

Liam wasn't surprised. It was David's favorite place for a burger and a beer.

Liam had met his business partner through his ex, and she had met David through his girlfriend, Alicia. The two women were regular volunteers at St. Ann's Church on Tuesday nights. They'd bring in snacks, set up chairs, and help direct visitors to the various addiction meetings—AA, ACA, Al-Anon, and so on. They were a comforting presence to new and returning attendees, alike.

Since their divorce, Catherine rarely showed Liam her good side. But he knew she still had one because she still volunteered.

The Crown's floor was covered in long sheets of gray porcelain tile. The tables were made of cherrywood and polished to a shine. Exposed filament lightbulbs hung from the ceiling at uneven heights.

David was sitting near a window in the back. He was a tall man who looked tall even when seated. He was wearing gray slacks and a blue button-down. His suede jacket was draped over the back of the chair. With him looking down at his phone, Liam could see the bald spot forming on the top of his head and his large nose seemed especially pronounced.

"Can you believe these assholes?" David said, without taking his eyes off the screen.

"Who?"

"The *Tribune* says next year the mayor's going to put more meter maids on the street. He thinks it will bring in another four million in revenue. As if the city doesn't tax us to hell and back already. I take it you're feeling better?" He was referring to the message Liam had left the night of the murder. He still didn't know what had happened.

David tucked his phone into his pocket and finally looked across the table at Liam. His face contorted into an expression of surprise. Liam didn't look like himself. He hadn't shaved since Thursday, his hair was a mess, and he was wearing a pair of jeans and an old sweatshirt, which were well outside his usual attire.

"You're not sick, are you? What's going on?"

"It's Elise."

"You guys broke up?"

"She's dead."

David leaned in, his lanky frame casting a shadow across the table. "Really?"

Liam nodded.

"What happened?"

Before Liam could answer, a waitress came over. "Are you gentlemen ready to order?"

Liam asked for a glass of water. He wasn't in the mood to eat and alcohol didn't seem like a good idea right now. David ordered the same burger and beer he always got from The Crown, a medium-rare slab of meat with onions and bacon and a Budweiser on draft.

When the waitress was gone, Liam glanced over his shoulder to make sure no one was within earshot and told him the story.

"That's awful," David said, and, even though it sounded trite, it seemed to Liam perhaps the most honest thing he could say. It *was* awful. It would always be awful. Even when it hurt less.

The waitress arrived with their drinks. From the look on her face, he thought she might have been eavesdropping, so after she'd left their table for the second time, he made sure to speak softer. "There's one more thing. After Detective Wyatt was done questioning me, I asked if he thought Elise had been murdered. I just kinda got the feeling he was leaning that way. He said he didn't know. That sounded a lot to me like a yes."

David considered this while he sipped from his beer. "If she was, I'm sure they'll get to the bottom of it."

"I hope so. I just can't figure out why anyone would've done it. I've been running the scene through my head over and over. The place hadn't been ransacked, so it wasn't like it was some run-of-the-mill robbery, you know?"

"I get it. Sometimes something like this—it's hard to understand."

"Do you think there was something going on? Something I didn't know about? Detective Wyatt asked if anybody was mad at her. Do you think somebody could've been mad enough to kill her?"

David sighed. "I don't know."

Liam slumped further into his seat. He was merely asking David the same questions he'd asked himself. He needed to stop thinking about the murder, at least for a while, so he willed the conversation toward work-related matters, and didn't even mind when David, following his lead, once again pitched his plans for their firm. He wanted to turn ConnectPlus into a full-fledged advertising agency. TV and radio spots, billboards and print ads. "We don't have to limit ourselves to digital advertising," David explained. "We could become a one-stop shop for all of our clients."

It was what he always said when pitching the idea. In response, Liam said what he was always said: "I don't think that's something I can deal with right now."

But this time, it was more true than ever.

Liam Parker

THE NEXT DAY, THE department heads crowded into the conference room at ConnectPlus for their regular Monday meeting. Liam took his seat at one end of the table, David took his at the other.

Liam's secretary popped her head in to ask if anyone would like coffee or water before they got started. After she left, Liam pressed a button and the glass wall that separated the conference room from the rest of the office clouded over.

The meeting was scheduled to last exactly an hour. It never went over and was not to be interrupted. Those were the rules. But not long after they started, while the director of IT was advising the team on a change to release dates, Liam's secretary opened the door. "Mr. Parker, there's someone here to see you."

Annoyed, Liam gestured to the department heads around the table. "I'm not sure now's the best time, Maggie."

Maggie blushed, clasped her hands together, and looked down at her shoes. She scurried across the room and whispered in Liam's ear, "It's a cop."

It had to be Bash, Liam figured, renewed sadness clawing at his chest. He could only think of two reasons the detective would have come to his office. Either he'd found the killer or had more questions. (Whichever it was, the mere fact that he was here meant suicide was off the table.) Liam was, of course, hoping for the former. Knowing who had done it and why wouldn't make her death any less painful, but at least it would take the mystery out of it.

He stood up, trying not to let his emotion show on his face. He straightened out his jacket, buttoning it and pulling the cuffs of his shirt into place. "I won't be long."

He followed Maggie to the lobby. Bash was standing in the middle of the room with his back to Liam, facing the windows. He had his hands in his pockets and appeared to be admiring the view. From those floor-to-ceiling windows, he could see clear across the city's skyline. It was half the reason Liam had rented this place.

"Detective Wyatt," Liam said, to draw his attention.

Bash turned around. "Do you have somewhere we can talk privately?"

"Sure." Liam led Bash to his office. The entire suite had been decorated by Midwest Design not long after Liam and David had signed a lease. It was how he and Ava had met. She'd done his office with an eye for grays and blacks. The large desk she'd selected dominated the space and was stained a color she'd called driftwood. A matching credenza had been placed by the door. Liam had art deco chairs for guests and an executive leather one for himself.

"Do you mind if I close the door?" Bash said.

"Be my guest." Liam sat down behind that monster desk. Although he liked it, he didn't like the distance it put between him and his guests. "How's the investigation going?"

Bash closed the door. "Mr. Parker, did you use Elise's phone while you were in the apartment?"

That seemed like a strange way to start the discussion. Liam couldn't see the relevance. "No. Why?"

"Are you sure?"

"Absolutely."

Bash stared at Liam for a couple of seconds, as if he was giving Liam a chance to change his answer. Then he said, "Because we found your fingerprints on it."

Liam wasn't surprised. His prints had been on file for twenty years. He, along with six others, had been arrested for a bar fight in college. Liam wasn't involved, he wasn't a fighter. But the police thought he was, and that was enough. He was slapped with a fine and community service. The whole thing was stupid. But facts were facts. He'd been arrested for fighting, his prints were on file, and, while he hadn't used Elise's phone, he had touched it.

Liam could see how his answer might look less than honest, so he clarified. "I left my phone in the car and tried to use hers to call 911 when I found her body."

"According to our notes, the call came from *your* cell."

"Her phone was locked, and I didn't know the code, so I went out to my car to get mine."

"Why didn't you use the emergency button on the lock screen?"

Liam didn't remember seeing one, but if the detective said it was there, it must be. "I didn't notice it."

Bash leaned against the credenza and crossed his arms over his chest. "So, you didn't use her phone to delete your text messages."

Delete his text messages? The question was so absurd that it didn't register at first. Once it did, Liam said, "What are you talking about?"

"Mr. Parker, we know that there were messages deleted from her phone. We got a court order and had the records sent over from AT&T. Based on the texts you two exchanged that night, it sounds like you might have been having some problems."

To a degree, the detective was right. They had been having

problems—or, at least one. But, even out of context, Liam didn't see how Bash could read much into those messages. People "had to talk" every day. Still, that seemed to be what Bash was doing, and the whole conversation was quickly making Liam uneasy. "I just needed her to give me some space."

Arms still crossed over his chest, Bash drummed his fingers on his bicep. "It looks like the last message she sent you was thirty-two minutes before you called 911. Does that sound right?"

"I guess." Liam rolled his chair back a foot, putting a little more distance between him and the detective.

"So, to recap, the door was unlocked when you arrived."

"Yes."

"Nothing was taken."

"Not that I could see."

"And there was only thirty-two minutes between the time of her last text to you and the time you called 911." Bash was rapidly firing one thought after another.

"I suppose," Liam said, responding just as fast.

"Your text messages were deleted."

"If you say so."

Bash pointed at Liam. "But you didn't delete them."

"No."

The detective opened his palm. "Mr. Parker, do you mind if we take a look at your phone?"

Liam pulled his phone out of his pocket, then hesitated. He realized handing it over might not be a good idea. To get into Ava's at night, he had to request permission to play through an app she provided. He didn't want the detective finding out about the gambling which, if he clicked on the app, he surely would. Besides, if Bash could twist a simple text message exchange into something suspect, what might he do with the rest of Liam's life? "Do you have a warrant?"

Bash let his arm fall to his side, and the silence that followed was uncomfortable.

On the credenza, a small collection of first edition novels from Ray Bradbury and Phillip K. Dick were framed by a juniper bonsai tree and a model biplane made of metal and wire. The plane had come from the Chicago Arts Festival last year. Liam had taken his kids on a Sunday morning before the crowds settled in. His son Charlie, who was seven at the time, had said it would be perfect for his office and, even though his son had never seen his office, he was right.

The detective picked up the plane and spun the propeller with one finger, watching the blades rotate until they stopped. The whole thing irked Liam—Bash coming into his office, touching the plane his son had picked out for him, and all but outright accusing him of Elise's murder.

Bash put the plane back down and rocked off the credenza. "Thanks for your time, Mr. Parker."

"You know, if you're thinking I killed her, you're wrong."

Bash opened the door without a response of any sort. It was almost as if he hadn't even heard Liam. Before leaving, however, he stopped, glanced over his shoulder, and said, "One more thing. Why did you tell the officers that night her last name is Whitman?"

"What do you mean? It *is* Whitman."

"It's Watson." Bash stepped through the doorway. "Well, don't worry. We'll get it all sorted out." Then, as he headed toward the lobby, he called out, "See you soon, Mr. Parker."

Liam Parker

BASH LEFT LIAM WORRIED and confused. The detective had all but outright accused him of murder. As if that weren't enough, his visit had also raised questions Liam couldn't answer. They swirled around in his head at an ever-faster rate. Why had Elise told him her last name was Whitman? And what had happened to his text messages? Had she deleted them or had the killer? He couldn't imagine she would have deleted them, but he couldn't imagine the killer would have either.

None of it made any sense.

The only thing he could say for sure was that he needed to hire a lawyer.

He called the man who'd handled his divorce for a reference. After a brief exchange in which Liam summarized the situation, the lawyer gave him the name Patricia Harrison.

"She's a partner at Flores and Washington. Probably the best criminal attorney I know. She'll be able to help you. Hold on. Let me get you the number."

"No need," Liam said. He was already at his computer, typing the firm's name into Google. A link for the Flores and Washington website came up right away. He ended the call with a "Thanks" and dialed the number at the top of the site.

A perky-sounding receptionist greeted him almost immediately. "Good morning, Flores and Washington. How may I help you?"

"I need to schedule an appointment with Patricia Harrison as soon as possible."

"Are you an existing client?"

When Liam said he wasn't, the receptionist sighed, mumbled, and began clacking away at her keyboard. A moment later she said, "Patricia has a small window open in thirty minutes. There is nothing else this week. She isn't accepting a lot of new clients."

Liam made the appointment and returned to the conference room. Through the fogged glass, he could see the shadows of the men and women inside, quietly tending to their own affairs, occupied with their phones and laptops. "I'm sorry," he said as he opened the door, "but something urgent has come up." He looked at David. "Carry on without me." Without waiting for a response, Liam headed straight to the elevator and, from there, to the garage.

Flores and Washington was located in the Loop, less than three miles from ConnectPlus. Patricia showed Liam into her office, directing him to a small collection of button tufted chairs positioned around a glass coffee table in the corner. Her office was located along an interior wall and had no windows. A large framed photo of the ocean hung behind her desk.

"It's more comfortable," Patricia said, as she glided to a seat. She had mousy features, but a large frame, and that large frame made the grace with which she moved all the more unexpected.

"So, why are you here?" she said, all business. Liam liked that.

"My girlfriend was murdered. I think the police think I did it," he said, also getting straight to the point.

"Did you?"

"Of course not."

The coffee table was bare save a pen and a yellow legal pad. Patricia picked them up. "Tell me what happened."

Liam started by repeating the same story he'd told David. He found his girlfriend dead in the bathtub. He tried to get her out. He grabbed her phone to call the police, but it was locked, so he ran out to his car to get his. In the lobby, he encountered a resident who must've been shocked by all the blood—yes, he got the blood on him when he tried to get his girlfriend out of the tub—because she started screaming. The police came right away and designated the apartment a crime scene. Liam thought Elise had killed herself, but she hadn't; someone had just tried to make it look that way. Then, about an hour ago, Detective Wyatt came by his office with a whole bunch of questions. Why didn't Liam use the emergency button on the lock screen of Elise's phone? Why did he say her last name was Whitman when it was Watson? Why did he delete his text messages? No, he hadn't deleted the messages—like he said, he couldn't get into her phone. Clearly, the detective didn't believe him.

Patricia scribbled furiously as he talked. When Liam was done, she was looking down at her notes and tapping the end of her pen against her chin.

After ten, maybe fifteen, seconds, Liam asked, "Don't you think it's strange that she told me her last name was Whitman when it's Watson?"

Patricia shrugged. "Not necessarily. Maybe she was married for a while and planned to start using her maiden name again or—"

"Elise wasn't married." Liam was sure about that. Bash would've known if Whitman was her maiden name and, if it was, there would have been no reason to ask the question he'd asked.

Patricia put her notepad and pen on the coffee table. "Okay, well, sometimes people change their name when they're looking for a fresh start. It doesn't happen often, but it does happen. These days, it's about the only way to outrun your digital footprint."

Liam shook his head, doubtful. "I don't know."

"Let me guess. You don't think she needed one."

"Honestly, no. Not based on what she told me."

"If that's why she did it, then that's the whole point, isn't it? Change her name. Change her past. A fresh start."

Liam unconsciously started tapping his heel against the carpet. "Let's say you're right. Why wouldn't she change her name legally?"

"Maybe she hadn't gotten around to it yet. Or maybe she couldn't. If she's got a record, it can be difficult."

"She doesn't have a record."

"You're sure about that?"

Actually, he wasn't. He had one, albeit the bar fight was the only thing on it. Maybe Elise had one as well.

When Liam didn't answer, Patricia added, "Look, regardless of her reason, one thing you're going to have to face is that there was something Elise didn't want you to find out about."

Liam's foot slowed to a stop. A fresh start. Was it possible? Could the "bad people" Elise worried about have been specific people instead of criminals in general? Maybe. He'd have to think that over later when he had time. Either way, it did nothing for answering the other question Bash had raised. "Why do you think my text messages were deleted?"

"Well, that is strange. I'll tell you what, when we're done here, I'll make a call. We've got a PI we use sometimes. Ryan Reyes. I'll ask him to shine a little light on Elise's past for us. I doubt he'll be able to tell us why your text messages were deleted, but he might be able to figure out why she was using a different last name."

It wasn't the answer he was hoping for, but what else could he expect her to say? There was no explaining what had happened to those text messages. Liam would have to take the wins where he could get them. If Ryan could uncover the reason Elise had changed her name, that would be something, at least. Then an idea occurred to him—while the PI was doing his thing, Liam would see what he could find out about *Elise Watson* online. It probably wouldn't lead anywhere, but it couldn't hurt to look.

Jacob Reed

JACOB HACKED HIS WAY into Christopher Bell's life only as far as he needed to find out where the man banked. Fingering the safety deposit box key in his pocket, he showed up at the First National on State Street wearing a suit, a wig, a Cubs baseball cap, and a pair of horn-rimmed glasses that didn't actually do anything for his vision.

First National was a massive building with polished floors and tall ceilings. Jacob's footsteps echoed through the cavernous lobby. A bank representative greeted him, asked why he was there, and directed him to a group of leather chairs situated near a series of offices, doors closed.

Jacob waited patiently to be seen. He watched the line for the tellers shrink and then grow again. He listened to their conversations. One customer was there to deposit her paycheck, another needed a cashier's check, a third had come to make a withdraw. The conversations were dull, and Jacob quickly lost interest. He tapped his fingers together as he sang the chorus to a pop song in his head. When he realized with disgust it was the newest hit by boy band Fresh Sync, he pushed it away and read the covers of the magazines spread out on the coffee table in front of him instead.

The one on top was a *Better Homes & Gardens.* It featured a smiling woman with two small kids beside her, sitting in a posh living room. Like so many photos, it made him think about the life that someday might be his.

A personal banker opened one of the office doors and invited him in. She was an attractive woman in her late twenties. She smiled at him and he smiled back. He crossed the lobby, keeping his head down, using the cap's bill to mitigate the risk that one security camera or another would catch a clear shot of his face. He told her he was there to get into his safety deposit box. She asked for his account information which, of course, he, Chris Bell, could provide. She checked his ID (a fake, with his picture and Chris's name). She had him sign a form. Boilerplate stuff.

Jacob made sure the only thing he touched other than his ID was the pen, which he slid through his fingers to smear any prints before returning.

Satisfied she had fulfilled her obligation to protect her customer's property, the banker accompanied Jacob to Chris's safety deposit box and together they unlocked it. "I'll be right outside if you need me," she told him, as she left him alone to peruse the contents.

Jacob flipped open the box's lid and found none of the items he'd expected to find: deeds, titles, birth certificates, a will. What he found was a ring. He didn't know much about jewelry, so he couldn't estimate the ring's value by looking at it. But since Chris Bell had gone to the trouble of putting it in a safety deposit box, he figured it had to be worth a lot.

Karma's a bitch, he thought, amused, and pocketed the ring. Then he wiped the box down with a handkerchief and slid it back into place.

"Thank you," he said to the personal banker on his way out. "I'm done here."

Liam Parker

LIAM ARRIVED AT THE Oakbrooke Cemetery at 3:15 on Tuesday for Elise's funeral. He went with the hope of learning more about the woman he'd fallen in love with and, if Elise had indeed been after a fresh start, the past she'd run away from. Maybe he would even stumble upon a clue that would point Bash in the right direction.

The service had been announced in the *Chicago Tribune's* obituaries. It was the only thing Liam had found online about Elise under the name Watson other than a dormant Facebook account.

The cemetery was an expansive green landscape, anchored by groves of oak trees along its southern and western borders, the tombstones neatly organized in rows. A narrow road meandered in from the east through an arched wrought-iron gate and then forked to the north and southwest, extending across the grounds in a misshapen Y.

As Liam marched through the headstones, he counted just under half-a-dozen mourners gathered near the burial site. Three men, two women. They stood in front of four rows of foldout metal chairs with programs on them. The men wore suits, the women black dresses. The casket was closed and suspended above the grave. A priest, dressed in white and holding a Bible, was standing at its head. He looked in Liam's direction, nodded, and waited for Liam to arrive before he began.

"I am the resurrection and the life, saith the Lord. He that believeth in me, though he were dead, yet shall he live; and whosoever liveth and believeth in me shall never die."

Some of the mourners glanced curiously at Liam. He pretended not to notice. He put his hands in his pockets and lowered his head.

When the priest finished, he asked if anyone would like to speak. There were only two people there who were old enough to be Elise's parents. They stood side by side, barely an inch between them. The man was slumped over and bald, his eyes bloodshot. He was thin everywhere except his stomach, which strained against the buttons of his shirt. The woman was taller than him by a good two inches. Her gray hair was pulled into a bun. With the arch of her eyebrows and high cheekbones, she bore a strong resemblance to Elise.

The woman elbowed the man, who fervently shook his head.

Liam could imagine what they must be feeling. For him, losing Elise was hard, but they'd only been dating for two months. If he lost one of his kids, he'd be shattered.

After the body was lowered into the ground and the priest said his parting prayer, Liam approached the couple. "I'm sorry," he said as the other mourners closed in around him. He got the feeling they were all related.

"You knew our daughter?" the man asked.

"I did."

The woman grabbed her husband's hand. The little bit of blood coloring her pale skin receded. "How did you know her?"

"We were dating."

All three mourners who'd gathered around Liam were quite a bit younger than Elise's parents. One of the men was short, with a mess of curly blond hair he'd been unable to tame. The other, whose features were also sharp like Elise's, was thin and lanky. His face was pitted from acne.

"How long?" the second one asked.

"A couple of months."

"What do you do?" the man with the curly hair said. It was an odd question, considering the circumstances, and the words were delivered in an equally strange tone. In another situation, Liam would have said the man sounded angry. He might have even gone so far as to say the man seemed to blame him for something. He must be mistaken though. What could he blame Liam for?

"I work in advertising, like Elise."

"Yeah, right," Curly Hair said, while at the same time the young woman with them said, "Elise didn't work in advertising. She didn't even go to college."

She had her hands clasped in front of her. An old scar marred her left check, extending nearly all the way from her earlobe to the corner of her mouth. Her dress was fitted at the waist and had satin buttons that ran down from the collar.

That news hit Liam hard. He'd decided the two men were likely Elise's brothers and the woman her sister. From what he could see of her family, she hadn't lied about them. But if the woman was right about Elise's education, and Liam had no reason to doubt her, then she was also probably right about her job. It was unlikely an advertising firm would have hired Elise if she hadn't gone to college. If that was true, it would mean she hadn't only been lying to hide her past.

"He's probably one of the dirtbags she was hanging around with before she disappeared," the second brother said.

It took a second or more for his words to register. Liam was still thinking about the newest lie, and all the subsequent ones it had spawned: stories about co-workers and campaigns, budgets and timelines. It had all sounded so legit. "What do you mean?" he asked.

"I mean she took off."

"How long ago was that?"

"She was twenty-two, so"—the curly haired brother mumbled to himself like he was trying to calculate the time—"a while ago."

The husband pinched the bridge of his nose with his thumb and first finger. He squeezed his eyes shut, holding back tears.

"He blames himself for her running away," the wife said, cupping one hand around the side of her mouth and speaking in a stage whisper.

Liam looked from one spouse to the other. *Maybe*, he thought. The only thing he could say for sure was that *she* blamed him and wasn't going to miss an opportunity to remind him of that.

"Let's go home," the husband snapped.

"I'm sure it's not your fault," Liam said. Even to his ears, the sentiment sounded like the cliché it was, but it was all he could come up with on the fly. Somehow, he had to stop Elise's family from leaving. They had barely started talking and there was so much more he wanted to know.

"Damn right it's not," Curly Hair said.

"Please. I would like to talk to you," Liam pressed as the husband turned and, still holding his wife's hand, dragged her along with him.

It was clear nothing he could say would stop them. Liam urgently took a business card out of his wallet. "All of you." He held out the card, offering it to each of the siblings as they passed. "I just want to know more about her. I miss her." Almost feebly, he added, "I loved her." That was true no matter what she was lying about.

Elise's mother turned toward him. She looked Liam up and down before her eyes landed on the business card. She plucked it from between his fingers as her husband jerked her forward a step and said, "Come on."

As Liam watched them head toward the road, he noticed something out of the corner of his right eye. Reflexively, he turned to look. It was a smudge of a person at the edge of the cemetery. Liam thought it might be Bash. He wondered if the detective was following him. Since there was no reason to chase down the family, he moved toward the observer. As he did, the observer strolled toward the nearest exit.

Liam was too far away to catch up to him on foot (not that he knew what he would do if he did), so he went back to his car and circled the block. He saw nobody besides the family walking along the cemetery's perimeter. The observer was gone.

Liam Parker

LIAM HAD JUST ENOUGH time after the funeral to get to his ex-wife's. Every Tuesday night, he had dinner with the kids. They also spent every other weekend with him. Although he often listened to one Spotify playlist or another while en route, right now he opted for silence. He needed to think.

Elise hadn't seen her family in six years. Liam figured she could have gone to school in that time despite what they believed. But he wanted to know for sure.

She'd said she worked at Out Front Media. He called their main number and asked for HR. A woman picked up and asked how she could help.

Liam started by introducing himself and his company and ended with a request for verification of employment.

As he merged onto I-94 North, he could hear the woman punching keys on her keyboard. "Hmm." She asked him to spell the name "Whitman" and then said, "Sorry. She's not in our system."

"How about under Watson?"

"Elise Watson?"

"Yes."

Silence.

This had to be the first time an employer had ever called to do a background check and given two last names. Sensing he needed to say something fast, Liam provided the only explanation he could think of. "It was her maiden name."

He held his breath until he heard more typing.

The woman again asked for the spelling. "Nobody by that name either."

Liam sighed. He thanked her and ended the call. At the funeral, he'd been surprised. Now he was angry. Elise had lied about her name, her job, her school. What else had she lied about? What the hell was going on?

Liam pulled up to Catherine's two-story brick house in Winnetka, about thirty minutes north of downtown. With quiet, safe neighborhoods and manicured yards, Winnetka was one of those suburbs that drew an affluent crowd.

He rang the doorbell and waited. It didn't take long before Tommy opened the door. "Dad!" Barely eight, he wrapped his arms around Liam's waist and hugged as tightly as he could. Most of the time, he was a giggling Energizer bunny, with hair never brushed quite right and wearing one wrinkled tee or another. Today it was a worn-out green job featuring the Teenage Mutant Ninja Turtles. When Liam was growing up, he was pretty much the same, only it was all Transformers, all the time.

"How's it going, buddy?" Liam said, giving his son a one-armed hug back.

Tommy let go. "Good. Hey, did you know, um, did you know that if you ever have to outrun a crocodile, you shouldn't run in a straight line? Because crocodiles can run fast, but they can't turn very well. So you should go like this." He demonstrated how Liam should evade a pursuing crocodile by balling his fist and moving it back and forth. "Like in a zigzag. Hank told me that."

"He did, did he?"

"Uh-huh. At lunch. He went down to Florida last week with his family. They went to Disney World. Can we go to Disney World?"

"Maybe over summer vacation."

"Hank said they went now because it wasn't as crowded."

"One day Hank's going to be serving you fries at McDonald's, so let's not use his family as role models, shall we?" Catherine said, appearing behind Tommy.

Liam glanced up at her. She was lean and dressed all in white. She looked younger than she was thanks to the miracle of Botox. She stood with her shoulders back, head high, always aware of her posture. Her mother had developed a stoop as she'd aged, and Catherine had said she was afraid the same thing would happen to her. "Beauty starts in the back," she'd told Liam more than once.

"I wouldn't mind serving fries at McDonald's," Tommy said. "I like fries."

Liam patted the top of his head. "Go get in the car, son."

Tommy darted down the brick steps and Liam watched him until he was belted into the back seat of the Tesla.

"Liam, we have to talk."

Before he could say anything, Liam's daughter appeared in the doorway. It was cloudy out, but that hadn't stopped her from putting on a pair of oversized sunglasses. Quite the opposite of Catherine, Alice dressed in ratty flannels and looked down at her feet when she walked. Liam suspected she was aware of her mother's feelings on posture and beauty and was doing both to piss her off.

Headphones on and blasting music loud enough that Liam could have sung along, she passed by with barely a "Hi, Dad" on her way to the car. Alice still blamed Catherine for her parents' divorce and didn't try to hide her feelings. She would become more talkative once they got to the restaurant.

For some reason, thinking about how the divorce had affected Alice caused Liam to think about the conversation that had proceeded it. Catherine had approached him in the kitchen and, as far as he was concerned, the whole thing had come more or less out of the blue. She told him she wasn't happy, hadn't been happy for a long time. After a while, they moved to the living room and stayed there until there'd been nothing left to say. She'd already made up her mind. She'd blamed it on his long hours at work and the gambling and had said something like, "Even when you're at home, you're not at home." Liam remembered packing a bag and going to a hotel and Alice crying; she wasn't much older than Tommy was now. He remembered the divorce itself and how things had turned mean, with Catherine squeezing every dollar out of him she could. But he couldn't remember exactly how the conversation had started. Perhaps it had been with the same three words he'd texted Elise. *We need to talk.* Oh, well. Liam figured it didn't matter now. Things started, things ended.

"What about?" he asked.

Catherine glanced at her daughter, then back to him. "I'm putting the house up for sale."

"Good for you." It was hers now, after all. She could set it on fire for all he cared.

"We're moving."

"Probably a good idea. I don't think the new owners would want you hanging around here after they move in."

Catherine shifted her weight from one leg to the other, annoyed.

"No, Liam. You don't get it. We're not staying here. We're moving to Mississippi. I'm going back to Jackson."

Liam was stunned. His mouth dropped open a little and stayed that way for a second or two before he said, "Wait. What? You can't do that."

"Mom's getting old. She needs me around. Besides, this isn't the kind of place I want to raise my kids. Alice has been sneaking out lately. Did you know that? Who knows what kind of trouble she could get into."

Liam wasn't surprised Alice was sneaking out. (He'd done it plenty of times growing up—going with his friends to the playground behind Ives Middle School to smoke cigarettes and, when he was older, drink Pabst.) He didn't like it. He'd talk to her about it. But teenagers did things like that. Alice was a good kid, so no matter what Catherine thought she was up to, he could be pretty sure he'd done worse.

The car door opened up behind him and Tommy shouted, "Dad, are we going?"

"In a minute, son," Liam said, putting on his best everything's-okay smile.

Tommy got back into the Tesla.

"I've already spoken to my lawyer about it."

"But—"

"I just wanted to give you a heads up."

"They're my kids too."

Her lips curled into a nasty grin as she placed one hand on the door handle. It was the same grin she'd shown him when the judge had ruled on the division of assets. "And that's the only reason you get to see them, at all."

Catherine closed the door before Liam could say anything else.

Liam thought she'd made it sound like she was doing him a favor. Could she really take the kids to Mississippi without his permission? He'd have to look into that.

He stepped off the stoop and, on the way back to his car, his cellphone rang. He glanced at the Caller ID. It was Patricia. He pressed a button to answer.

"What's up?"

"First things first. You were right. Elise was never married."

Clearly, Patricia hadn't believed Liam when he had told her as much in her office. But at least she was being thorough.

"That said, remember how I told you Elise might have a record?"

"Yeah."

"She does. Reyes got a copy of it."

After everything else Liam had learned, he wasn't surprised. But he didn't expect Patricia to read off the charges she did.

Jacob Reed

THE HEARTLAND NURSING HOME was a sprawling behemoth of stone and brick surrounded by gardens that had gone dormant. Jacob slipped past the reception desk, hoping he wouldn't be noticed, and made his way up to the third floor where his mother had a private room. She was the only family he had, and after the dementia had taken hold, he hardly even had her anymore.

While he waited for the elevator, Jacob pulled a faded, cracked picture out of his pocket. He'd found it in a wallet he'd stolen four months back, and had kept it for the same reason he'd kept the picture he'd found in Chris Bell's wallet—to fuel his dreams about the life that might one day be his. Though the woman and infant posing Christmas-card style with the man he'd robbed were two-dimensional strangers, he had imagined a rich, fulfilling life for all of them. One full of love, where the parents read stories to their child at bedtime and the whole family spent summers on the lake and nothing bad ever happened. He didn't try to square this with stealing the man's wallet.

His childhood had not been anything close to that, not that it was bad. His mother was always working. She left early, came home late. She cleaned houses for Maids Around Town, bagged groceries at Treasure Island, and worked the cash register at McDonald's part-time. While it was enough to keep the lights on, she depended on food stamps to keep Jacob fed and the good will of the neighborhood to make sure he stayed out of trouble.

Jacob never knew what had happened to his father. He had never seen a picture or heard a story. His mother refused to talk about him. Whenever he had asked, she'd said it was just the two of them now and the past didn't matter.

Sometimes Jacob imagined his father was dead, and perhaps he was. Sometimes he thought his father might not have known his mother was pregnant, and that could be true too. Whatever the reality was, it amounted to the same—the man never sent a check.

Jacob had decided a long time ago his life wasn't going to be like that. His mother had followed all the rules; she had raised a child in a hard world and done a damn fine job of it. Now that she needed him to take care of her, he made sure she had the best care available. She deserved that. But that was what following all the rules got you, wasn't it? A tough life. If Jacob followed them, too, hers would have been a tough life with a tougher end.

The rules were for suckers. He would take care of his mother, make his fortune, and raise a family the right way. If he had to screw some people over to make that happen, so what? Family was all that mattered. Besides, most of them probably deserved it.

When the elevator doors opened, he put the picture back in his pocket. It wouldn't hold together much longer.

He put his phone on silent. Since his mother had started suffering from dementia, he tried to keep distractions to a minimum. Especially those she found unsettling, and the phone was without a doubt the most unsettling distraction he'd introduced. The one time it rang, playing a portion of The Rolling Stones' "Sympathy for the Devil," she first looked confused, then alarmed when he pulled the device out of his pocket. She didn't know what it was, and trying to explain it to her only upset her more.

Jacob followed the hallways to his mother's room. Residents shuffled past him, some with staff help, some on their own. With each visit, he recognized more of them, but only one did he know by name. Natalie Winder. She was a small woman who moved slowly, a friend of his mother's. Ms. Winder—she didn't like to be called Natalie by anyone a generation younger than her—was headed in the same direction he was. She was wearing a white sweater, tan slacks, and white slippers. As far as Jacob could tell, her bouffant hairstyle hadn't changed since the sixties.

He said hello as he passed. Another thirty paces down, he reached his mother's room. The door was closed. That was unusual. She liked to see the people crossing back and forth. It made her feel like she wasn't alone. He turned the knob. The door was also locked. That was even more unusual. Jacob told himself she could be in the cafeteria or any of a dozen other places she might visit on a good day, but that still didn't explain the locked door.

He knocked and, instead of his mother's voice, heard Ms. Winder say, "You're looking for Lizzy?"

It was a stupid question, Jacob thought. Elizabeth was his mother. This was her room. Of course he was looking for Lizzy. But he kept his answer to a simple, "Yes."

She closed the distance between them and craned her neck up so she could look him in the eyes. "You don't know? I would have thought they'd have told you. They moved her downstairs. End of the hall. Do you know Ms. Locklear?"

Jacob shook his head.

"They put Lizzy with her. She's got these little paper flowers stuck to her door. You can't miss it. Personally, I think they look stupid. I told her to take them down. But she likes them and won't listen to me."

Jacob thanked Ms. Winder, then took the stairs down one flight and quickly found the door with the flowers on it. His mother was alone, sitting on one of two beds inside, a photo album open in her lap.

"Mom, what's going on? What are you doing here?"

She looked up. He could tell from the way she smiled today was one of her good days. "Come sit with me. Do you remember this?" She pointed to one of the pictures. In it, much younger versions of himself and his mother were standing at the top of the John Hancock Center. Beyond the windows behind them, miles of city stretched out in miniature. They had been on one of their "vacations." Lizzy could rarely afford to take them anywhere beyond the suburbs, but she did her best to make up for it with trips like those.

Jacob often found her looking at old photo albums on her good days. She loved to reminisce. Although he thought she colored the past in a way that made it seem better than it was, where was the harm in that?

"I remember it." Jacob sat down beside his mother. He gently took the photo album from her, closed it, and placed it on the bed. "Mom, what's going on? Why are you in this room?"

"They moved me."

"When?"

Felix Winkler, the nursing home administrator, appeared in the doorway. He had an arrogance about him Jacob had never cared for. "This morning," he said. "We've been trying to reach you for days now."

Jacob knew that was true. He'd been avoiding their calls. However, their reason for calling, and his reason for not answering, didn't justify what they had done. "You can't just move her."

"Let's talk in the hall."

Jacob reassuringly cupped one hand over his mother's two. "I'll be right back." He followed Felix into the hall and closed the door. "What are you doing putting her in there?" he asked.

Felix was somehow both slight and pudgy, a wisp of hair brushed across his bald spot as if that would be enough to hide it. He didn't look like he was good at confrontation. But he held Jacob's gaze firmly when he said, "You're two months late. Private rooms are in high demand. If you can't afford to pay for yours, we can't keep her in it."

"I'll get you the money."

"Please do. We can keep her in this room for a month or two, but if the account isn't brought current by then . . ." Felix let the threat hang in the air. He didn't have to mention the word "eviction" explicitly. It had all been spelled out in the paperwork Jacob had signed when he moved his mother in.

"I said I'll get you the money."

"I hope so." Suddenly Felix's mood changed. His eyes brightened and he smiled. "Anyway, they're serving Chicken Florentine in the cafeteria tonight. It's quite good. Stick around if you can."

Jacob snorted and returned to his mother's room.

Liam Parker

PATRICIA TOLD LIAM THAT Elise had been arrested twice, once
for prostitution and once for possession. She'd avoided jail time for the
prostitution charge but did one year at the Redwood Penitentiary for
the drugs.

He didn't ask any questions. He needed time to process the news.
He thanked Patricia for the information and told her he would call
later. Then, after an uneventful dinner with the kids at Chili's, he
headed over to Ava's to blow off some steam.

It was becoming increasingly clear that Liam knew very little about
Elise. If all the secrets he'd learned after she died had been revealed
sooner, he might have walked away from the relationship. No, he *would*
have walked away from the relationship. But with Bash gunning for
him and no relationship to walk away from, Liam was bound to Elise's
ghost for the time being.

At a red light, he pulled up Ava's app and requested permission to
play. While he waited for a response, he called the attorney who'd
handled his divorce. Ever since he'd stepped off Catherine's stoop, he'd
been planning on making that call in the morning. He hated to bother
the lawyer after hours. But her threat was only compounding his stress
and he needed to take action where he could.

The lawyer assured Liam that Catherine wouldn't be able to take
the kids without a hearing and no judge was likely to grant a move

during the school year as long as they had another capable parent in the city. "She's trying to push your buttons," he said. "You know how she is. If I were you, I'd focus my attention on the criminal case for now, okay? That's what matters. If it goes sideways, you're not going to see the kids much no matter where they're living."

"You're right." Even though Liam thought the advice could have been delivered without reminding him what was at stake, the bluntness of it also took some of the sting out of Catherine's threat. In that respect, it was exactly what he needed to hear.

He got off the phone and, a couple of seconds later, a barcode for the elevator appeared. Liam was in business.

He parked in the garage, took the elevator to the ninth floor, punched the PIN he'd received through the app into the keypad mounted next to Midwest Design's glass door, and navigated his way to the back of the suite. The bodyguard who patted him down was sporting a gray t-shirt tucked into black slacks and a pair of wingtips. He had a gold medallion featuring St. Christopher on a chain around his neck. When he was done, the bodyguard gestured toward the room with an open hand and said, "Have good time, sir."

Ava Perez was sitting quietly in the corner. She looked from the players to Liam and nodded a welcome.

Liam took a seat at the table.

"How's life treating you?" Jacob asked in his usual upbeat tone.

Normally Liam responded with a "pretty good" or "better than yesterday." But since he couldn't bring himself to gloss over everything that had happened lately, he settled on the most benign news he could. "My daughter's been sneaking out."

Jacob offered a tsk-tsk, and added, "Kids will be kids, I guess, right?" On the next hand, he dealt Liam in.

The Grunter was back. So was Emily, her short black hair again plastered to her head with gel. The only other player Liam knew by name was Eric Ricci. Liam had played with him on several other occasions—he had been among those to leave early the night Elise died—but he'd known about Eric long before their first game.

Eric had been a star football player at Northwestern and had gone on to play a couple of seasons with the Bears. During that time, he'd racked up endorsement deals faster than any other player Liam could recall. He was on billboards selling cologne and in magazines selling clothes. Even now, more than a decade later, he was still a celebrity of sorts, making minor appearances on TV and in films.

Liam did his best to concentrate on the cards and watch for tells. He knew Emily would tap her fingernail on the table when she had a bad hand. Eric's right eye would twitch. Eventually, he figured out the Grunter, whose real name was Tom Morgan, had the most obvious tell of all—he grunted.

Despite those insights, Liam didn't play well. He kept thinking about the last time he was here, the messages from Elise, the things he might have done differently. If he'd left thirty minutes earlier, just thirty minutes, she might still be alive. If he hadn't come here at all, she would be, for sure. They could have gone to a movie (Elise wanted to see *Jurassic World*) and stayed at his place. Maybe when he dropped her off the next day, they'd have found her door broken in or other signs of an unwanted visitor. Maybe that would have been enough for her to tell him about the bad people. Maybe if she'd told him everything in her own words, he would have understood. Maybe they'd still be together, and maybe one day she could have been Mrs. Parker. Maybe, maybe, maybe.

One thing was for sure: those maybes were all he had left.

Liam thought about them throughout the night and was still thinking about them when a knock on his door got him out of bed early the next morning and drew him cautiously to the door of his condo. He should have gotten a call from the concierge announcing the visitor. Dressed in his boxers and white tee, he quietly slid the chain on the door into place. He had his cell phone in one hand, ready to dial 911. He looked through the peephole and saw Bash, flanked by uniformed officers.

Bash knocked again, harder. "Mr. Parker, I know you're in there. I need you to open up."

Liam instantly felt weak. He placed his free hand against the wall to steady himself. There was only one reason Bash would be here before seven a.m. Liam stepped deeper into the condo so he could call Patricia without being heard.

"What's wrong, Liam?" she said when she answered, sounding surprisingly alert for the hour.

"Bash is outside. I'm pretty sure I'm about to get arrested."

"All right, we knew this could happen. Don't fight it. Do what they tell you to. I'll find out where they're going to take you and meet you there."

With the demands for Liam to open the door intensifying, he did just that. The uniformed officers charged in first, guns pulled and clearing the unit. Bash entered waving an arrest warrant.

"Get dressed," he said.

Liam Parker

LIAM SAT IN AN interview room at police headquarters, handcuffed to a table.

Bash sat across from him. "We know you weren't at home when you sent the text messages to Elise."

Liam didn't respond.

"You were in Lakeview. Why did you lie to me?"

"I'm not saying anything until my lawyer gets here."

Bash shrugged. "If that's how you want to handle it, that's fine with me. But she's going to tell you to keep quiet, go to court. And every hour you spend in jail she's going to be out there working *on your behalf.*" He made air quotes around the last three words. "All the while she's charging you—what? Two hundred dollars an hour? More? I know you can afford it, but you have to ask yourself, do you really think she's looking out for your best interest? If you go to court, you're going away for life. I can guarantee you that. But, if we can put this thing to bed now, I believe I could get the DA to drop murder one to manslaughter."

Liam leaned back in his chair, panic welling up inside him. Still, he knew he was being played. He kept his mouth shut. He'd already said everything he had to say for now.

"No matter how careful somebody is, a murder is a hard thing to cover up," Bash said. "And it's never a good idea to try to make it look like a suicide. When you strangle someone, there are a lot of little clues you leave behind. Pressure marks behind the ears, burst blood vessels under the eyelids, stuff like that. Not to mention the bruises you left on her neck. And cutting her wrists after she died?" He shook his head. "Since the body wasn't pumping blood anymore, that was never going to fool anyone.

"Look, I'll admit I don't know what you were doing in Lakeview. But if it was something you felt you needed to lie about, I can be damn sure it's not going to make your situation any better. And it doesn't change a thing about what you did to Elise."

Bash crossed his arms over his chest and stared at Liam until Liam said, "Lawyer."

"Let me tell you what I think happened. I think you found out Elise was cheating on you. I think you went over there to tell her to cut it out. She said she wouldn't. Maybe she broke up with you. Either way, you got mad, things got out of hand. You didn't mean to kill her. It just happened. Then you freaked out. You had to cover it up. So you dumped her in the tub, cut her wrists, and took off. Like I said, the prosecutor's going to go for murder one. But if that's how things went down, you don't need to spend the rest of your life behind bars. People make mistakes, right?"

"Lawyer."

"I also think I know why you placed the call from your phone instead of hers. After all, if you could get into her phone to delete your messages, you could have dialed 911 instead."

Liam restrained himself from reminding the detective that he hadn't deleted the messages. If Bash hadn't believed him the first time, he wasn't going to believe him now.

"You nearly knocked over a resident when you were fleeing the scene. Remember her? I think that's the real reason you placed the 911 call from your phone. Once someone had seen you, you couldn't just disappear, right? And you want to know something else? I'll bet you a jury's going to think the exact same thing. Especially since you were the only one seen going in or out of the apartment."

An officer opened the door and Patricia stepped inside just in time to hear the end of Bash's sentence. She introduced herself, then said, "Mr. Parker did ask for his lawyer, didn't he?"

"I did," Liam said. "Several times."

"You mind telling me what you're doing in here, Detective Wyatt?"

"Passing the time."

"Uh-huh." She gestured to the door. "Do you mind?"

Bash looked from the lawyer to Liam and back. He got up slowly and, without trying to hide his disdain for Patricia, left the room. She took his seat and placed her briefcase on the floor beside her. "Did you say anything?"

"No."

She nodded. "Good."

"Detective Wyatt said something to me before you came in that doesn't make any sense though. I encountered only two people when I went to see Elise—the woman who held the door for me and the one I ran into when I was going to my car to get my phone. Both of them were in the lobby. But he said I was the only one seen going in or out of her apartment. Nobody saw me go in or out of her apartment."

"Are you sure?"

"I'm sure." Liam moved his cuffed arm a little bit, trying to make it more comfortable.

"All right, let me see what I can find out about the building's security. Maybe they have footage of you on the floor. If they do, and you really are the only one going in or out of that apartment . . ." She shook her head. "Do I need to be prepared for that possibility?"

She'd held his gaze when she asked the question and he held hers when he answered. "If they've got footage of that floor, I won't be the only one on it."

Liam Parker

PATRICIA TOLD LIAM HE'D be arraigned in a couple of days. Until then, he'd have to sit tight. After that, the police fingerprinted and photographed him. The routine was more or less the same as it had been when he was arrested in college. Now, however, instead of being kept in a large room with dozens of other men, he was outfitted with an orange jumpsuit and transferred to the county jail. He was assigned a cell and told he'd get an hour a day to shower and stretch his legs.

There was a small bed and a desk on opposite walls. A sink and a toilet. It looked like something out of a nightmare.

Liam sat down on the bed. The prison smelled like piss and vomit. He was scared and overwhelmed. He wanted to cry, and looked away from the other cells in case he did.

At least he was alone. Everyone on this wing was. It was where the guards housed those yet to be processed. He couldn't imagine sharing the forty-eight square feet with another man. Especially someone who *had* committed murder.

Jacob Reed

JACOB FOUND A BLACK-MARKET dealer online. Presenting himself to the public at large as an up-and-up businessman, the dealer ran a jewelry shop on Halstead called Forever Diamonds. He had told Jacob through secure messages exchanged on the dark web they would make the deal there.

The store was unassuming and small, nestled between a bakery and a clothing boutique. Inside, three long cases of jewelry had been organized in a U formation. There were no customers when Jacob arrived.

The dealer showed him to a back room. He silently examined the ring with a loupe while he made his assessment, then placed the ring on a piece of brown felt that had been laid out on the table between them and made his offer.

Although Jacob wasn't sure what the ring was worth, he was certain the man was offering a fraction of its true value. "I don't know," he said, feigning reluctance in hopes of driving up the price. "That seems low."

The dealer crossed his arms over his chest. "Think you can do better?" He gestured to the ring. "Take it."

Jacob knew he couldn't do better. The offer was more than he was getting from the pawn shops and, most importantly, it would be enough to pay off his debt to the Heartland Nursing Home. He made the deal, pocketed the cash, and while waiting on the metro, pulled out his phone to check his news feed.

Jacob didn't care much for the news and normally paid little attention to it. But since he'd seen the first story detailing Elise's death, he'd been watching his feed closely for further updates. With cold, trembling fingers, he clicked a story titled "Suspect Arrested in Logan Square Murder."

When he was done reading it, he knew what he needed to do next. He needed to get into Liam's apartment.

Christopher Bell

CHRIS HAD BEEN DATING Emma for five years and living with her for eighteen months before he'd worked up the nerve to ask her to marry him. Actually, he hadn't asked. He'd only bought a ring, but that was a big step forward for him.

The jeweler had described it as a French Pavé diamond eternity engagement ring with a round three-carat diamond clocking in at over fifty-three thousand dollars. Except for the price, that all meant nothing to Chris. But it was pretty. Emma would love it.

What Chris knew well were stocks. He was a broker for Ellison Trust with a solid track record. He could predict the movement of the Dow better than most. It was a reputation that had gotten him booked on CNN and MSNBC, as well as quoted in *The New York Times* and *Wall Street Journal*.

To say he was good because he did his homework would be an understatement. All the brokers Chris knew did their homework, though few stayed at the office as late as he did and even fewer took stacks of documents to bed with them to read before going to sleep.

Emma couldn't understand how anybody could put that many hours into a job. Nor could she understand why, if he brought his work home anyway, he would so often stay at the office well into the night. Although Chris had told her he could concentrate better there, she didn't buy it. On more than one occasion, she'd accused him of having an affair.

That was something he would never do. Making her believe that, though, wasn't always easy. Emma would snoop through his drawers, open his credit card statements, check his email. Chris knew all this and loved her anyway. He had no secrets. Not until he'd bought the ring, and that one secret he couldn't let her uncover before he was ready.

He'd carried it around in his jacket for the first two weeks, telling himself one night or the next, or maybe this weekend, he would pop the question. Perhaps he'd take her out on his boat for a candlelight dinner and do it under the stars. But the weekend came and went and one night folded into the next and still he hadn't asked.

Chris wasn't concerned about her answer. Emma had been hinting at marriage for a while. If he'd came home one day, dropped the ring on the table, and said, "You wanna?", he was confident she would have said yes. Although in practice Chris had given up the single life long ago, he was reluctant to make it official. Marriage came with a string of entanglements, not the least of which was financial. Emma had already announced she wasn't going to sign a prenup, and that never sat right with him.

When Chris had come to terms with the reality that he wasn't going to propose yet, he'd decided he better put the ring somewhere safe until he was finally, actually, and truly ready. He'd selected the First National on State Street because it was close to his office. Then he put the key in his wallet where Emma wouldn't find it, and in the eight months since had thought about it exactly three times: Christmas, New Year's, and their anniversary.

After his wallet was stolen, he promptly replaced his credit cards and went by the DMV to get a new license. The photo of Emma was digital; he could reprint that when he got around to it. But the cash was gone forever. That irritated him the most. On some level he never thought about he believed people were replaceable. Even Emma. She hadn't been his first girlfriend, and if she left, she wouldn't be his last. Money, on the other hand, was not. A dollar stolen was a dollar gone. When he came into possession of another, it did not fill the void of the one he no longer had.

He remembered the key to the safety deposit box several days later. He and Emma were lying in bed. They'd been making love not minutes before. Emma clung to him, one arm draped over his chest. She asked if their relationship was going anywhere, which of course meant marriage, and, more immediately, a ring, a safety deposit box, and a key.

Chris told himself not to worry. A pickpocket wouldn't have any interest in a safety deposit box or any way to get into it. They were opportunists, that was all. He'd have taken the cash. *Bastard.* Perhaps he'd have charged up the credit cards if he'd had the chance. But a key? It would have gone in the trash with everything else.

Chris decided he would stop by the bank in the morning and replace it. Everything would be fine.

But it wasn't fine. The personal banker went pale when Chris told her he needed to replace the key to his safety deposit box. She called her manager over. They spoke privately for a while, and he took the brunt of Chris's explosion. Nobody knew whether the man posing as Chris Bell had taken anything out of the safety deposit box; they only knew he'd been inside it.

Chris didn't have to check the box to know the ring would be gone, but he did anyway.

"Certainly the ring is insured," the manager said, huddling with Chris and the personal banker in her office.

"I thought it was safe here," Chris snapped. He wanted to break something. He wanted to hurt someone. Fifty-three thousand dollars—gone. Emma should have agreed to sign a damn prenup.

"Okay, relax. We'll call the police. We have security cameras. I'm sure they can get to the bottom of this."

The police reviewed First National's CCTV footage. Views of their suspect were obscured by a Cubs baseball cap, a mop of hair they thought might be a wig, and glasses they weren't sure he needed. Dusting the safety deposit box for prints only turned up ones that matched bank employees.

The police put the photo out on the wire anyway because, as one officer said, "You never know."

Chris could tell he wasn't optimistic and spent the next two days on a slow burn. He blamed everyone: the police, the bank, the thief, but most of all, he blamed Emma. This was her fault, after all. If she'd agreed to sign a damn prenup, none of this would have happened. Finally, he told her as much.

The confrontation happened in the living room. It was nearing midnight and they'd both had too much beer. He paced the room, decorated with black leather sofas and a multicolored rug with no discernable pattern.

Sitting on the sofa closest to the fireplace, Emma let Chris talk until he had nothing left to say. He called her stupid and selfish. He could tell a part of her was delighted that he'd gotten so close to a proposal he'd bought a ring, and that only made him angrier.

When he was done, she waited a beat, letting the tension in the room defuse a little, then got to her feet. "Honey, you should have come to me about this sooner. We're a team."

"What could you do about it?" he spat.

"You said the guy who stole the ring is the same guy who stole your wallet, right?"

"So?"

"Did you tell the police that?" Emma asked, gently placing a hand on Chris's arm.

He shook her off. "Of course I told the police."

She took a step back. "You shouldn't have done that."

"Why not?"

"What do you think is going to happen if they arrest him? He'll deny everything. Without fingerprints, a confession, or any good way to visually ID him, will they even charge him with the robbery at the bank?" She shrugged. "No doubt they'll set a trial date for the theft of your wallet, but he'll get bail. Then what? If he hasn't sold the ring already, he'll sell it then, for sure. It'll be gone for good."

"You have a better idea?"

Her lips stretched into a Cheshire cat grin. Chris had only seen that expression on a few occasions, and only when she was up to no good. "I might." Then it fell away and she said gravely, "If it's not already too late."

Liam Parker

DURING THE HOUR OUT of his cell, Liam placed a collect call to David from a wall-mounted pay phone (he hadn't seen one of those since he was a teenager) and asked him to watch Elise's dog until he got bail. God, he didn't even want to think about what would happen if he didn't get bail. After he hung up, he headed to the yard to walk around.

There was a basketball hoop on one side, free weights on another. Liam stuck to the perimeter, walking along the fence line and keeping his head down. He was there not twenty minutes before a fight broke out right in front of him. In a flurry of activity, the inmates surrounding the two fighters backed away. Some, who egged the men on, did it to make room. Others, like Liam, just wanted to get the hell out of the way.

The fight lasted only seconds before a team of guards broke it up. But that was long enough. One man was sent to the infirmary with a broken nose and a gash deep enough to need stitches. The other was taken to solitary confinement.

Liam didn't hear what started it, and it left him even more on edge, certain a fight could break out over anything. He asked to be returned to his cell and decided that, from then on, that was where he'd stay. To hell with stretching his legs. At least there he was safe.

Jacob Reed

JACOB ENTERED LIAM'S BUILDING carrying a box perhaps two feet in diameter. He was dressed in a brown pair of pants and a matching coat with a UPS logo stitched into the right breast pocket. He made his first attempt to get past the concierge by ignoring him, but that was a no-go.

"Excuse me," said the man in the blue blazer and black tie sitting behind a marble desk.

Jacob kept walking.

The concierge stood up and shouted, "Excuse me, sir!"

Jacob kneeled, awkwardly supporting the box with one knee, and pulled the earbud out of his left ear. There wasn't any music playing. The earbuds were just part of the show. "Yeah?"

"Can I help you?"

Jacob nodded to the elevator. "Package for 2100." Then he started walking again.

"Sir!"

There was only one right away to pull this off. Jacob needed someone to show up and make a fuss while he tried to sweet-talk his way inside. If someone made a fuss loud enough and long enough, Jacob was certain the frustrated concierge would eventually send him on his way. Who needed to be bothered with the protocols of a UPS delivery when there was a crazy person cussing up a storm?

Actually, if Jacob had someone who could show up and make a fuss, he wouldn't need to be here at all since the plan would be entirely different. But he didn't, not anymore, so he'd have to make the best of it. He detoured toward the concierge and placed the box on the desk next to the sign-in log.

"You can leave it here," the concierge said.

"No can do. Got to get Mr."—he glanced down at the label— "Parker's John Hancock for this bad boy."

"It's fine. I'll sign for it."

The concierge reached out his hands to grab hold of the package and Jacob pulled it away. The box was empty, that much would be obvious to anyone who picked it up. "I was instructed to hand it directly to Mr. Parker and Mr. Parker alone."

The concierge eyed Jacob suspiciously. "Let me call up and see if I can reach him for you."

"Sure," Jacob said. What did he care? Liam was in jail. The concierge could place as many calls as he liked to Liam's condo. But he also knew the jig was up. He was never getting past the lobby. Everything he did from here on out would simply be about exiting the con gracefully.

While he waited for the concierge to get off the phone, Jacob put the box on the floor and feigned impatience. He placed his hands on his hips, tapped his foot, checked the time on his cellphone, groaned. Anything to seem like he was a man on a schedule, just someone trying to do his job.

"No answer," the concierge said when he hung up.

"Fine," Jacob said, sounding annoyed. He scooped up the box, did a one-eighty, and headed for the exit. "You know, this is the second time this has happened to me today." He pushed through the revolving glass door, ignoring the concierge's request for a delivery notification slip.

This wasn't over. Jacob was going to get into Liam's condo. He had to.

Liam Parker

PATRICIA SHOWED UP AT eleven o'clock the next day. In a small room similar to the one in which Bash interrogated him, she told him his hearing would be Friday and that the judge assigned to his case was more likely than most of his peers to grant bail.

I only have to make it one more day, Liam thought, and then said it aloud as if he needed to hear the words for them to feel real.

"That's right," Patricia said. "That's the good news. Now, as far as who saw you going into Elise's apartment, I checked with the management office at her building. The only security camera they have is in the lobby. Unfortunately, it was on the fritz. They said they had maintenance scheduled for Monday and that it's working now. But, for us . . ." She shrugged. "Nothing. So Detective Wyatt must have a witness."

Liam shook his head. "Nobody saw me go in or out of her apartment."

"The prosecution will have to hand over a witness list at some point. We will find out who it is. The problem is it will become your word against theirs, and when the jury weighs their testimony with the totality of the evidence, it's hard to know who they'll believe."

Liam Parker

LIAM WAS GRANTED BAIL and Patricia told him to come by her office next week so they could get started on his defense. Liam said he would, then took an Uber home. He was tired and numb, looking forward to a shower and sleeping in his own bed.

When the driver pulled up to Liam's building, there were reporters everywhere, all hoping to snap a photo of the crime scene circuit's rising star. One saw him and pointed. They swarmed the car, snapping photos, shouting questions.

The driver cracked his window. "Get away from the vehicle! Hey!" He slammed on his horn, but it didn't make any difference. The reporters crowded in closer, shouted their questions louder. "Don't touch the vehicle!"

"Keep going," Liam said.

Happy to oblige, the driver pressed on the gas, then the brake. The car lunged forward a couple of feet. Finally, the reporters jumped back, clearing a path. "What was that about?" he said, when they'd left the melee behind. "You somebody important?"

Liam shook his head. "Not particularly."

The driver seemed to rightly understand that Liam didn't want to talk about it. "So where are we going now?"

Liam wasn't sure. He wanted to be somewhere that felt safe and familiar. Next to his own condo, the only place like that was David's.

When ConnectPlus was in its infancy, they'd spent many days there plotting their success. David had always lived alone, so unlike Liam's house in the suburbs, which at the time was overrun with the chaos that was small children, it was also always quiet.

Liam pulled out his cellphone and called his friend.

"Of course, come on over," David said. "You shouldn't be alone right now."

When Liam arrived, Elise's Pomeranian greeted him at the door and Liam felt a strange mix of anger and betrayal, somehow directed at the dog even though the dog was a victim too.

"I've made up the guest room." David handed Liam a glass of wine and directed him to the kitchen. He was wearing an apron with "Chefs do it with Spice" printed across the front. Even tied in place, the apron hung loosely on his lanky frame. "I thought a nice meal might do you some good. Feed the body, feed the soul. Lasagna's still your favorite, right?"

"Yeah, sure," Liam said halfheartedly. He didn't have much interest in food right now.

David washed his hands. He cracked two eggs into a small plastic bowl and beat them with a whisk. "How are you holding up?"

Liam took a sip of his wine and placed the glass down on the kitchen island. While David worked, mixing the eggs with a variety of cheeses and cooking a pound of ground beef in a skillet, Liam talked about his time in jail. He was terrified of losing at trial, of going back, of—dare not think it—spending the rest of his life there. Eventually he worked his way around to the witness Bash had mentioned.

"The detective told me I was the only one seen going in or out of her apartment, but it's not possible. It's just not. The building doesn't have any cameras on Elise's floor, and nobody was there to see me. I mean *nobody*. I even tried knocking on the neighbors' doors after I found her body. No one was home."

David, who was sprinkling Parmesan cheese on top of the lasagna, looked up from his dish. "You haven't seen the article in the *Tribune*, have you?"

"What article?"

David wiped his hands on his apron. He looked up something on his phone, then hesitated. "Huh. Looks like they've already got a story out about your release." He tapped the screen, presumably to navigate to a different page, and handed the phone to Liam. "Anyway, read that."

Liam took the phone and read:

Suspect Arrested in Logan Square Murder

Elise Watson, a twenty-eight-year-old female, was found dead in her Logan Square apartment on October 2. While Ms. Watson's murder could be seen as just one more in a series of killings that has already topped 300 this year, the circumstances surrounding it and the only suspect are noteworthy.

According to unnamed sources within the Chicago Police Department, lead detective on the case Sebastian Wyatt has arrested and charged local businessman Liam Parker with the murder.

Mr. Parker, co-owner of downtown advertising agency ConnectPlus, is the last known person to have had contact with Ms. Watson and was found on the scene when the police arrived. There was bruising on the victim's neck, leading investigators to believe Ms. Watson had been strangled.

"There was a lot of noise coming from next door," said neighbor Ashley Carlson.

Ms. Carlson went on to say that she looked through her peephole and spotted Mr. Parker outside the apartment. "He was the only person I saw come anywhere near [Ms. Watson's] apartment that night. He was covered in blood. He looked crazy."

Mr. Parker's fingerprints were the only ones found on the body. His fingerprints were also found on her phone, from which his text messages were deleted. It is believed these messages were deleted to conceal any communication Mr. Parker and Ms. Watson had before her death.

Ms. Watson's wrists had been slit post-mortem which, also according to unnamed sources within the department, was an attempt to disguise the murder as a suicide.

Liam put the phone down on the island and took another sip of wine. He didn't know what to say. That had to be the witness Bash was talking about.

"That article was making the rounds at the office on Wednesday. I had to hold an all-hands to quell the alarm. I told the staff not to worry and to direct any questions concerning your"—David hesitated, looked down at the lasagna—"*situation* to me."

His *situation*. Liam found a dark humor in the euphemism. David had made it sound like he was dealing with an ailing parent or any of a hundred other things that might go wrong during his life. This was nothing like that. If anything, "giant shit show" would've been more accurate.

"How'd they take it?" he asked.

"They're shaken. No surprise. How would you feel if you found out your boss was charged with murder? But they're working."

"That's good."

David slid the lasagna into the oven and set the timer. Then he leaned forward, gripping the edge of the kitchen island. "This isn't an easy thing to say."

Liam's pulse quickened. *Oh, God. What now?*

"I think you should stay away from the office for a while. Let me run things. Your presence there isn't going to do anyone any good, is it?"

That's it? Liam thought. Perhaps because of everything he'd been through lately, he was expecting worse. If anything, Liam might have suggested the same thing, had he thought of it. "Sure. I mean, of course."

David looked pleased. He nodded toward the phone. "So what are you going to do about that woman?"

"What do you mean?"

"What do I mean? You need to talk to her, Liam. You need to straighten her out, make her understand why you were knocking on her door. She needs to see the situation from your point of view. You think the police are going to help her do that? There's no way she can reliably say you were the only one at the apartment that night. But she seems to think she can, and you need to find out why."

"Shouldn't Patricia do that?"

"Your lawyer?"

"She's got a PI—"

David threw his hands up. "Oh, that's even better, isn't it? What would you think if you were her and some private dick came around asking questions? I can tell you, if it was me, I'd be more suspicious. No, Liam. You need to do this yourself." He took a breath, then came around the island and put a comforting hand on Liam's shoulder. "Speak to her from the heart. Trust me. It's the best way to handle this."

Christopher Bell

EMMA AND CHRIS HAD come from different worlds. In high school, Chris kept his nose in his books, while Emma rarely opened hers. Chris kept an eye toward Harvard. Emma didn't think any further than the next party. Chris had few friends, but they were carefully selected and principled. Emma hung out with anyone and everyone, and still had phone numbers of people Chris would have called "morally flexible."

One such individual was a man named Arkin Prichard. Arkin worked in the Chicago Transit Authority's IT Department. Emma didn't elaborate on how the two knew each other, but she did say that in high school he was the kind of person who could get you things and, as it turned out, still was.

When Chris showed up at the transit authority's headquarters, he could see Arkin pacing around the empty lobby on the other side of the glass doors. He was alone, which Chris had expected.

Chris rapped on the glass.

Arkin, sporting a buzz cut and a CTA jacket, zipped up, scurried over to the door to let him in. "Bastards turn off the heat at night," he said after he opened the door.

Chris didn't mind. It was warmer in here than it was on the street, and he'd be back in his car soon enough.

A stack of bills changed hands and disappeared into Arkin's pocket.

Arkin didn't insult Chris by counting the money.

"Come on," Arkin said, and led Chris to a door on the third floor. A placard on the wall beside it read *IT Department*. Arkin swiped his badge in front of the security reader. There was a click and a red light on the reader turned green.

Inside were a series of long white tables in rows with translucent partitions dividing them into workstations. Arkin sat down at one of the workstations and gestured to the chair at another.

Chris wheeled the chair over so that he could see Arkin's computer screen.

"What time frame you lookin' for?" Arkin asked as he brought the computer to life and logged in.

"Friday morning. Let's begin at two o'clock. Belmont Station."

"Coming up," Arkin said, and went to work. A fisheye view of the station's entrance appeared on the screen with a clock in the lower-left corner that read 02:00:00. As he fast-forwarded the black-and-white image, he said, "Tell me when to stop."

From the camera's angle, Chris could tell it was attached to the underside of the tracks. It looked down on the road that ran beneath them, a station map mounted behind glass near the entrance, a Dunkin' Donuts with walk-up windows, and cement pillars with cartoonish faces painted on them.

For a while, that's all he saw. Then, a homeless man pushing a shopping cart zipped back and forth a couple of times at high speed. A group of college kids raced down the sidewalk. A blur of gray transformed into a man as he ran toward the entrance and stopped to pull out his metro card.

"Pause it," Chris said.

Arkin did.

Chris couldn't make out the face of the man standing in front of the turnstile and wasn't entirely sure he remembered what the thief looked like anyway. But he could see another man entering the camera's view from the right and that man he recognized as himself. He pointed at the guy who had stolen his wallet. "Who's that?"

"Let's see if we can find out." Arkin minimized the video and brought up a different application. "I just have to match up the time on the video to the time he scanned his Ventra card," Arkin explained, his voice trailing off as he quickly navigated to a search form and filled out the required fields. He pressed Enter.

The screen refreshed. The personal details of the man who'd stolen Chris's wallet appeared: name, address, phone number.

Chris couldn't believe it. Emma was right. Arkin had been able to provide him with everything he needed. "Do you know if the police have been by to take a look at this yet?"

"I don't know. That would've gone through security."

Chris chewed on his lip, digesting the news. In the end, he knew it didn't matter. Either way, he had only one choice. He had to go by the thief's apartment now. The longer he waited, the greater the odds were he'd never get the ring back.

But he didn't feel comfortable visiting the thief's apartment alone at night. He needed backup. The people Chris called his friends would not be suited for such a task. He needed somebody with Arkin's moral flexibility. And since Arkin was already here, sitting not two feet away, he asked, "You want to make a little more money tonight?"

Jacob Reed

JACOB WAS SITTING IN the dining room of his basement apartment, his laptop open on the small wooden table in front of him. He began digging into Liam's life through his social media accounts and public records. He found a birth certificate, a marriage certificate, information on his divorce and the birth of his children, which led him to other social media accounts and other records. After enough digging, he believed he had found a way into Liam's condo. It wasn't going to be easy. It would mean becoming a new kind of criminal. But it had to be done.

With his plan formed, Jacob closed the lid of his laptop, ready to call it a night. He crossed the dull, creaking floors that once might have been called mahogany, turned off the light, and made his way to the bathroom to pee. He looked forward to soon having a bathroom that was wider than the length of his outstretched arms.

While he was peeing, he thought he heard a knock and, when he stepped out of the bathroom, he was sure he heard another. Jacob was immediately on edge. Very few people knew where he lived, and none of them dropped in unexpectedly.

He quietly moved to the door to listen for voices on the other side. There was a large bay window beside the door, but he always kept the blinds closed, so there was no chance of being seen. He leaned in close, trying to pick out any small sound he could. It turned out, he didn't have to listen very hard.

"Open the damn door!" a man shouted.

Jacob jerked back like he'd been struck, then retreated several steps deeper into the apartment. His first instinct was to run, but there were only two ways out of the apartment—his front door and his bedroom window, both of which opened onto the courtyard. He was trapped. Maybe if he could figure out what the visitor wanted, he could talk his way out of the situation.

But even with his mind working on overdrive, he came up empty. Then another demand from the other side of the door. "I want the ring back, you son of a bitch!"

With that, Jacob no longer had to wonder who it was. He didn't know how Chris had found him, and now wasn't the time to figure it out.

Think. What do I do?

He'd been quiet. So far, there was no way for Chris to know he was here. If Jacob stayed quiet, maybe he would go away.

Christopher Bell

THE STONE PATIO OUTSIDE the thief's door was four steps below ground level. Although there was enough room for a table and chairs, the patio was empty except for a long-dead fern in one corner and a bed of leaves that hadn't been raked since they began to fall months earlier.

"You think he's home?" Chris asked Arkin.

Arkin ran his fingers through his greasy, unkempt hair. Without a word, he climbed the stairs that took him from patio to street.

"Where are you going?" Chris demanded.

Arkin didn't respond. He walked to the small yard in front of the building, examining the ground. Then he picked something up, which Chris realized was a rock as big as his fist when Arkin returned.

"You can't—"

"Do you want the ring back or not?" Arkin wound up like a pitcher and heaved the rock through the window beside the door. It shattered the glass, tore open the blinds with a clatter, and thudded across the hardwood floor. The single pane of glass that was never designed to be opened was now open for good.

Chris saw a flash of a man running through a doorway that, in an apartment this small, he suspected led to a bedroom. That had to be his thief. Although he would never have broken the window himself, he was emboldened by Arkin's actions. He reached through the hole, careful not to cut himself on the shards of glass that still clung to the frame, and felt along the inside of the door until he found the deadbolt.

Jacob Reed

SECONDS EARLIER, JACOB HAD heard Chris say, "You can't—"

Then there was another voice. "Do you want the ring back or not?"

His fingers flexed like they did when he was about to steal a wallet. This time, though, the energy driving that flex was terror, a feeling of being trapped. Chris wasn't alone. More important, the man he was with planned on getting inside, whether or not Jacob answered the door. Standing still like this didn't seem like such a hot idea anymore. He scooped up his laptop and disappeared into his bedroom just as a rock crashed through the bay window and thudded across the floor.

He toppled the dresser to bar the door, slid the bed across the room to reinforce the blockade. He knew this wouldn't keep the men out forever. That was okay. He had a plan.

"Get out of here or I'll call the police!" Jacob didn't expect that to discourage them. But he wasn't sure if they had seen him duck into the bedroom and he wanted them to know where he was.

A second later they started pounding on the door, trying to force it open, again demanding he return the ring. That was the moment Jacob had been waiting for. With the men distracted, like a magician's audience looking to the left side of the stage while the real trick was performed on the right, he opened the bedroom window and crawled through it. He crouched low, keeping the laptop clutched to his chest as he passed beneath the bay window.

Once he made it up the four steps to the street and around the corner, he considered his disappearing act complete. Sooner or later the men would get into his bedroom. They'd find him gone and probably trash the apartment looking for the ring.

Jacob didn't care. With his laptop in hand and the envelope of cash he'd gotten from the jeweler in his pocket, there was nothing there of value. Besides, if everything went according to plan, he had no reason to ever return.

Liam Parker

AS THE EVENING WORE on, the lasagna brought Liam a small degree of peace, first through its smell and then its taste. After a second glass of wine, he went to bed. He needed to stay sharp.

Chloe scratched at the door until Liam let her in and then whined until he picked her up and put her on the bed with him. Sometime during the evening, his anger with her, his irrational feeling that the tiny Pomeranian should have been able to prevent the attack, had dissipated.

Chloe curled up beside Liam and put her head on his calf. The two stayed that way the rest of the night. Liam slept deeply. In the only dream he'd remember later, he was running through the jail, chased by guards and prisoners alike. They were screaming at him, blaming him for Elise's murder. Each hallway led to a fork. Each choice he made seemed to be wrong. There was no escape, and every cell he looked in, he saw Elise, struggling to get out of her bathtub, begging for his help.

Just after seven, Liam woke up with his forehead damp from sweat and terrified of going back to jail. David was right, he should speak to the neighbor. Nobody would be able to tell his story better than he could. If she would listen to him, she would probably realize she was mistaken.

Elise's building looked dirtier, older, even monstrous and forbidding in a way it hadn't before. Liam could feel the six stories of gray stucco and glass looming over him as he approached the entrance.

He scrolled through the directory until he found a listing for *Carlson, A.* He thought about buzzing her apartment, asking her to let him up so they could talk, then reconsidered. Even if she said no, he wasn't going to go away. This was too important. Liam needed to speak to Ashley face to face, right from the very beginning. She needed to see him as he was now—in a pressed blue button-down and a black overcoat, his hair styled and his clothes blood-free.

Liam buzzed other apartments at random until somebody let him in. He took the elevator to the fourth floor, rising slowly in fits and starts as it always did, and navigated the ugly yellow halls back to Elise's apartment. He half-expected to see police tape strung across her door, but there wasn't any. In fact, there was no indication at all that something horrible had happened there.

Liam looked at the doors of the two closest apartments. These were the ones he'd knocked on looking for help. Ashley had to be behind one of them. Guessing which one seemed like a coin toss.

While there was probably no harm in knocking on the wrong door, Liam didn't like being here. He wanted to get in and out as fast as possible. He studied the doors, looking for clues, not expecting to find any. Then he did. Elise's apartment was on a corner. One door was across the hall from hers and farther from the elevator. The other was along the perpendicular hallway he had to travel to reach Elise's apartment, and the last anyone would encounter before doing so. With an eye to the peephole or the door open, that resident would be able to see anybody who visited Elise.

That had to be it.

Liam knocked and waited and knocked again. It was still pretty early on Saturday morning. He hoped Ashley hadn't spent that night at a boyfriend's or gone out for an early breakfast.

Finally, a woman's voice said, "Go away."

Liam was afraid she might say something like that. Still, he persisted. "Ashley Carlson?"

"Go away. I don't want to talk to you."

"I saw the article in the *Tribune*. I won't take up much of your time. I just wanted you to hear my side of the story. I wanted you to know what happened. Please open the door."

Silence followed. Liam heard the deadbolt turn, and the door cracked open a couple of inches. The security chain was still in place.

Ashley looked as if she had just woken up. She was wearing a pink bathrobe over a pair of sweatpants and a tee shirt. Behind her, clothes and magazines were scattered about the floor. She held up her cell phone so Liam could see she'd already pressed the numbers 911. "You try anything, and I'll hit Send."

Liam took a step back, held out his hands. "No, no. I promise. I only want to talk to you."

Ashley raised her eyebrows as if to say *Get on with it.*

"I didn't kill Elise. She was already dead when I got here. I tried to pull her out of the bathtub, but I couldn't. That's how I got her blood on me. When I knocked on your apartment door, I was looking for help. I had left my phone in the car. I was going to ask you to call the police. I'm not sure what you . . ." He was going to say *"thought I was doing,"* but of course, he already knew. The article had made it crystal clear, hadn't it? Elise had been killed only minutes before Liam had arrived. Ashley had said she heard a lot of noise coming from next door. At the time, her mind wouldn't have jumped straight to murder. But when a stranger showed up covered in blood, knocking on her door, demanding she open up, could she be blamed for thinking he was a madman on a killing spree or a killer seeking out witnesses?

"I did call the police," Ashley snapped.

Later, Liam would realize that was why they had arrived so soon after he had called them.

Right now, though, all Liam could think was that he'd made a mistake. He shouldn't have come here. Ashley was never going to change her mind. "I'm sorry," he said, trying to make a quick exit. "I know this has been hard on you. I wanted you to know what happened, that's all. I won't bother you again."

Liam turned around and, before he made even one step down the hall, he heard the door slam and deadbolt lock.

He dropped his head and sighed. He was starting to understand why the police thought he was guilty. The text messages pointed to motive. The means and opportunity were both easy enough to establish. As for timing, if his cell phone records alone didn't tie that up, Ashley's testimony would.

He didn't know what Patricia had planned for his defense, but it better be good.

The Tall Man

THE TALL MAN FOLLOWED Liam to Elise's building at a safe distance, always keeping at least one car between them. He watched Liam enter the lobby from inside his car. He checked the digital display above the elevator to see which floor Liam had gone to. He scouted the hallways of the fourth floor. Slow and silent. He peered around a corner and saw Liam standing in front of a door, knocking. He pressed his back flat to the wall and listened.

A muffed voice spoke from the behind the door. The Tall Man couldn't make out the words.

"Ashley Carlson?" Liam said.

Another muffled response. Eventually, Ashley opened the door. He listened to the exchange and was pleased with how it went. When Liam apologized, signaling the end of the conversation, the Tall Man returned the way he had come, hiding in another hallway until Liam left. Then he, too, stopped by Ashley's apartment and knocked.

"I'm done talking to you!" she shouted. "If you don't go away, I really will call the police. You hear me?"

"He's gone."

The Tall Man saw the peephole darken as Ashley looked through it. He heard the rattle of the security chain, the click of the deadbolt.

She cracked the door and made eye contact with him.

"You handled that well," he said.

"What are you doing here?"

"Just keeping an eye on things. Doing my civic duty. I think the police might want to know about Liam's visit, don't you?"

Squeezed between the door and the frame, Ashley continued to stare at the Tall Man, but said nothing.

That was okay. She didn't have to. He could tell from the look on her face that she'd gotten the message. Since he had nothing else to say, the Tall Man turned and walked away.

Liam Parker

LIAM WAS BARELY TWO blocks away from Elise's building when his phone rang. He answered, routing the call through the Tesla's speakers.

"It's Anita," the caller announced. "You came to my sister's funeral."

Liam remembered the family gathered around Elise's grave. This had to be the young woman with a scar on her cheek. "My mom's been pretty upset. I mean, she hasn't been herself since Elise disappeared. But since her death—well, I'm sure you can imagine. Anyway, she wanted to talk to you. I guess she's looking for closure or something."

Liam was surprised to hear from anybody in Elise's family, and not just because of how they had acted at the funeral. Certainly they knew he had been charged with Elise's murder, even if they hadn't seen it in the paper. Bash would have told them.

After a couple of seconds, he settled on a simple, "Why?"

"You mean why does she want to speak to you?"

"That's exactly what I mean."

"We haven't seen Elise in six years. We haven't even gotten so much as a phone call. But, Mom and I, we don't think the person who killed her would come to her funeral, passing out his business card and asking to talk to us. There's a place to eat at the corner of Park and Third. It's called The Griddle. Are you free this morning?"

Liam felt a warmth well up inside him that nearly brought him to tears. Sure, David believed him. But Liam had started to wonder if he might be the only one. Even Patricia had her doubts; she'd basically said as much at the jail. But Anita and her mother more than anyone had reason to blame him and they didn't. "Yeah, I guess so. I can be there in an hour."

The truth was, Liam didn't know how much help he could be. The more he learned about Elise, the less he knew. But, as one parent to another, he wanted to do what he could to provide Elise's mother some solace.

Liam arrived at The Griddle ten minutes early. The diner was chrome-everything and had an honest-to-God jukebox. Anita and her mother were already there. He joined them at their booth. Anita's mom looked frail. Her eyes and nose were red from crying. Once again the arch of her eyebrows and her high cheekbones reminded him of Elise.

Anita was wearing a black motorcycle jacket, zipped up. Her skin was darker than her sister's. She had long black fingernails and a don't-fuck-with-me look that seemed to have more to do with genetics than attitude.

Both women were drinking tea. A collection of discarded tea bags, wet napkins, and open sugar packets had been pushed to the corner of the table.

The mother held out her hand and Liam shook it. In a high-pitched voice that had a bit of a quiver, she thanked him for coming. She didn't tell him her name, which he figured was an oversight and let it slide. This would probably be the only conversation he ever had with her.

She looked at Anita. "Remember not to say anything to your father about this."

Anita patted her mother's forearm. "I know, Mom."

The mother turned her attention back to Liam. "He would not like me to talking to you."

Liam wasn't surprised. He couldn't expect everyone in Elise's family to believe in him. "So what do you want to know?"

"You and Elise were dating?" the mother asked.

"Yes, for two months."

"And you said she was working in advertising?"

Liam nodded. He had decided it would be best to keep up the lie.

"She came a long way," the mother said to Anita proudly. "What was she like?"

"She was one of the nicest people I ever met," Liam said. He could tell from the mother's face she wanted something more meaningful. What boyfriend wouldn't say that? So he elaborated. "She had this sort of motherly instinct when it came to animals. There was this one time when we had dinner reservations and were running late. When we stepped outside her apartment building, I didn't pay any attention to the stray cat that was circling the bushes. All I could think was that if we didn't get to the restaurant soon they'd give away our table. But she did. She stopped and asked me to be quiet. 'Did you hear that?' she said. I didn't hear anything. I said we needed to hurry, but she wouldn't let it go. She told me to hold on while she shooed the cat away and looked into the bushes, where she found this small gray bird. Elise was worried it was hurt, so we took it to McAllister Animal Shelter." Liam paused the story as he remembered the night and smiled. "Our dinner ending up being McDonald's, and we ate it at the shelter while we waited for them to examine the bird. They said we didn't have to stay, but Elise wanted to know it would be all right before we left."

"Was it?"

"They said it'd be fine."

The mother smiled too.

"And Elise was smart. She was always reading. It didn't matter what it was. Newspapers, paperbacks, biographies. Just about everything. I think her favorites were books on psychology. She had two shelves dedicated to them, and those were just the ones she liked enough to buy. Most books she checked out of the library. One of her favorite authors was Patrick Ainsworth."

"Really?" her mother said, surprised.

"She never read when she was living at home," Anita added. "She was always out with her friends doing who-knows-what. There's all kinds of trouble you can get into in Uptown."

Uptown was a neighborhood north of The Loop, and a good long way from Oak Park, which was where Liam had grown up and where Elise had told him she had.

"Uptown? When did you live there?"

"Why?" Anita asked.

Liam shrugged. "Just curious."

"We always lived there," the mother said. "Still do."

Liam hadn't expected this conversation to reveal another lie, but there it was. He wasn't sure what to do with it, so for now he filed it away with the others. When they were done talking and on their way out of the diner, Liam asked the women if they'd be willing to stop by Patricia's office one day.

Anita was holding her mother's arm to steady her as they headed toward a beat-up VW Jetta with a missing headlight. "What for?" she asked.

"I think she'd be interested in talking to you about my defense. She might even want to put you on the stand. That is, if you wouldn't mind. Since you two believe I wouldn't come to the funeral passing out my business card if I was guilty, the jury might, as well."

"I don't know," the mother said. Anita opened the passenger door for her and she directed her gaze at her daughter. "I'm not sure it'd be such a good idea. Your father wouldn't like it."

Anita rolled her eyes and closed the passenger door after her mother got in. With her mother out of earshot, Anita said defiantly, "I'll do it."

Liam had expected that a no from the mother was a no from both. "Are you sure?"

"I might not know what happened to my sister that night, but I know you didn't kill her. I'll help you."

Liam Parker

LIAM HUNG AROUND DAVID'S condo, killing time. His only breaks from the monotony were the walks outside with Chloe and his meeting with Patricia on Tuesday. Ryan Reyes was also in attendance. This time, Patricia had only introduced him as her PI, but the alliteration had made his name easy to remember.

The three of them sat around a large conference table. The doors to the conference room were closed, sealing them off from the rest of the Flores and Washington suite.

Ryan, who was leaning back in his chair, legs and arms crossed, looked to be in his early thirties. He was lean and in good shape. His hair was neatly parted to the right. He was dressed in a suit, sans jacket. His tie was loose, his shirt sleeves rolled halfway up his forearms. A tattoo peeked out from underneath one of them.

Patricia sat perched at the edge of her chair, laptop in front of her and fingers poised over the keyboard. She recited the facts of the case and said their best defense—their only defense—would be the truth.

Ryan listened quietly, his eyes darting between Patricia and Liam as if he were watching a tennis match.

"The best thing you have going for you is your credibility. You run a reputable firm that employs over a hundred people. You're likable. You're trustworthy. Except for a bar fight in college, you have no history of violence."

"That was a mistake. I wasn't—"

"The case the police have built is entirely circumstantial," Patricia continued, barreling forward. "If we can make even one member of the jury doubt the prosecution's story, we can get a mistrial at a minimum."

Liam didn't like the way that sounded. He was expecting something more aggressive than honesty. An alternate theory, perhaps. Maybe even a guess as to who the real killer was. Wasn't that why Ryan was here? To dig up some information they could use to finger someone else?

"Are you sure that's the best way to go?" he said. "If we get a mistrial, can't they try me again?"

"Yes, but it doesn't mean that's what will happen. And even if it does, it's better than a guilty verdict."

"Would it help if we put Elise's sister on the stand?"

"How would that help?" Patricia said.

"She thinks I'm innocent. I thought if—"

"How do you know she thinks you're innocent?"

"I met with her over the weekend, and—"

"You *what?*" Patricia's ruddy complexion darkened. "I don't want you out there talking to anybody. It's a bad idea. Trust me."

"You don't think she'd be helpful?"

"Unless she was there when Elise died, then no, I don't. Let's set aside the reality that her opinion is just that—an opinion, but what happens if she gets up on the stand and changes her mind? We need to focus on your reputation and the facts. There's no debating that Elise was alive shortly before you arrived, that you were found with her blood on you, or that you were the only one seen coming or going from her apartment."

Liam shifted uncomfortably in his seat, thinking about his

conversation with the neighbor. He should tell Patricia about that at some point, too, but this didn't seem like the best time.

"The only people we need to put on the stand are those who can cast doubt on the prosecution's theory—forensics experts, people who can speak to your reputation and, this is what we need to be focused on, your whereabouts. Because we have two big problems with our defense. First, you told the police you were at home, which you weren't. So where were you?"

Liam leaned forward. He clasped his hands together, intertwining his fingers, and squeezed. He had to tell them. "Okay, look, there's a woman who hosts a poker game over in Lakeview. I was there."

If the news concerned Patricia, she didn't show it. "All right. We'll figure out how to deal with that later. Let's discuss our second problem. The prosecution is going to claim you found out Elise was seeing someone else and killed her because of it."

Liam wasn't surprised. He remembered Bash laying out that same theory for him after he was arrested. Although there wasn't anything to say, he felt like he needed to say something, and the words that came out were: "You know that's not true." They sounded defensive and he regretted them as soon as he said them.

"Ryan has been doing some digging on our behalf. Elise doesn't have much of a paper trail. No credit cards, no bank statements, no work history. The one and only apartment he found in her name was the one she died in."

"I did get ahold of her phone records," Ryan added, finally speaking.

"And?" Liam pressed.

"Apparently the theory isn't so farfetched," Patricia said.

"What do you mean?" Liam said. Although the implication was clear, it seemed impossible to him. Despite all her lies, he still believed their relationship had been real. He figured he had to be missing the point.

But he wasn't, and when Ryan said, "Looks like she was indeed seeing someone else," a powerful cocktail of shock and denial powered through Liam's system like a locomotive.

Christopher Bell

CHRIS PUSHED THE THIEF'S bedroom door open far enough to see the cracked window and knew he was gone. He was livid. He didn't think about the risk he was taking by being in this apartment. (If the thief called the police to report a B&E, his career—his whole life— would be over.) All he thought about was the ring and where the thief might have put it.

He and Arkin turned the apartment upside down, dumping everything out of the drawers and cabinets, toppling furniture, checking every pocket in every article of clothing. They found several loose coins, mostly pennies, and came across a folded and worn photo in the back pocket of a pair of jeans, but no ring. Or not the ring he was looking for, anyway.

Chris hadn't gotten a good look at the thief on the CTA video and barely remembered what he looked like—skinny, white, average height. He wasn't a redhead and his hair wasn't jet black either. To be any more precise than that, he'd be guessing. But that alone was enough to know the thief wasn't among those in the photo he found. The man in it was older, balding, sitting next to a woman who held an infant in her lap.

When Chris gave up his search, he felt defeated. Emma chastised him for his failure. She told him he should have expected the thief to go out the window. "If I'd been there," she said, "I would've told Arkin to wait outside, just in case something like that happened."

"You're going to Monday-morning quarterback this thing?"

"Call it what you want, but you screwed this up royally. We're never going to get that ring back now."

Although Chris didn't say as much to Emma at the time, he refused to accept that. He'd get the ring back. If he couldn't, he'd get revenge. It only seemed fair. When the thief had stolen it, Chris felt violated. He'd wanted the thief to go to jail and had wanted the ring back because it was expensive. Now he had a more personal reason, as well—Emma. She was disappointed in him. If he didn't make things right, she'd always be disappointed in him.

The only question was how.

Liam Parker

LIAM COULDN'T STOP THINKING about the mystery man Elise had been dating. Ryan hadn't been able to tell him much but the quantity of texts and phone calls the two had exchanged. As far as suspects went, though, it didn't make any difference. The police had questioned him and ruled him out.

After two more days stuck in David's condo, watching TV and thinking about Elise, Liam couldn't take it anymore. He needed to direct his attention elsewhere for a while. His trial was six months away and he couldn't put his entire life on hold until then.

He decided to swing by ConnectPlus to pick up his computer. A quick in and out. Although he'd agreed it was best to let David run the place on his own for the time being, that didn't mean he had to remain entirely uninvolved. If Liam had his computer, he could monitor the business in a way he couldn't without it. Unlike David, he knew how to use the data to look for sales opportunities and warning signs. It was only smart he use that knowledge to help David steer the ship in his absence.

Liam made it to his office with little more than a few awkward hellos. He unplugged his laptop, stuffed it into his computer bag, and was about to leave when his phone rang. He pulled his cell out of his pocket and answered.

"What the hell were you thinking?" Patricia demanded. "You spoke to the state's witness. Are you crazy?"

"Who are you talking about?"

"Who am I—Jesus, Liam, how many people did you talk to?"

Then Liam realized Patricia had to mean Ashley Carlson. Before he could say as much, Patricia said, "Elise's neighbor. Did you go by her apartment to try to get her to change her story?"

"I wanted her to know what really happened," Liam said defensively. He had left the door to his office open. Several employees on the other side had stopped what they were doing to listen.

"I told you not to speak to anybody."

"I know. This was before—"

"Why didn't you tell me? It doesn't matter. The judge is revoking your bail."

He turned toward the tall windows behind his desk, seeking privacy. "He can't do that."

"If he thinks you were trying to influence her testimony, he absolutely can."

Liam pressed one hand to the glass to steady himself. He saw a line of police cars two blocks away and headed in his direction.

Patricia took a deep breath to calm herself down. "Are you at home?"

"No, not right now."

"Okay, I think Detective Wyatt's going to let you turn yourself in. I want you to go home, get your affairs in order, and then call me back."

Nearly frozen with fear, Liam watched the police cars get closer and closer still. He nodded and, feeling like he had responded, hung up.

He left his laptop on his desk and hurried to the elevator, ignoring the eyes on him. As he descended the floors alone, he told himself he was going home, following Patricia's instructions. But something deep and primal was screaming out, demanding he run as far and as fast as he could.

The police have somebody watching you, that voice said. Despite what Patricia had told him, they knew where he was and they were coming.

The elevator doors opened. As Liam stepped off and rounded the corner toward the lobby, the four police cars he'd seen from a distance pulled up to the curb, lights flashing. Any doubts he had they were coming for him were gone. Bash stepped out of one, uniformed officers stepped out of the others.

Liam moved back into the alcove that housed the elevators before anybody saw him. That primal instinct to run was growing stronger. He needed a second to think. Giving in to that instinct would be crazy. If he ran, if he dodged and weaved and managed to avoid getting caught, he would become a criminal for real, even if evading arrest was his only crime.

But so what? He had unwittingly destroyed any chance Patricia's defense had by talking to the neighbor. And she herself had said she didn't have a better strategy. If he went to jail now, he might never get out. That terrified him. He couldn't imagine living the rest of his life the way he had those two days awaiting his arraignment. His only chance was . . . was what? Then it came to him—his only chance was to find the real killer, and it looked like he was going to have to do that on his own.

From the elevators, Liam only had access to the twentieth floor. Returning to ConnectPlus would be as useless for his escape as staying where he was. He needed to find another way out.

He glanced around frantically, seeing nothing that would help him and reconstructing the layout of the ground floor in his mind. On the other side of the alcove, closer to the lobby, there was a mail drop. Along the back wall, partially visible from the street, was a stairwell.

That might work, he thought.

Reaching it without being seen would require a little luck. But since he had no other choice, Liam made a run for it. There was no reason to be cautious, peering around the corner to see where the cops were and weighing his odds of success. Either they'd see him or they wouldn't, and if they did, a full-out sprint was his best chance of getting away.

He slammed through the door and took the stairs down. He hoped they would lead to a loading dock at the back of the building or a basement where he could hide. And perhaps they did indeed lead to one of those places. But since for Liam, they stopped at a door secured by a wall-mounted scanner, it didn't matter where they went.

He stayed there for a minute or so, crouching down and doing his best to hide, in case any of the cops came in after him. When they didn't, Liam was confident he had made it to the stairwell unseen.

He quietly eased back up the stairs to the ground floor. He wiped the sweat off his forehead using the sleeve of his overcoat. He placed one hand on the doorknob, slowly turned it, and hesitated. He imagined coming face-to-face with Bash when he cracked the door open to see if the coast was clear. But having ruled out the stairwell, the lobby was his only way out. He breathed in through his nose, out through his mouth, and pushed the door forward an inch. No cops. Another inch. Still no cops. He had been certain there would be at least one—a lookout Bash had left behind—but they must all be on their way to the twentieth floor.

A group of well-dressed office workers stepped out of the elevator alcove. Acting on instinct, Liam blended in behind them, keeping his head down and the collar of his overcoat up.

As he approached the revolving door, he noticed two cops standing outside by their cruisers. So that was where Bash had placed his lookouts. If Liam was going to make a clean escape, he was going to have to get past them unnoticed. He kept his pace slow so as not to draw attention, pulled out his phone, and held it to one ear to further obscure his face. Out of the corner of his eye, he could see them watching him as he turned left onto the sidewalk and melded into the throngs of foot traffic.

One tapped the arm of the other and pointed in Liam's direction. Liam picked up his pace. He glanced over his shoulder and saw the second cop had pulled out his radio. He didn't have to be a genius to know the cop was saying something about him.

Liam pushed his way through the pedestrians and around the corner. The cops started to move, closing in fast. They shouted for people to get out of the way, for Liam to stop.

There'd be no losing the cops on foot. Thankfully his car was parked in a four-story lot at the end of the street. If he could get to it, he'd be home free. Until then, the best he could do was stay far enough ahead of them so that they couldn't catch him.

Liam slammed through a gray metal door that took him into the parking lot's stairwell. Last time he'd looked back, he had a forty-foot lead. The time before that it had been fifty. He took the steps two at a time. The stairwell smelled like urine. The handrail was chipped and sticky. Once on the third floor, Liam went through another metal door. This one was red and was marked with a large "N3."

His car was parked midway along the back row. He reached it without getting caught, jumped in, slammed the gearshift into reverse, and took off. As he wound his way down to the first floor, ignoring the directional signs that would take him longer to reach the exit, he was overcome with the uneasy feeling that he'd been outmaneuvered. The cops should have been right behind him. Liam should have seen them when he was backing out of his parking spot. He should have heard them on the stairwell. But he hadn't, and when he reached the exit, he found out why.

Liam Parker

STANDING BEHIND THE MECHANICAL arm that separated the parking lot from Michigan Avenue, the two officers drew their guns. Liam slowed to a stop.

"Get out of the car, Mr. Parker! Get out of the car, now!"

Liam licked his lips and tapped his fingers on the steering wheel. He squinted in the sunlight that reflected off the Bank of America across the street. There wasn't anywhere for him to go but through that gate. He was either doing it on foot with the cops or alone in his car.

One of the officers stepped forward. "Mr. Parker!"

When Liam had decided to run, he'd imagined an easy escape and a hero's welcome after he showed the police who the real killer was. The first part of that fantasy had already been blown to hell. The second part might be also, if he kept running. Because the only way to keep running would be to slam his foot down on the gas and trust those two cops to get out of the way.

He tightened his hands on the steering wheel. There was really only one choice, wasn't there?

In case the cops didn't move fast enough, Liam tapped the brakes as the mechanical arm splintered. They dove safely into the bushes that flanked the exit and Liam careened onto the road. Drivers honked, slammed on their brakes. He slowed at the red light in front of him, but didn't stop. There was a gap in the crossing traffic. He seized it, and turned right, heading for Lakeshore Drive.

While Liam figured the police would put out an APB for his car, he wanted to put some distance between himself and the scene before dumping it.

The city was dirtier and uglier on the west side of Chicago than it was along the river. Liam pulled into a cracked parking lot that was shared by CVS and Petco. The frigid air had blown discarded shopping bags, candy wrappers, paper cups, napkins, and other trash up against the fence surrounding it. A sign at the entrance said spots were reserved for shoppers only. "ALL OTHERS WILL BE TOWED," it announced in big red letters.

That was going to include Liam's Tesla sooner or later. It had been thirty-eight minutes since he'd left his office. As much as he didn't want to leave his car there, he couldn't risk holding onto it any longer.

Liam withdrew a few hundred dollars out of the ATM. His phone chirped an alert. He pulled it out of his pocket to take a look. He had a voicemail from David and a text message from a number he didn't know. Liam didn't have to listen to the voicemail to know it had something to do with Bash showing up at ConnectPlus.

The text message read: *U need to disappear. Call me. I can help.*

Liam looked at it for several seconds, trying to figure out who might have sent it, when his phone rang. The number calling him was the same one from which the text had come. This wasn't right. He needed to disappear, but who would be calling him offering help? It smelled wrong. Liam turned off his phone and put it in his glovebox. He wasn't sure the police could trace the phone's location if it was off, but holding onto it seemed like too big of a risk.

He went into the CVS and asked where he could find a hotel. The cashier told him there was a Comfort Inn six blocks away.

But the Comfort Inn wanted an ID and a credit card on file. Since Liam planned to check in under an assumed name, he walked to two more hotels—both names he didn't know. While one called Holiday Home didn't care to keep a credit card on file, they both wanted IDs. Going with the lesser of two evils, he checked into Holiday Home. At least it mitigated his risk. The clerk gave him the key to a room on the second floor and told him the elevator was out.

The room overlooked an alley where a homeless man slept, bundled up in blankets and leaning against the side of a dumpster. There was peeling paisley wallpaper along the edge of the ceiling and an unidentifiable stain on the carpet Liam made sure to step around.

He sat down on the corner of the bed, reluctant to touch even that much of it. The room was unusually hot. He undid the top button on his shirt and rolled up his sleeves. For the first time since he'd decided to run, Liam had a chance to think. If he was going to find Elise's killer, he'd have to start with what he knew, and what he knew was this: Elise had run away from home. Before that, she'd been hanging with a bad crowd. Something had happened that caused her to change her name. Patricia Harrison was probably right—Elise had probably done it to leave her past behind. So far, everything tracked.

What about the text messages though? Why were those deleted? And why did she lie about her job and where she grew up?

Liam still couldn't answer those questions, so he decided not to dwell on them. He had to focus on the pieces that made sense for now.

He thought some more about why Elise had changed her last name. Since she hadn't done it legally, she wasn't hiding from the possession or prostitution charges. Those would show up on any criminal background check. That meant she wasn't necessarily hiding something about her past but hiding from something in it.

Perhaps some*one*.

He needed to talk to Elise's sister. He had to find out more about the crowd she was hanging out with before she ran away from home. If he could trace her life from then forward, he believed he could find her killer.

But first he needed a new ID, not to mention a new look and name to go with it. He had no idea where this investigation would take him. If he ever had to get into a building like his, he wasn't going to get past the security desk simply on his charm. These days, he couldn't even rent a room in a sketchy hotel on only his charm. And since the odds were good he'd make front page news for a while, he couldn't keep flashing his real ID around town.

Liam didn't know anything about fake IDs or where to get one. People who could get him something like that didn't advertise. Well, not anywhere Liam had ever seen.

He thought about the text—*U need to disappear*—and the call that had come in seconds before he turned off his phone. Both unnerved him, but that message sounded a lot like somebody who could help him get what he was after. Perhaps they wouldn't seem so strange if he knew who was trying to reach him. He should have answered the call.

Maybe . . .

He double-timed his way down the stairs without finishing the thought.

"What's the rush?" the guy at the front desk said as Liam ran toward the double doors at the front of the hotel. It had been an hour since he left his car in the lot, and a truck from XF Towing was already there. The driver had hooked up Liam's Tesla and was sitting in the cab, working the controls that would pull it onto the bed.

Liam banged on his door. "Hey! Hold on!"

Startled, the driver jerked his head up. There was a screech and a hiss and Liam's car stopped moving. The driver rolled down the window. His thick, unkempt beard hid the collar of his plaid shirt. "I gotta do it, buddy." He held out a business card. "You can come get it later today."

"Yeah, I know." Liam took the card. "I have to get something, okay?"

The driver shook his head. "I don't know. Not supposed to do that. How do I know it's your car?"

Liam pulled his keys out of his pocket. He held them up so the driver could see him press the lock button on the fob. The Tesla beeped and its lights flashed.

The driver mulled it over. He nodded toward the back of the truck. "All right, go ahead."

"Thanks." Liam scrambled over to the Tesla and grabbed his phone out of the glovebox. "That's it. I'm done. She's all yours."

Without a word, the driver rolled back up his window and started the crank.

Liam found the text and moved to the other end of the parking lot for some privacy.

Liam Parker

"HELLO, LIAM," A VOICE said.

Liam recognized that voice immediately. It was the dealer from Ava's. "Jacob?" He had so many questions that they tumbled over each other, cutting each down to a word or two, until he landed on, "How did you get my number?" His phone number was unlisted.

"That's not the question you need to be asking."

A cold breeze cut through the lot and Liam turned his back to it. "How did you know—"

"About the arrest?" Jacob said. "It doesn't matter. Now, listen to me. I can help you disappear, but you don't have a lot of time. Sooner or later, the police are going to find you. There's a bar downtown called Backstage. Meet me there at nine o'clock."

"You can get me a fake ID?"

"Bring a thousand dollars in cash and I'll take care of you."

It sounded like a lot for what Liam wanted, but he wasn't in a position to haggle over the price. He glanced around the trash-strewn parking lot in front of the CVS, saw the brake lights on the back of the tow truck flash as the vehicle started to move. "Okay." Jacob hung up, and Liam glanced down at his cell, staring at it as if it were a foreign object.

The whole thing felt surreal, and he asked himself the same question he'd asked Jacob: *How did he know about the arrest?* Then he asked himself another: *Why is he offering to help?* He knew he wasn't going to get an answer to either question—not at the bar, not even if he called Jacob back and demanded one. Besides, what would it change if he did? He still needed that ID and Jacob was the only person he knew who could get it for him. Maybe, when this was all over, Jacob would fill in these mysterious blanks. For the time being, Liam would have to let them go.

He tried to decide what to do with his phone. The tow truck was gone, so there was no putting it back in his car. That left only one option. Liam reluctantly turned it off and dropped it into the trash can in front of the CVS.

At least my data is backed up, he thought, and went into the pharmacy to buy a TracFone with one hundred prepaid minutes and Internet access. (He'd realized he'd need to stay connected if he wanted to get anything done.) He also bought black hair dye and a pair of sunglasses.

After he withdrew more money from the ATM, he stopped at a More Than Sneakers for Nikes and a Goodwill for clothes.

Liam found a pair of jeans that fit, which was the only requirement he had, and an oversized army jacket. He was flipping through shirts on one of a dozen circular racks, looking for something nondescript and preferably gray, when he ran across a Teenage Mutant Ninja tee similar to the one his son had been wearing, and wondered if he'd ever see Tommy again. If he was arrested before he could prove his innocence, he doubted it. Catherine would take the kids straight to Mississippi, and by the time Tommy could come see Liam on his own, she might have convinced him it wasn't worth his time.

Liam couldn't think about that. It wasn't going to do him any good. He had to focus on the task at hand. He moved on to the next shirt and flipped past ten more before he found what he was looking for.

Christopher Bell

CHRIS'S OFFICE WAS A shrine to sports fandom. Among the collection of paraphernalia, he had a pair of mint-condition baseball cards—"Shoeless" Joe Jackson and Pete Rose—framed and hanging behind his desk; a Michael Jordan Bulls jersey, also framed; a photo of Wayne Gretzky closing in on the goal, and a football signed by the entire Northwestern team, including Eric Ricci.

He had four computer monitors mounted to stands on his desk and a fifth on the wall above his door that monitored the movements of selected stocks in real time.

Chris closed the door and pulled up an internal application that would let him check the thief's credit report. This wasn't something Chris was supposed to do, but he doubted anybody at Ellison Trust would find out.

Ellison Trust had made an aggressive push to expand their credit card business two years ago. They'd offered cards with limits as low as five hundred dollars and had run an advertising campaign through every regional media outlet. Chris was hoping his thief had signed up for one.

As luck would have it, he had.

It appeared to be one of two credit cards the man carried, and it had a zero balance. Chris called over to Retail Banking and said he had a client who wanted to sign up for alerts. Any amount. Then he provided an email address that was, in fact, his, and prayed the thief would use his card soon. One charge might be all Chris needed to find him.

Liam Parker

LIAM DYED HIS HAIR in the hotel bathroom, changed his clothes, and killed time watching CNN, which spent most of their airtime talking about the war in Syria and a congressional spending bill. A guest named Christopher Bell commented on the state of the stock market. Liam's name didn't come up.

He left the hotel looking and feeling like a new man. His disguise wasn't so thorough that he was entirely unrecognizable. But with black hair spiked up, eyebrows dyed to match, sunglasses, and clothes he wouldn't normally wear, even his friends would have to look twice to know for sure it was him.

Backstage turned out to be a dimly lit hole in the wall. There was a coin-operated pool table in the back. Neon signs advertising a wide variety of beer hung behind the bar and in the windows. He found Jacob sitting at a table in the corner.

Before they could get down to business, a waitress appeared to take Liam's drink order. He asked for a Heineken just to get rid of her.

"You look like a douchebag in those sunglasses," Jacob said once she was gone.

Liam shrugged. He was pretty sure Jacob was right.

"You got the money?"

Liam pulled an envelope of cash out of the pocket of his army jacket and handed it over. The envelope he had gotten from the hotel's front desk and had the name Holiday Home printed in the upper-left corner. The bills inside were loose, impossible to count at a glance, but Jacob appeared satisfied with barely a peek.

"So, how do we do this?" Liam asked. "Do you have a guy—"

Like Liam had pulled the cash out of his coat, Jacob took a stack of items from the pocket of his and placed them on the table. They included a driver's license, a plane ticket, and a passport.

Liam had assumed the bar was simply a meeting place, that they'd go from there to another location where his picture would be taken and any documents prepared. He was also only expecting a driver's license. A thousand dollars didn't seem like so much when he considered everything on the table.

He picked up the license. The name on it was Richard Hawthorne. Liam recognized the photo as a headshot from the ConnectPlus website. He hadn't realized until now how much it had in common with those used on government IDs.

Jacob had used the same photo for the passport. The ticket was for Belarus. "They don't have an extradition treaty with the US. You leave tomorrow night. After that, you'll figure it out."

If Liam was going anywhere, he probably *would* figure it out. He'd get to Belarus, then transfer the money from his bank accounts in the US through a series of countries until it became untraceable. Not exactly easy-peasy, but doable.

Of course, he'd never be getting on that plane. That was not why he started this.

The waitress showed up with a bottle of Heineken. Liam scooped up the documents and palmed them under the table. She smiled, giving no indication she'd noticed the suspicious behavior. "Here you go, hon."

Liam took a sip of the beer.

"Where are you staying?" Jacob asked.

He shrugged. "Don't know." With a new name at his disposal, he didn't have any reason to go back to the hotel he was in before, and why would he want to?

"Then I've got one more thing for you." Jacob placed the keycard for a room at a Best Western on the table. "State Street. It's already paid for. You can stay there until it's time for your flight."

The extent of his generosity made Liam uncomfortable. "Why are you doing all this?"

"You paid for it."

"It's a lot more than I expected."

Jacob stood. "If I were you, I wouldn't think too much about it, okay?" He zipped up his jacket. "Just say thank you." Then he left. He weaved around a couple of biker types at the pool table and dropped some cash on the waitress's tray on his way out the door.

Liam, on the other hand, wasn't in any hurry. Sitting in this bar was the safest he'd felt in a while. He considered what Jacob had said—*don't think too much about it*—and looked at the license again, this time examining it closely. It passed the eyeball test. He placed it side by side with his real one for a closer examination. Every detail checked out.

He wondered if Ava had something to do with this. Liam wouldn't be surprised if she was paying off the cops to make sure they didn't bother her, and that would mean she had contacts inside the department. Maybe Ava's app also gave her access to his phone number.

But the theory strained credulity to the point that even Liam, who wanted an explanation, couldn't buy it. If Ava had contacts in the Chicago PD, how would they know Liam was one of her players? And if they did, why would they tell her they were going to arrest him? Even more importantly, why would Ava care?

Jacob Reed

JACOB DIDN'T OWN A car, but since he knew he would need one after his meeting with Liam, he had rented a black Ford Focus. It was in that Ford Focus, half a block from Backstage, where he sat now. He had a clear view of the entrance to the bar. While he waited for Liam to exit, he fiddled with the heat, turning it up, down, and back up again. The temperature was never too hot or too cold. The act of adjusting it was something akin to a nervous twitch.

Liam appeared and got in a cab. Jacob followed from a safe distance, always keeping at least one car between them. While he didn't expect to be made since Liam had no reason to think Jacob was following him, he wasn't taking any chances.

The cab pulled up in front of the Best Western and Liam got out. With the momentum of traffic pushing him along the congested downtown streets, Jacob couldn't stay where he was long enough to watch Liam go inside, but he didn't need to. It was obvious Liam had decided to use the hotel room Jacob had rented for him.

Satisfied, Jacob returned to his own hotel. He had rented a room at a Best Western for himself as well, only his was on the other side of town, close to Liam's condo.

The room was clean and quiet. It had red carpet, a single queen bed, dressed all in white, and a small desk with a leather chair and a matching dresser on the other side of the room.

Jacob sat down at the desk, opened his laptop, and went to work. There wasn't a photo of Richard Hawthorne anywhere online. He'd never been on Facebook, Twitter, or LinkedIn. He'd never posted a picture on Instagram.

It was time for that to change.

Jacob spent a lot of hours opening accounts and adding strangers as friends. (It was amazing how many people would accept friend requests from someone they'd never met.) He posted pictures of Liam under Richard Hawthorne's name. He commented, liked, and shared until he felt like Richard had a solid web presence.

Then he set his alarm for nine a.m. and got four solid hours of shut eye.

Liam Parker

LIAM'S ROOM WAS A mirror image of Jacob's. He anxiously paced the carpet trying to figure out what to do. He had the TV on for company and the curtains closed.

Twice, he picked up the phone to call his kids and decided it was a bad idea. Then he decided it would be a bad idea not to. Depending on how all this played out, who knew how many more times he'd get to speak with them? He dialed his wife's home number.

His son answered. Liam asked how school was going and Tommy said fine. Yes, he was keeping up with his homework. Yes, he was paying attention in class. "Our teacher taught us how storms are made. Do you know?" Liam said he did, and Tommy told him anyway.

When they were done, Liam told Tommy he loved him and asked to speak to his sister. Alice answered each question with as few words as possible and a distracted tone. She sounded like she had something else on her mind. Eventually, Liam found out what it was.

"Dad, what's going on? Did you . . . Why are you accused of . . . ?"

He knew what she was trying to say and did his best to put her mind at ease. "They got me mixed up with someone else. Don't worry about it. Everything's going to be fine."

The answer didn't satisfy Alice. She pressed for more details, which Liam refused to give. But he did give her the number to the phone he was using, having decided at least one of his kids should have it in case there was an emergency.

As he was getting out the word "emergency," Catherine took the phone from her daughter.

"What the hell have you gotten yourself mixed up in?" she asked.

He tried to answer, to calm her down, but she barely let him get out two words before she was tearing into him again.

"I don't want to hear it. I wish I'd never met you. I can't wait to get the kids as far from you as possible. You're a hot mess."

Catherine hung up. Liam dropped the phone onto the desk. Well, that didn't go the way he'd hoped it would. At least he'd gotten to tell Tommy he loved him. For now, that would have to be enough.

It was time to call Anita. But, he realized Anita's number was, along with his iPhone, in the CVS trashcan, so he logged into Facebook using his burner, searched for her name, and scrolled through a long list of results until he found one with a photo that matched the woman he was looking for. Liam sent a friend request and a message asking if she would be available to meet at the diner tomorrow morning.

After a moment of deliberation, he added: *I'm going to find Elise's killer. I need your help.*

He hoped the addition would generate a quick response, but none came.

While Liam waited, he took a shower and ordered a burger from room service. Even with his new look, he wasn't interested in being out in public more than necessary. He ate his dinner in front of the TV, then, still without an answer from Anita, reluctantly went to bed.

Liam stared at the ceiling for a long time. He wasn't sure what he would do if she never responded.

Liam Parker

LIAM SAW A FACEBOOK message from Anita when he woke up saying she would meet him at the diner at eleven. He checked the digital clock on the bedside table. That was two hours from now.

I'll be there, he responded.

He took the same booth he'd sat at before and ordered coffee to keep the waitress at bay. He watched the window. Anita's VW was easy to spot. The missing headlight was not the only thing wrong with it. The car was tan, but the rear door on the driver's side was blue, suggesting it had been a junkyard replacement. Two hubcaps were missing and one of the mirrors was cracked.

She drove into the lot, taking the corner a little too fast, popping one wheel up and over the curb, and parked by the door.

Liam went out to the parking lot to meet her. He wasn't sure Anita would recognize him and didn't want to draw attention by waving to her when she came inside.

Anita got out of the car. She looked Liam over. "What's going on with all this?" she said, gesturing in such a way as to suggest she was talking about Liam's appearance.

"You don't want to know," Liam said.

"I think I do."

With his hands in his pockets, Liam nodded toward the diner. "Come on. I'll buy you something to eat. I need to know what you can tell me about the people Elise was hanging around with before she ran away."

Anita grabbed his arm. "Whoa, whoa, whoa. That's not why I'm here. You think I came to give you information? Think again. I want to know what happened to my sister that night as much as you do. If you're serious about looking for her killer, I'm in."

Liam glanced over both shoulders. "I'm not looking for a partner here."

"Too bad, because it's all or nothing."

She was serious. She wanted to help, and who could blame her? But if he was caught, anyone with him might be charged with aiding and abetting. He didn't want that to happen to Anita. She and her family had suffered enough already. Maybe if he told her, she'd let go of the idea.

"There's something you have to know."

"You mean that you're on the run?" She gestured to his clothes again. "I kinda figured that out."

The door to the diner swung open and two teenage boys exited. They both looked at Anita. One winked. She flipped them the bird. They chuckled and walked away, but were still within earshot when they stopped to light the cigarettes one had taken out of a pack.

"So, do you want my help?"

"You know how it's going to look if I get caught," Liam whispered.

"Do you want my help?" Anita repeated firmly.

Of course he wanted her help. In fact, the more he thought about the idea, the better it sounded. Liam didn't know what he was up against and Anita might prove more valuable than a mere conduit to Elise's past. If she was willing to take the risk, then yes, yes, a thousand times, "Yes."

She gestured to the car. "Get in."

She drove them to Uptown. The neighborhood was being revitalized. New midrise apartment buildings and scattered pockets of upscale shopping were popping up along Lake Michigan. Everyone wanted a view of the water.

They spent most of their time cruising the streets that hadn't seen this influx of cash. Graffiti marred the facades of gas stations and convenience stores. A particularly active artist (if Liam could call him that) had tagged more than two dozen businesses with the handle "Red Bear." Half the pedestrians looked sketchy and a quarter of them looked homeless. Everything seemed a little gray and sagged under the weight of neglect. Although Liam had grown up on streets not much better than these, he still felt out of his element.

"Why does your dad blame himself for Elise?" he asked, remembering that her mother had said as much at the funeral.

"Oh, that. He shouldn't, you know. He just kept telling her to go to school or get a job or do *something* with her life. He said she couldn't keep going out at all hours and sleeping until noon. Nothing good would come of that, he insisted. Elise complained about it a lot, said he needed to stop nagging her. She told me over and over that if he didn't stop she was going to leave and we'd see how he liked that, but I didn't think she really would. I thought it was all talk. Then, one day she was gone. None of us believed it at first. We kept thinking she'd hooked up with some guy"—her eyes cut from the road to Liam— "Sorry. Anyway, we kept thinking she'd come back after a little while. But, you know, she didn't."

"That's not your fault. Or your dad's."

"I suppose. But we all kind of blamed ourselves for a while. I could have helped her get into nursing school, like I did, or gotten her a part-time job at the jewelry shop where I worked before that. I should have done more than just listen to her complain."

Liam knew there was nothing he could say to assuage her guilt. But he said, "I'm sorry," anyway.

Anita wasn't having it. She shot Liam a look that said *Whatever*. He let it go.

They came to a red light. Somebody on a bicycle whizzed past, traffic be damned.

"You're a nurse?"

"Night shift over at Rush Medical. Any idea who you want to talk to?" she asked.

"Not really." Liam realized he was going to have to tell her about the arrests, and now seemed like as good a time as any. "Look, since you're doing this with me there are some things you need to know about Elise that I didn't tell you and your mom at the diner. Before she straightened out her life, she went to a dark place . . ."

Liam paused long enough for Anita to ask, "What do you mean?"

"She was arrested on charges of prostitution and possession."

"That sounds about right," Anita said in a matter-of-fact way. "My brother thought that might happen." She gently touched the scar on her cheek. "He wanted to make sure I didn't do the same thing."

Liam wasn't sure which brother she meant, but the inference was as unmistakable as it was horrifying.

They drove for a while in silence.

"We should talk to Dale," Anita eventually said. "If that's the kind of life she was living, he's probably our best bet."

Liam nodded. "Okay." He expected her to give him more than a name. When she didn't, he asked, "Who's Dale?"

"Back in those days he managed some girls who worked the

Streeterville neighborhood. He and Elise spent a lot of time down at Brewskis. It's a bar a couple of miles from here. That's the kind of stellar company she kept in those days."

Managed some girls. Liam found that to be a charitable description for a pimp and figured Dale had to be the one who had pushed Elise into prostitution. Ever since he'd set out to find her killer, he had known he might come face-to-face with that man.

Anita parked along the curb in front of Brewskis. The bar was on the corner of Madison and Wilcox. The front door faced the intersection. The side they were on backed up to a smoke shop. The only way you could tell where one ended and the other began was by looking in the windows. Those belonging to the bar were tinted so dark Liam could hardly see anything inside. The ones belonging to the smoke shop featured a display of bongs and e-cigarettes.

"He still hangs out here?" Liam asked, as he got out of the car.

"He owns the place now," Anita said.

Brewskis was almost as dark inside as it had looked through the windows. The bar jutted out from the back wall and took up a lot of the floor space. It was surrounded on three sides by stools. Booths lined the walls with windows and neon signs adorned the rest. A few scattered customers drank their lunch. "Route 66," performed by The Rolling Stones, was playing over the speakers.

Anita directed Liam's attention to a man behind the bar. He was crouched down, distracted, his head barely visible. "That's him." She walked up to the bar and Liam followed. When they got closer, they saw Dale fiddling with a keg.

"Hey," she said.

Without standing up, Dale's focus shifted from the keg to Anita. His lips parted into a reptilian smile. "How's it going, beautiful?"

Anita did not smile back. "We wanted to ask you about Elise."

His gaze cut to Liam. "Who's this?"

"He was her boyfriend."

Dale stood up, wiped his hands on his jeans. "She's a real bitch, you know."

"I'm not—"

"She's dead," Anita interrupted.

"Really?" Dale asked.

"Really." Liam leaned awkwardly back, settling onto one of the stools. The man in front of him was skinny and bald and didn't look like much of a pimp. But he had no reason to doubt Anita, so Liam pressed forward with his question. "You mind telling us if she ever worked for you?"

"Here? No. I only bought this place a few years ago. It's been a long time since I've seen Elise."

"Not here."

Dale's brow furrowed. Then his eyes lit up and his reptilian smile was back. "Oh, you mean . . ."

"That's exactly what I mean," Liam said, sickened by the thoughts he imagined going through Dale's mind.

"Sadly, no. She thought she was too good for me. Didn't mind coming around here to let me buy her drinks, but work for me?" He frowned, shook his head. "No way. She wasn't having it. Believe me, I asked."

"Are you sure?" Anita said. "She was busted for prostitution."

"No shit," Dale replied, in a way that suggested he already knew.

"Who was she working for?" Liam said.

"She didn't work for anyone. The prostitution charge was bullshit. She was just getting out there on the street and hustling her way into guys' cars to rip them off. Who are they going to tell, right? I don't know how long she was up to that crap. Once I found out, I told her to knock it off or I'd bust her up proper and then nobody'd be asking to go balls deep. She was messing with my cash flow, you know? People didn't want to stop."

Liam thought about what Anita's brother must have done to her, how his reason had been different, but his goal the same. His disgust with Dale grew into anger. "Did you do something to Elise?"

"No way. I liked Elise. I'm not sure what I would've done if I had to make good on my threat. I just wanted to give her a good scare. Apparently it worked, too, because after we had our little chat, I never saw her again. Why are you asking about her, anyway?"

Liam looked at Anita and she nodded, as if to say it was okay to tell Dale. "Elise was murdered."

"And you two are trying to figure out who killed her?" Dale almost laughed. "What are you, like, Cagney and Lacey?"

Liam ignored the sarcasm. As tempting as it might be to reach across the bar, grab Dale by the shirt, and throw a hard right into his jaw, that wasn't who he was. Sometimes he wished he could be that person, but wishing wouldn't make it so, and besides, he wasn't done asking questions.

Anita did not have the same problem. She unzipped her leather jacket to reveal a Beretta strapped underneath her shoulder. "Hey, dickwad, knock it off. This guy's been through a lot and the last thing he needs to deal with is your BS."

Dale's amusement subsided a little, but not entirely. "Yeah, okay. Calm yourself down, Inspector Gadget," he said to Anita. "What else do you want to know?"

Anita looked at Liam, raised her eyebrows questioningly.

Liam, who had instinctively hopped off the stool and back a step when he saw the gun, pulse quickening, tried to pull himself together. "Um, do you know anybody who might have wanted to hurt her? What about any of the guys she ripped off?"

"No, don't know any of them. Anything else?"

Liam tried to think of another question. There had to be something this man could tell him. There just had to be. But he couldn't think of one, so he reluctantly shook his head.

"Best of luck to you two on this little detective thing you got going on." Dale winked. Then, as if Liam and Anita had already left, he returned his attention to the keg.

"This was a waste of time," Anita said. "Let's go."

Liam slid out between the stool and the bar. He felt a little foolish thinking he could solve Elise's murder, and after seeing the gun, further out of his element than he'd expected to be.

Maybe it wasn't just coming here that was a waste of time. Maybe this whole thing was.

As he and Anita turned to leave, Dale said, "Wait. I'm sorry. I don't know what you two think you're going to accomplish, but if you want to talk to somebody who might be able to send you in the right direction, give Karen Bennett a ring. Last time I saw Elise, those two were living together."

"You know where we can find her?" Anita said.

"Pretty sure she works over at Barking Good. It's like a kennel for rich people or something. Used to, anyway."

Liam Parker

THE LOBBY AT BARKING Good was small. A wooden kiosk occupied most of the floor space and every inch of the kiosk was covered with toys and treats for sale. Leashes hung on the wall to the right. Half-a-dozen monitors mounted by the door broadcast indoor and outdoor play areas where dogs, grouped by size, roamed free.

Liam and Anita maneuvered around the kiosk to the counter and rang the bell. A short, stocky woman entered from the back. Her hair was trimmed to her ears. She was dressed in a Barking Good tee shirt and carrying a handful of rawhides. "Can I help you?"

"We're looking for Karen Bennett," Anita said.

"You found her. What can I do for you?"

"Do you remember Elise Watson?"

Karen dropped the rawhides into a jar on the counter. "Oh, God. What has she gotten herself into now? Whatever it is, I didn't have anything to do with it. I haven't seen that girl in years."

"It's nothing like that," Liam said. "We just need to ask you some questions." On their way over, they had decided it would be best to avoid mentioning to anyone else Elise had been murdered. They didn't need any more *Cagney and Lacey* wisecracks. They also agreed that if they could frame their conversation in such a way that led Karen to think they were cops, so much the better. Anita had even gone so far as to suggest they *say* they were cops, but Liam wasn't comfortable breaking any more laws than he had to and was pretty sure they could accomplish the same thing by simply implying it.

Judging from the way Karen was regarding them at that moment, Liam thought it might be working, too.

"Elise lived with you, right?" Anita asked.

"For a while."

"I gather you two don't talk anymore," Liam said.

Karen made a face while she began arranging the rawhides, spreading them out along the lip of the jar. "You gather right."

"Why did you two part ways?"

"She met some guy and, I'm not sure how to say it exactly, but she . . . changed. She started flashing around cash she shouldn't have."

"Do you know where it came from?" Liam asked.

"Nope. I told her I didn't even want to know what it was about. The whole thing made me uncomfortable."

"That's why you kicked her out? Because of the money?"

"I let her live with me because I thought it would do her some good to get out of her parents' house. But whatever she was up to, that wasn't what I signed up for. I told her she needed to knock it off, that whatever she was doing was going to make things worse for her." Karen slid the jar with rawhides to the edge of the counter. "She didn't listen, so eventually, yeah, I asked her to leave."

Anita nodded. "Do you know where she went?"

"No, I don't. Honestly, at that time I didn't care. For a while I thought she had gone to stay with that guy she was hanging around with, but . . ." She shrugged.

Liam and Anita waited. After several seconds, Liam said, "But what?"

"Well, the thing is, Elise came home with a black eye one night. I asked her who did it and all she said was that it was some jerk at a bar. She didn't give a lot of details."

Liam wondered if that might have been Dale. He'd said he hadn't hurt Elise when he found out she was hustling the johns that stopped to pick up his girls, but was it true? Or had this happened sooner? Maybe he did it when she refused to work for him and that was why she had started hustling the johns in the first place. "Do you know if the man she was talking about was named Dale?"

"That slime ball? I doubt it. This was long after she stopped going to Brewskis. I never found out why those two fell out, but I was glad he was out of her life."

Karen pulled a slip of paper out from under the register, wrote $9.99 on it, and stuck it to the jar. "She told me a couple nights after it happened it was this other guy," she continued. "We were watching the news and this financial dude came on and she just kinda muttered, 'That's him.' I believed her at the time. But after she left, I started thinking about it. Why would someone like that go punching Elise for no good reason? Hell, you look at the way he was dressed and you frankly have to wonder what they would have even been doing at the same bar. Nah, if you want to know the truth, I think it was probably that guy she was hanging around with when I kicked her out. God bless her if she really did go live with him."

"Do you remember who that was? The man she was hanging around with?"

Karen shook her head. "Sorry."

"What about the guy on the TV?" Anita asked.

"Now that I do know. I see him on the news pretty regularly. His name's Christopher Bell. But like I said, I don't think he had anything to do with it anymore. She just told me it was him because I was pestering her for more information about what happened. Guess you shouldn't always listen to your first instinct, right?"

Liam and Anita sat in the car outside Barking Good, the engine running. Liam briefly wondered if Karen and Elise had built their friendship on their shared love of animals. He held his hands up to the vents to warm them up. "We need to figure out who she was hanging around with," he said. "Who else can we talk to?"

"I think we should go see Christopher Bell," Anita replied.

"Why? You heard Karen. There's no way he had anything to do with this."

Anita was holding onto the bottom of the steering wheel, perhaps just because it was somewhere to put her hands, and tapped her thumbs against the worn plastic. "I'm not so sure. When we were growing up, Elise would sometimes say these quiet little things that, if you weren't listening, you'd miss. They were always the truth."

"What do you mean?"

"I remember once when we were children Dad brought all us kids into the living room and demanded to know who took ten dollars out of his wallet. Elise swore up and down it wasn't her and Dad believed her. He ended up blaming one of our brothers instead. Dad grounded him, sent him to his room, and a little while later I saw Elise . . ."

Anita stopped talking for a few seconds. She was looking straight at Liam, but he could tell that the only thing she actually saw was in her memory. "She was standing in the hall right outside our brother's bedroom. She didn't know I was there. She gently placed one hand on his door. I wasn't sure why at first. Then she whispered, 'I shouldn't have done that,' and I understood. It was like she just needed to say it, whether anyone heard her or not."

"So you think that's what happened here?"

"I don't know. But it sounds a lot like it to me. If it was Christopher Bell who hit her, maybe if we find out what she did to piss him off we'll know a little more about the kinds of things she was up to when Karen kicked her out."

Anita didn't go so far as to say that finding out what Elise was up to might lead them to their killer. But Liam was sure she was thinking it. And what the hell, since it sounded like it could have been the truth, why not talk to Christopher Bell?

Liam Parker

LIAM AND ANITA ENTERED a tall glass building. He nervously handed his fake ID over to the security guard in the lobby while at the same time, Anita handed over her real one. The moment of truth had come. Although the ID looked good to him, was it going to pass muster when it mattered? Nervous energy thrummed in his legs, ready to turn into momentum, to send him running, if it didn't.

Standing behind the security desk in her gray and black uniform, the security guard typed his information into her computer, registering the visit, and handed it back. She then directed them to elevator six, which she had authorized to provide access to Ellison Trust.

When the elevator doors opened onto the Ellison Trust lobby, Liam and Anita found themselves standing less than twenty feet from the receptionist. She was a young woman with picture-perfect makeup, sitting behind a sleek oak desk with a glass top. The Ellison Trust name had been etched into black marble behind her. Moving almost as one, Liam and Anita crossed the porcelain tile.

The receptionist looked at them, appraising Liam's oversized army jacket and Anita's leather with disgust. Liam gathered they did not look like the firm's usual visitors. She did her best to smile and said, "Welcome to Ellison Trust. How can I help you?"

"We're here to see Christopher Bell," Liam said.

"Do you have an appointment?"

"No, we don't. But we only need a few minutes of his time."

"We don't usually see people without an appointment. Would you like to make one?"

"This is urgent," Anita said. "Go get him."

"Miss . . . ?" The receptionist hesitated, waiting for Anita to provide her name. Anita shifted her weight onto one hip and crossed her arms over her chest. The receptionist continued, "He's not in right now. So I couldn't *go get him* even if I wanted to."

"Do you know when he'll be back?" Liam asked.

"I do not."

Anita nodded at Liam in a way that suggested they step back from the receptionist so they could talk privately. "What do you want to do?" she whispered.

"If you're sure he's our best lead—"

"I am."

"I guess we need to wait."

The receptionist watched them have a seat in a pair of leather chairs in an otherwise empty lobby. She rolled her eyes, then her phone rang, diverting her attention.

Liam and Anita sat in silence for nearly twenty minutes. Liam knew what Christopher Bell looked like from TV and none of the men who came in or out could be mistaken for him.

In that forced moment of calm, where Liam had a chance to think not about where the next clue led, but about the puzzle of Elise's life as a whole, he wondered if there might be a more efficient way to fill in the blanks. Until now, he'd believed the only way to find the killer was to start with Elise's past and move forward. Her name was a lie. Her job was a lie. Liam had believed there was nothing from the present to go on. But was that true? Since he'd started asking questions, he'd learned one thing about the last year of Elise's life that was not in dispute: she'd spent part of it in jail.

That meant she had a cellmate. It wasn't hard for Liam to imagine that if he'd never gotten bail, he might have said all kinds of things to his while he awaited trial. But how were they going to find her? Even if they did, there was no way Liam was going to walk into a prison to visit her. That seemed like it would be tempting fate.

He didn't have to, though, did he? Anita could do that. Since she was a free woman, she could go anywhere she wanted. Even—and that was when it occurred to him how they could find Elise's cellmate—to see Ryan Reyes.

No doubt, as a PI, he knew how to get that information.

Liam couldn't risk going into Ryan's office any more than he could risk visiting a prison, so if Anita was game, he'd have to send her off to do both.

That might be for the best. Divide and conquer. Liam could stay here to follow up on the lead Anita thought was important while she went to chase down the one he thought was.

Whispering, Liam explained his idea to Anita.

"That makes sense," she whispered back.

He gave her the number to his burner, and she asked him to escort her to the elevator, where she reached for her gun.

"What are you doing?" Liam said.

She pressed the Beretta into his hand. "Put it in your pocket. I can't take it with me into the prison and I'd feel better if you have it. Just in case."

"Just in case what?"

"I don't know. Just take it, all right? It's not going to hurt."

Liam didn't care for guns. He wasn't comfortable handling them.

But the receptionist was watching. Even though Anita's body shielded the weapon from her view, he could see growing concern on her face. Perhaps simply that they were standing on the far side of the room whispering was enough to alarm her.

He took the gun to end the conversation, discreetly sliding it into a pocket inside his jacket. Anita looked pleased. She pushed the elevator button. The doors opened immediately. "I'll call you when I'm done," she said, and stepped on board.

Anita Watson

RYAN WORKED OUT OF his home. He welcomed Anita into a large living room with mahogany floors. The only furniture was a pair of white leather sofas, facing each other and separated by a glass coffee table. He was wearing a pair of loose cotton pants, sling sandals, and a black sports tee. His yoga mat was laid out on the floor, facing the windows and the view of the lake beyond.

"Don't mind my appearance," Ryan said. "I was in the middle of an afternoon stretch." He went to the kitchen. "Would you like a glass of cucumber water?"

"I'm fine," Anita said. She'd been surprised when Ryan gave her an address in The Gold Coast, one of the city's most expensive neighborhoods, but was even more so now that she was inside Ryan's apartment. This man and his home were not what she was expecting from a PI.

Ryan returned to one of the two sofas and gestured for her to have a seat on the other. "So what can I help you with?"

All Anita had told him on the phone was that the matter was urgent, figuring the details would be better delivered in person. "You were hired by Flores and Washington to work on Liam Parker's defense."

Ryan's whole energy changed. His spine straightened. He lowered his head, leaned forward. He had transformed from an easygoing yoga enthusiast to a man on edge, ready to react to the slightest threat. Anita wasn't surprised. She was a stranger, showing up out of nowhere and discussing a murder suspect who'd gone on the run. But Anita hardly cared whether she'd put him on edge. Now that she was here, she wanted to get straight to the point.

"I'm Elise's sister. I'm helping Liam figure out what happened to her. We need your help."

"You know Liam is on the run from the police."

"I know."

Ryan looked Anita over in a different way than he had when she arrived. She could tell he was trying to decide whether to believe her. He sipped from his glass of cucumber water and leaned back. "What do you need my help with?"

And with that, Anita, too, was able to relax a little. Ever since she'd left Liam waiting alone for Chris in the lobby of Ellison Trust, part of her had been afraid she'd have to go back to him with the news that she'd failed to find out who Elise's cellmate was. That was something she just couldn't do. They both needed this. But if Ryan had sent her on her way, she might not have had any choice. Ryan was more likely to believe in Liam's innocence than anyone else she could hire, and it wasn't a good idea to go around announcing to strangers that she was helping a wanted felon evade the police.

"Can you find out where Elise did her time and who she shared a cell with?"

"You think they might know something?"

"We don't know."

Ryan rubbed his face, then ran his hands through his hair as he thought some more. "Patricia Harrison asked me to do a routine background check on Elise, see if anything popped up she could use. But if you guys are serious about finding the killer, you should let me help. I'm good at what I do."

"It's not my decision to make. Can you get the answers or not?" In truth, Anita didn't want to hand the investigation over to a stranger, and she didn't think Liam would want to either.

"Give me a minute." Ryan got up and disappeared down the hall.

As soon as he was out of sight, Anita worried he was going to call the police. She was tempted to tiptoe down the hall so she could see what he was up to. But she wouldn't be able to make it back to the sofa if he returned unexpectedly, and he likely wouldn't take kindly to being spied on. It was better to stay where she was. Ryan seemed sincere when he'd offered to help, and she needed this information.

While she waited, she looked out at the cold waters of Lake Michigan. From here she could see the languid waves crashing onto a beach that was all but entirely deserted this time of year. Elise would have liked this view. Elise would have liked this whole apartment. It was the kind of place she'd talked about living in before she ran way.

I should have done more to help her, Anita thought for the umpteenth time.

Ryan returned, carrying a manila folder. He placed it on the bar that separated the kitchen from the living room and flipped through it until he found what he was looking for. "Elise was housed at the Redwood Penitentiary," he said. "It's a private prison just outside the city. Her cellmate was a woman named Julia Santora. She's still there."

It hadn't occurred to Anita—or, she assumed, Liam—that Elise's cellmate might also have been released.

Ryan removed a piece of paper and returned to the sofa. "Give Liam this."

"What is it?" Anita asked, taking it from him. Ryan didn't respond, and once she looked at it, she understood why. The answer was obvious. It was a photocopy of an Illinois ID with Elise's first name and picture on it. The last name, however, was not Watson. It was Ross.

"I came across it after my last meeting with Liam and Patricia," he said. "I assume you know Elise had been going under an alias when she was killed."

Anita didn't. Liam hadn't mentioned that to her. But she thought it would be better to pretend she did, so she nodded.

"This was found on her when she was arrested last year. It didn't seem to be linked to any criminal activity, so the prosecution agreed to drop the charge of possessing it in exchange for a guilty plea, which is why it didn't show up on her record. While I don't know if this has anything to do with who killed her, this makes for at least two aliases."

"What do you think it means?"

"I don't know. But from my experience, if there were two, there were probably more."

Anita looked at her sister staring back at her through time. She'd thought she had a pretty good picture of what Elise's life had been like when Liam told her about the arrests. But after she'd met with Dale, she wasn't so sure. Now she found herself wondering anew what Elise had gotten herself into.

Christopher Bell

CHRIS RETURNED FROM LUNCH in a bad mood. Emma had been on the phone with him, squawking into his headset while he ate, asking him again how he'd let the thief get away after cornering him at his apartment, and when he was going to get her a new ring, and, since he'd bought the ring because he was going to ask her to marry him, when they were going to start making wedding plans.

Making matters worse, when the elevator doors opened onto the lobby of Ellison Trust, he was accosted by a man wearing a worn-out army jacket and tee shirt who had dyed his hair black and spiked it up like he was a damn teenager. To Chris, he looked poor and dirty.

"Hey, can I talk to you for a minute? It's not going to take a lot of time, I promise. I just need to ask you some questions."

Chris held up a hand to keep the man at bay. He didn't want Army Jacket getting too close. He could almost feel the grime and disease on the stranger transferring to him merely by their proximity. He looked at the receptionist, accusingly. "What's this man doing here?"

The receptionist shrugged, her mannequin-like face inscrutable.

"Something bad has happened to someone I care about," Army Jacket continued. "I think you might have met her once."

"I'm quite sure I don't know anybody you know."

"Her name was Elise. You might have run into her in a bar a while back."

"I never met anybody by that name. You need to get out of here."

"Wait." Army Jacket pulled a cheap TracFone out of his pocket, which surprised Chris only insomuch that this stranger had a phone at all. His thumbs tapped rapidly at the digital display.

Chris turned back to the receptionist. "Can you call—"

"Please. Just one second." Army Jacket turned the phone around so Chris could see the screen.

The stranger had brought up a Facebook page and zoomed in close on the profile picture. Chris recognized the woman immediately. She'd tried to rob him several years ago. He remembered the incident well. He'd hit her hard, pushed her to the ground. He hadn't cared that she was a woman. Why should he?

He didn't let on, though. There was something off about this whole thing, and he didn't like it. Why would this stranger be here, asking about a long-past and failed con job?

"Call security," Chris said to the receptionist. "Get this man out of here." He turned and headed toward his office.

"Do you know her?" the stranger shouted after him.

"I've never met her in my life," Chris lied without looking back.

Liam Parker

LIAM WASN'T SURE WHETHER Chris was telling the truth. There was something in his eyes, some flicker that might have been recognition, when he saw the picture. But with Chris heading for his office and the receptionist on the phone with security, his opportunity to pursue this lead had come to a close . . . at least for now.

It was disappointing, but not surprising. Their encounter (if it had even happened) had been a long time ago. Chris might have been drunk. Or he might have forgotten it. If he did remember it, he probably didn't want to own up to a hitting a woman.

Either way, Liam was confident Chris wasn't the killer. All he'd hoped to get out of their discussion was some insight into Elise's life, something that would take them one step closer to figuring out what had happened the night she died.

Besides, with Anita pursuing the name of Elise's cellmate, it wasn't even all that important.

"I'm going," Liam told the receptionist.

She either didn't hear him or didn't care, because she said into the phone, "Someone's on their way now? Good. Thank you."

Liam pressed the button for the elevator. He wasn't particularly concerned about the security guard that was on his way. A security guard would do nothing more than force him to leave the building. Still, he had no reason to stick around and didn't want to draw unnecessary attention.

As Liam exited onto the sidewalk, his phone rang. It was Anita. He moved out of the flow of pedestrian traffic, squeezing close to the building.

"I got it," she said. "Elise was housed at Redwood Penitentiary. I'm going to talk to her cellmate now. Have you seen Chris yet?"

"That was a dead end. He didn't remember her."

Anita was quiet for a moment, and in that moment, Liam started to feel exposed. He couldn't stand here like this. A cop could walk by any second. Someone could recognize him. The more faces he saw, the more danger he was in. He had to keep moving. He had to get off the street.

He started to walk.

Christopher Bell

CHRIS STEPPED INTO HIS office and closed the door, still wondering about Army Jacket and his questions. He'd been so preoccupied by the man's appearance he hadn't thought to ask his name. Seconds ago, when he'd been approached in the lobby, it hadn't seemed to matter. Chris had just wanted to get as far away from Army Jacket as possible. Now, though, he had an uneasy feeling it might.

He returned to the lobby to ask the receptionist who said she hadn't gotten his name. At his insistence, she called down to the security desk and repeated to Chris the name they gave her: Richard Hawthorne.

The man didn't look quite like he did in Chris's memory. But Chris didn't entirely trust his memory. He tried to picture Army Jacket without the hair dye or sunglasses and, as he did, his blood started to boil. It didn't make sense that Richard would come here asking questions like that. Actually, it didn't make sense that Richard would come here at all.

Chris pressed the button to call the elevator. It took an unusually long time to come—or maybe it only seemed that way. In his agitated state, Chris couldn't be sure.

When the doors opened onto the lobby, he ran out, pushing past those who exited too slowly. Richard couldn't have gotten far. Chris charged through the revolving glass door toward the street. A security guard shouted for him to slow down.

Once outside, Chris looked in each direction, trying to figure out which way Richard had gone. With heavy foot traffic, it was impossible to see everyone clearly. Even those who were only a block away had melded into a tapestry of color and movement that threatened to make identification impossible.

Then he saw a flash of green to his left and started to move. He wasn't sure he was chasing the right person until the sea of pedestrians parted again and he saw Richard's spiky black hair.

Chris all but mowed over the people in his way. And he was close—so close—to catching Richard when a cab pulled to the curb and Richard got inside.

Liam Parker

"CAN I SEND YOU a picture?" Anita said.

"Sure." Liam flagged down a cab and climbed in. The driver asked where he wanted to go, and he gave the address for the Best Western. At least he'd be safe there until Anita was done talking to Elise's cellmate.

His phone vibrated and he checked the message Anita had sent him. "You got it?" she asked, her voice sounding tinny with the phone held out in front of him.

"Got it." He tapped on the picture she'd sent. It was a photograph of a piece of paper with something too small on it to see until he zoomed in. He recognized the picture in the photocopied ID as Elise. "What's this?"

"Look at the name."

He did, and realized this made for a second alias. "Where did you get this?"

"Hold on. You answer my question first. Why didn't you tell me my sister was living under a fake name?"

Liam wasn't sure what to say.

"Ryan told me."

He glanced at the rearview mirror, where he could see the cab driver's eyes. The man appeared to be watching the road, paying no attention to Liam's conversation. Regardless, Liam chose his words carefully. "It bothered me too when I first found out." Just like the deleted text messages had. Just like all the lies had. But also like the deleted text messages and the lies, he didn't think the alias would get him any closer to finding the killer and he didn't want to tarnish Anita's memory of her sister any more than he had to. "I didn't think you needed to know. It doesn't really matter, does it?"

"What do you mean? How could it not matter?" Anita's voice pitched up with annoyance.

Liam cupped one hand around the microphone and whispered, "Whoever killed her was probably somebody who knew her real name because they knew how to find her." He watched the rearview mirror as he spoke. No reaction from the driver.

"I think it might matter. I got the impression Ryan did also. He said, since there are two, there are probably more."

"Does he have a theory about them?"

"No. All he could say for sure was that the ID wasn't linked to any crimes. But think about the timing of it all. She had an alias before she was arrested and after. It's not something new. So what does it mean?"

Liam considered the possibility that the second alias pointed to identity theft. Then again, there was nothing on her record, and since Ryan hadn't found any crimes tied to the ID, he was back to his original theory. "I think Elise was hiding from someone."

Only now he wondered *how long* she had been hiding from someone.

Liam Parker

LIAM COULD FEEL A certain paranoia taking hold. A feeling that he couldn't let his guard down, not even for a second. Even after getting off the phone with Anita, he watched the driver's eyes in the rearview mirror. He listened to the radio calls to see if any sounded like a request for police assistance. He looked at every person in every car they passed to make sure that person wasn't looking at him and examined the few who did for signs of recognition or alarm.

To a degree, that paranoia had been present ever since he had evaded arrest. It was the whole reason he had dumped his cell phone in the trash. But it was getting stronger, and by the time Liam reached the hotel, he was exhausted. He couldn't understand how those on the run lived with that paranoia long-term. Maybe it was something you got used to.

He went to his room and hung the Do Not Disturb sign on the knob outside. (That should have been task number one after checking in.) Then he put Anita's gun in the small safe beside the mini fridge; he was more likely to shoot off his own foot than do anything else with it and didn't want to carry it around any longer than he had to.

He pulled out his phone and clicked on the photo Anita had sent him. He stared at it for a long time. He wondered if there might be a reason for the fake ID other than the ones he'd considered. What if the aliases were not to protect Elise from someone who was after her but the reason she was killed?

That theory had a ring of truth that sent chills through his body. Had he been looking at this whole thing upside down?

By itself, Liam didn't feel like the theory got him any closer to figuring out who had killed Elise or why. It did, however, introduce new questions that might. Like: What was she doing with the ID? Why did she have two aliases? Was Ryan correct—were there more? If so, why did she need more aliases?

Liam didn't know much about fake IDs. Other than buying alcohol as a teenager or running from the police, he certainly didn't know why anybody would want one. But he did know somebody who might be able to help him fill in the blanks.

Jacob.

Looking for him on Facebook would be pointless. He didn't know Jacob's last name, and it was too late to go digging his phone out of the CVS trashcan. It would have been emptied by now anyway.

Then he had an idea. He logged into his AT&T account from his phone. Navigating the website on the small screen was difficult and it ultimately took a detour to Google to find what he was looking for: a call log.

Jacob's number had been the last one Liam dialed, making it easy to find. He punched the digits into his burner and waited.

Jacob Reed

JACOB STOPPED BY THE Heartland Nursing Home with a check for Felix Winkler. "Get her back into her old room," he told the nursing home administrator when he handed it over. Then he found the door on the second floor with the paper flowers stuck to it. His mother was alone inside, watching Wheel of Fortune with the volume turned up loud.

Jacob stepped in front of the screen so she knew he was there and her face lit up. She muted the TV and used both armrests to push herself out of the chair—an act Jacob noticed had become considerably harder than it had been the year before.

"They're going to move you back," he said when she hugged him.

"You don't need to do that. I'm fine where I am."

Jacob knew she was lying, and he was glad that, on this—his last— visit to see her, he could do something that would make her happy.

He took off his jacket, planning to stay for a while, and hung it from a hook on the back of the door. He sat down on the footstool in front of his mother's chair and took her hands in his. "I have to go away for a while." Actually, he would to have to go away forever, but he couldn't bring himself to tell her that.

She looked concerned. "What for?"

"Work."

"They're sending you to another factory? Why?"

More and more often, Jacob's mother confused him with her brother, Howard, who had worked at a General Motors plant years ago. Today was one of those days. He wished he'd said goodbye on his previous visit, when she was lucid.

Normally, he'd play along, pretend to be Howard, say he had a message from her son, and usually that message would simply be that he loved her. He couldn't bring himself to do that today. He couldn't stand the thought that he would have to leave Chicago without her ever knowing, and he didn't want to pass such a message through "Howard," who had died last year. If he did that, he feared she would think he didn't care enough to say goodbye in person.

"No, Mom. It's me. Your son."

Confusion crinkled her face, folding the skin along deep wrinkles. She shook her head. "No, you're Howard. My son's just a boy. You're not a boy."

"I'm your son, Mom."

"Why are you saying that? Why are you trying to confuse me?"

Jacob's phone vibrated in his pocket. He ignored it. "I'm not trying to confuse you. I just wanted to say goodbye. I have to leave for a while and I wanted you to know I loved you."

"If you have to go, just go, Howard," she snapped, ripping her hands away from him. "I don't need you coming here and messing with my head. You were always mean to me. Always! Get out! My boy will take care of me. He loves me."

While Jacob knew his mother became agitated when confronted about her dementia, he'd never seen her like this. Was it because he told her he was leaving? Because once he was gone she wouldn't have any family left to visit her? He feared it was, that on some level she knew he wasn't Howard and that once he left Chicago she would be alone.

Maybe he wouldn't have to go away forever, he told himself. Maybe once things settled down, he could come back to visit her. Either way, he had to see his plan through. It would be as good for her as it would for him.

She pointed to the door. "Go!"

Jacob got up and grabbed his jacket. Standing by the door, he said one last time, "Mom, I love you."

"You're not my son, Howard! Go!"

Jacob left. He heard his mother call him a jerk after he closed the door. It hurt, but he convinced himself she didn't mean it. Then, on the way to the elevator, he pulled his phone out of his pocket to see who had called. The number was not one he recognized, and the caller hadn't left a message. Jacob didn't return calls from people he didn't know.

As he departed the hospital, ready to put the last steps of his plan into motion, he didn't realize that when he'd pulled his phone out of his pocket, something else had come with it: an ID he'd transferred from suit pants to jeans without thinking, an ID he should have gotten rid of days ago but hadn't.

Anita Watson

ANITA MADE HER WAY past the guard post and parked in a fenced lot. The Redwood Penitentiary was three stories, with guard towers at each corner of the property. From those towers, armed men surveyed the prison grounds.

She emptied the pockets of her leather jacket into a small plastic bin, then went through the metal detector. Eventually, she was directed to one of a dozen booths that had a phone built into the steel partition dividing her station from the next.

She sat on the stool, hands in her lap.

A minute later, Julia Santora appeared on the other side of a large plexiglass window. She was wearing an orange jumpsuit. Her matted black hair didn't look as if it had been combed in weeks. She was skinny—too skinny, Anita thought—and when she sat it was more like she collapsed.

When Anita had arrived, the three stories of barred windows and razor wire had hardly registered. This was not her home, would never be her home, and she wasn't worried that the women housed here could be a threat with the bars between them. Perhaps because of that it wasn't until she saw Elise's cellmate that she realized how hard this place must be. The guilt she felt for not doing more to help her sister compounded.

Julia picked up the phone and Anita mirrored the action. "What do you want?" Julia asked.

"I wanted to talk to you about Elise."

"Yeah? What for?"

"I'm her sister. I wanted to find out—"

"She didn't tell me she had no sister," Julia looked bemused. "She must not have liked you, huh?"

Anita wasn't sure she believed Julia, but quickly decided it didn't matter. Julia didn't care about Elise's relationship with her sister. She was trying to find out how much control she could exert over the conversation. To what end, though? Perhaps Julia pushed everyone she met, poking and prodding to find out who was weak, who could be manipulated.

Anita refused to take the bait. "Do you know anybody who might have had a problem with Elise?" she asked.

"If I tell you, what are you going to do for me?"

Anita recognized the question as another attempt to take control of the conversation. Well, if that's the way she wanted to play it, so be it. "What do you want?"

Julia frowned. "Two hundred dollars. Put it in my commissary account and then we'll talk."

"One hundred. And you tell me now."

Julia considered the offer, shrugged. "There was a girl over on Block C who didn't like her much. Called her a princess and shit like that because she thought Elise acted like she was too good for Redwood. And you know something? She was right. I didn't say it to nobody because I had to live with her and I didn't want her stink getting on me, but that girl of yours was always talking about how she was going to turn her life around when she got out of here, how she was going to *make something* of herself. As if."

"Did the girl on Block C get out?"

"No way. That bitch has got another three years or something."

161

Anita shifted in her seat, disappointed. She was certain she was on to something for a second. "Was there anybody else she talked about? Someone on the outside?"

"Not that I can think of. There was this one woman writing her letters. I found one of them tucked up under her pillow. As far as I know, that was the only contact she had with the outside world. Nobody ever came to see her. I guess she was about as well liked out there as she was in here."

"Do you know what they talked about?"

"Some shit about church retreats and books. It's what got Elise reading all that psychology crap from the prison library. That's what she called it, anyway. *Psychology.* Those books looked more like self-help garbage to me. I didn't pay any of it too much attention. It was all just the same sort of uppity BS I got from Elise about changing her life and I didn't need any more of that than I had to put up with already."

Everything Anita had learned about Elise's life since leaving home had sounded bleak. This was different. Anita couldn't quite say how it made her feel. Proud wasn't the right word. But it was something akin to that, because it meant Elise hadn't entirely given in to her worst impulses. Maybe the good part of Elise, the part that had felt guilty for framing her brother all those years ago, had finally begun to win out.

But if that was what she wanted, why didn't Elise come home when she was released? Why didn't she let her family help her?

Elise could be so stubborn.

"Do you know who the letters were from?" Anita asked.

Julia pushed her greasy hair from one side of her head to the other. "Think her name was Kate."

"There wasn't anything in them that made you think Kate had a problem with Elise?"

"Didn't seem like it. In one of those letters, she even offered Elise a job when she got out. Why do you keep asking if someone had a problem with her? Did something happen?"

"I'm not sure," Anita said.

"She's missing?"

Anita didn't answer.

"Well, I'll tell you this. I didn't see no problem between them in those letters. But they wasn't right to me. Some stranger writing you in jail and offering you a job? This ain't Disney World."

No, it certainly was not.

These letters sounded like something Anita would need to find out more about if she could. For now, she thought it was best to focus on the things Julia might be able to help her with. "What did she tell you about her life? Did she mention any names? Tell you about anybody she was hanging around with before she was arrested?"

"Not much. There was this one guy she mentioned a couple times."

"What'd she say about him?"

"She told me they'd been working together. She said they mostly hit the tourist areas over by the lake."

"What do you mean?"

"What do you think I mean?" Julia shook her head. "You don't know very much about your sister. She said they did all kinds of stuff, but what worked best for them was a variation of The Ring. She didn't tell me much about the specifics, though."

Anita didn't need the specifics to know that sounded like a con. She wondered if there might be a connection between it and the fake ID. She pulled the piece of paper Ryan had given her out of her pocket, unfolded it, and held it up to the glass. "Do you know anything about this?"

Julia leaned in, squinting so she could read it. Then her eyes widened and she smiled, showing all her teeth. "He does good work."

"Who?"

"This guy. Think she said his name was Hawk or Hank. I'm not sure. Said he runs a studio called Clix. Mostly does family portraits. You know, baby pictures and crap like that. But she told me if I ever need a fake ID, he's the guy to go to. I thought it was more BS." She leaned in to take another look at the ID. "I guess not this time."

Anita put the piece of paper back in her pocket. "So what else can you tell me?"

"I'll tell you how The Ring works for another hundred bucks."

"Do you know how it worked?"

"I know how the original version works."

Anita hung up the phone. She'd let Julia think she was running the show for long enough. Talking about things that didn't directly relate to Elise's life was pointless. Besides, armed with the name Clix, she had everything she needed. She could feel it.

As she got up, Julia banged on the glass. She looked annoyed. *Don't forget the money*, she mouthed.

Anita thought about nodding, assuring Julia she'd follow through on her end of the deal. But why lie?

Anita waved goodbye.

Julia flipped her the bird and pounded on the glass harder.

Jacob Reed

JACOB SAT IN HIS rented Ford Focus outside Aubury High. The bell would ring any minute and teenagers would come barreling through the double doors in front. He'd seen Alice in pictures online, but with hundreds of kids pushing through those doors at the same time, he might miss her if he wasn't alert.

Alice exited the building wearing a blue-and-red flannel shirt Jacob recognized from an Instagram photo and a large pair of sunglasses. She was in lockstep with a friend, a blonde who was shorter than Alice and clutched a pair of books to her chest as if they could shield her from the world.

The girls headed toward a parking lot off the side of the building. Jacob eased the Ford around the corner so as not to lose sight of them. They got into a white Volvo that looked new. Alice's friend took the driver's seat.

He followed the girls from the school to a McDonald's, where they met with other students. Jacob parked on the other side of the restaurant. He ordered McNuggets and a Coke, and sat with his back to their booth. He was far enough away that he didn't draw attention but close enough to hear most of their conversation. They talked a lot about boys and teachers. Nauseating teenage stuff. Alice mentioned the Fresh Sync concert tonight.

Jacob knew she was going from her posts online. There must have been a dozen or more across Facebook and Twitter, most of them linking to videos of the band's hit songs, full of emojis and exclamation points.

Fresh Sync was a pop band Jacob didn't care for. He was all about the classics. Pink Floyd. The Beatles. Queen. Real music. But he knew enough about the band even before perusing Alice's posts to name some of their hits (and, like he had at the bank, sing some of their lyrics). It was hard to turn on the radio these days without hearing something by the quartet.

Alice was sometimes quiet for long periods. But since she couldn't leave without walking right past him, Jacob wasn't worried about where she might be. When she and her friend broke off from the group and returned to their car, he did the same.

He'd gathered from the conversation that the two girls would go together to the Bowards Arena tonight and meet more of their friends there. That was okay with him. The bigger the group got, the easier it'd be to see them in the crowd.

They drove from the McDonald's to a nearby mall. Jacob kept his distance, watching them as they went into Forever 21, Charlotte Russe, and H&M. The girls seemed like good kids. He wondered if he might have a daughter like Alice someday.

When they stopped by Urban Outfitters, which was more Jacob's speed, he followed them in. He was some fifteen years older than Alice, but looked half that and hoped to use it to his advantage. He browsed through stacks of tee shirts while the girls selected items to try on.

Finally, Alice's friend disappeared down a hall leading to the dressing rooms with a large stack of clothes draped over one arm.

Jacob's plan for Alice involved two steps. This was his opportunity to implement the first one. He pulled his cellphone out of his pocket and held it to his ear, pretending he'd received a call. He meandered across the store, getting ever closer to Alice, keeping his attention on the clothes. Just a shopper talking to a friend. Once he believed she couldn't help but overhear him, Jacob provided his imaginary caller a glowing review of Fresh Sync. "Best band out there. No, really. Without a doubt. I saw them in Denver last year. Man, I can't even begin to tell you what a good show that was."

He bumped into Alice and, feigning surprise, dropped his phone. "Oh, I'm sorry," he said with a smile as he scooped it up. "I didn't see you there."

"It's okay," she said, and he noticed she was smiling too, or at least half-smiling.

He kept his eyes fixed on hers for a couple of seconds. He wanted to make sure she remembered his face. "I was—" He pointed to the phone. "I should've been paying attention to where I was going."

"It's fine."

"All right, well, thanks." Jacob grinned and waved. Another seemingly innocuous gesture that helped to ensure she'd remember this exchange later. Then he pressed his phone to his ear, started talking about Fresh Sync again, and walked away.

Jacob worked his way toward the exit at the same slow pace. He returned to his rental in the parking garage and watched the Volvo. An hour passed. He pulled the photo of Chris and his girlfriend out of his back pocket. He imagined himself in Chris's place, the woman a little less sleazy. He imagined a pair of kids just outside the frame, family dinners, Chris helping his son with homework.

An engine started up, and he looked over to see the Volvo pulling out of its spot.

Jacob followed the girls to Alice's home and parked at the end of the block. Here, with only residential traffic, he couldn't get too close.

Alice got out of the car. She grabbed her backpack from the rear seat and slung it over both shoulders. Her friend drove off. Jacob put his car in park and waited.

Alice Parker

ALICE HAD RECEIVED THREE phone calls and two texts from Catherine asking where she was. She hadn't answered any of them. She was out having fun and wasn't going to be bothered. At the front door, she hunched forward a little. It was uncomfortable, but she loved to get under Catherine's skin. She hadn't called Catherine "Mom" since the divorce.

She entered the house, heard Catherine's voice before she saw her.

"Where have you been?" Catherine bellowed, stepping from the living room into the foyer. Her hair was pinned up like it usually was and in a way that Alice thought must take hours. Her wrinkle-free blouse was tucked into wrinkle-free pants. Everything was perfect. Alice didn't know why she bothered. It wasn't like Catherine had a job. She lived on Liam's money.

"Chill out, Catherine."

"Don't call me that!" Catherine snapped. "I'm your mother."

Alice rolled her eyes and headed toward the stairs. Tommy was sitting on the landing halfway up, holding onto the balusters and looking down at her.

"Where do you think you're going?"

"To my room. Where do you think?"

"Get back here."

Ugh. What now? Alice didn't have any interest in what Catherine wanted, but since she knew Catherine would follow her upstairs, her voice getting increasingly shrill as she demanded her daughter's attention, Alice decided it was best to get the conversation over with. She stopped, one foot on the bottom stair and a hand on the banister. "What do you want?"

"Could you come into the living room, please?"

"Fine." Alice shrugged out of her backpack and followed Catherine into the living room, where she saw David standing by the fireplace.

"You look good," David said.

If Alice had given any thought to David's comment, she would have decided it was a lie. She most definitely did *not* look good. In fact, she made a *point* of not looking good. But Alice hadn't seen much of David since her parents' divorce, and the only thought she could manage was, *Something's wrong.* There was also the look on his face, a kind of worry and exhaustion that would have alarmed her in any environment. But here, where he did not belong, it troubled her even more.

"Your mom tells me you talked to Liam last night," David continued.

"Yeah. So what?"

"What did he say to you?"

If Catherine had been the one asking, Alice would've told her it was none of her business. But since it was David, and since David wouldn't be here looking like he did without a good reason, she tried to remember. The truth was, "Not much." They'd talked about school, mostly. Alice had asked Liam about the murder, but all he told her was that it was a mix up. She hadn't believed him. She'd pressed him for details. But he hadn't given her any, so what else was there to say?

David took a step closer to Alice. "Are you sure?" he asked, perhaps with more intensity than he meant to.

It scared Alice. "Yeah. Why? What's going on?" Then she thought about the phone number Liam had given her. It was for emergencies only, he'd told her. Why did he need a number just for emergencies? She'd wondered about that at the time, then decided that any strange behavior should simply be chalked up to the stress he was under. Now, with David here, she wondered about it again. "Did something happen to him?"

"Maybe you should sit down," Catherine said.

"What happened? Is Dad okay?"

"We don't know," David said. "The police revoked his bail and he took off. We need to find him. I need to convince him to turn himself in. Running like this is not going to do him any good."

With that, Alice did sit down. She couldn't believe what she was hearing. "Dad wouldn't do that."

"He did," Catherine said.

Alice shot her mother a hateful glare. "Of course you'd believe that."

"It's true," David said. "I was there when it happened. When you talked to him last night, he was already on the run. So if you know anything at all about how I can find him, it would mean a lot. He's running because he's scared, and he needs me right now to talk him down."

Suddenly the emergency number made sense. Liam had dumped his phone and was using one of those cheap pharmacy mobiles. Alice had seen it happen often enough in movies.

"I came across some important information," David continued. "It will clear his name."

Alice nodded slowly as she took in the news. She wasn't surprised David was out there trying to help her father. "He gave me a phone number. He said it was for emergencies only. You can reach him on that."

"What?" Catherine snapped. "You didn't think to tell me about that last night?"

"He gave it to *me*. If he wanted you to have it, he could have given it to you."

"Can I have it?" David asked.

"It's in my room. I'll go get it." Alice stood up and climbed the stairs to the second floor.

"What's going on?" asked Tommy, who was sitting on the landing and holding onto the balusters like they were prison bars. "Is Dad okay?"

"He's fine," Alice said. While she wasn't so sure that was true last night, she believed it might be now. She went into her room and grabbed a Mead spiral notebook off her desk. It had "English" scrawled across the front in black magic marker. She flipped to the last page, where her dad's number was written in the lower-right corner. The rest of the sheet was covered in doodles, mostly flowers and unicorns, that she had drawn during her teacher's last long-winded lecture. Before she tore it out, removing only enough of the paper to capture the number, she copied it into her phone. She went downstairs and handed the slip of paper to David.

"We're going to get this straightened out fast," he said. "This will all be behind us soon."

Liam Parker

LIAM HADN'T BEEN ABLE to reach Jacob and didn't want to leave a message. You never knew who might hear it. Probably not the police, but what if they did? For the time being, there was no harm in being a little paranoid.

He would call later. Or so he thought until Anita told him she had the name of the guy who'd made Elise's fake ID. Armed with that information, additional calls to Jacob seemed unnecessary.

The conversation with Hawk/Hank was one Liam would have to have on his own, Anita said. She'd spent much more time getting in and out of the prison than she'd expected and had to go to work. "I'll meet you at the diner at noon tomorrow and we'll get back to it. I think we're getting close to something," she said, right before she hung up.

Clix was properly called Clix Studio, as indicated by the name over the shop's door, and appeared to be a one-man operation. Although there was a lobby, there was no receptionist. Liam had an unobstructed view of a photographer shooting a mother and her baby against a roll-down backdrop of a park. As far as he could tell, there was no one else present.

The photographer, with his long gray hair pulled into a ponytail and a Fisher-Price rattle in hand, glanced over and said, "Have a seat. We're almost done here."

"No problem." Liam had already decided to wait until they were alone to ask his questions.

The photographer turned back to his subjects. With his finger on the camera's shutter button, he shook the rattle and made cooing sounds to draw the baby's attention. He told the mother to "Smile!" and "Hold the baby a little higher, if you can."

When the session ended, he cashed the woman out and said, "That baby is one of the best I've ever had."

Liam thought it was a lie but the mother looked pleased. She thanked the photographer and left. Chimes strung to the door jingled on her way out.

"Now, what can I do for you?" the photographer said to his prospective client.

Liam got up and approached the counter separating the lobby from the studio.

"You know, you look familiar."

"I get that a lot," Liam said, which wasn't true. He suspected the photographer recognized him from the newspaper or an online article about the murder. That was not something he needed the photographer thinking about, so he barreled forward with his first question. "Is your name Hank?"

The photographer's smile faltered. "No. Why?"

"Hawk?"

"It's Frank."

The name sounded enough like the one he was looking for that Liam figured this had to be the right guy. Time to try out the tactic he had settled on. "Elise sent us to see you."

"Elise who?"

"Dark hair. Skinny. Big blue eyes. You'd remember her."

"Doesn't ring a bell."

Liam pulled his phone out of his pocket and showed him the picture of the ID Anita had sent him. "You recognize this?"

Frank went pale. "I think you're in the wrong place."

"I don't think so," Liam said with a courage he wouldn't have expected. But he was scared and tired and, dammit, he needed some answers. "I'll bet in that room back there"—Liam pointed at the only closed door he saw—"there's all kinds of things that would interest the police, isn't there? Maybe a blue screen? A computer? Whatever it is you need to make a fake ID these days. If they're not there, they're somewhere around here, aren't they?"

Frank instinctively looked over his shoulder at the door, which confirmed to Liam he was correct. "Look, I'm just trying to make a living. You think glamour shots and prom pictures are enough to pay the bills around here?"

"I just need some answers."

Frank considered this, held up a finger. *Wait a second*, it said. He walked around the counter, locked the front door, and turned the open sign to closed. "What do you want to know?"

"Why did Elise have you make this ID?"

"I didn't ask. Sometimes they tell me. Like they need to justify it or something. Usually that's the kids, though. The ones looking to buy booze or get into a club. But she and that guy she was with, they were pretty quiet when they came in here." Frank squinted and wagged a finger at Liam. "I swear you look familiar. Why is that?"

"What guy?"

"Just some guy. No one special." There was a pause. Frank seemed to be thinking about something. Then he blurted out, "That's it! That's where I know you from. That guy. You must know him."

"I don't know who you're talking about."

"You have to. He came in here, had a driver's license and a passport made for you. I'm surprised I didn't pick you out right away. It was an unusual request. Normally I take the photos, myself. But he came in with a picture of you and insisted I use it. You must know about it, right? You've gotta know what I'm talking about."

There was only one person that could have been. "Jacob." Liam felt his world shift in a way he couldn't quite explain. It meant Elise and Jacob had known each other long before Liam had met her at Ava's. There was no way they were both there by chance. But *why* were they there? Liam had thought Jacob was helping him because of Ava. Was he actually helping him because of Elise? No, that wasn't it. But he couldn't put his finger on what the truth was either. Not right now. Besides, there wasn't any time to think about it anyway because Frank had already started to respond.

"No, that's not his name."

"It has to be," Liam insisted.

"I don't think so."

Liam pulled the fake ID Jacob had given him out of his wallet and handed it over. "This is the ID you're talking about, right?"

"That's it!" Frank said, pointing at the ceiling as if he were having a eureka moment. "Richard Hawthorne. Rick. That's what was so unusual. Well, aside from the fact that he provided the picture."

"What are you talking about?"

"That," Frank said, pointing to the ID. "He wanted the ID in his name. But hey, like I said—I don't ask questions."

Liam sat on a bench outside Clix. It was cold, but he felt overwhelmed and needed a second to think. He pulled the army jacket tight, then took out his TracFone and searched the web for Richard Hawthorne. He wasn't sure exactly what he was looking for, he just wanted to see what he would find.

The search results were ordinary at first. Google presented a list that included Facebook, Twitter, and Instagram. There were also listings that mentioned a failed state senate race, a hot dog eating contest, and an obituary. The remaining results on the first page referenced a Mike Hawthorne, The Hawthorne Foundation, and a site called MyLife that promised all sorts of background information on Richard.

Liam clicked on Facebook first, perhaps simply because it was at the top of the list. Suddenly, the results no longer looked so ordinary. Richard Hawthorne had north of a hundred and fifty friends. He'd reposted memes and jokes; nothing personal. His profile picture was Liam's—the same one, in fact, Liam now had on his fake ID.

Feeling more overwhelmed now than when he sat on the bench, Liam clicked on the Twitter and Instagram accounts, and discovered a disturbing trend. All three accounts in Richard's name had Liam's picture.

But why? There was no obvious answer. The only way Liam could find out would be to ask Rick.

Rick—who had known Elise, who'd bought fake IDs with her, who'd sold him an ID after he was charged with Elise's murder. . . . Had Rick killed her? Was he trying to frame Liam? The fake ID in Richard's name didn't fit that story. But Rick knew something. He had to. Liam had to talk to him.

Getting in touch with Rick, though, was another matter. Liam couldn't just call him up. If Rick was interested in telling him the truth, he'd have done it already. No, this had to be handled in person. How was Liam going to find him?

He tried the MyLife site, only to be presented with a lengthy list of Richard Hawthornes, identified by age, city, and family members. Refusing to be deterred, he began scrolling through the results. While Liam felt comfortable ruling out anyone over forty, he found several that could be the right age. Two were even from the Chicago suburbs. Then he wondered whether the information on the site was current or even accurate. He didn't have time to go tracking down one Richard after another, hoping he'd eventually find the one he was looking for.

Fortunately, he realized that wasn't his only option.

Alice Parker

AS DAVID LEFT, ALICE wished him luck. Catherine closed the door. She looked up at Tommy, who was still sitting on the stairs. "Go to your room." He didn't move right away, so she added, "Now!" and Tommy scurried off. "Why didn't you tell me about the number last night?" she asked her daughter.

Alice crossed her arms over her chest. "I told you. He gave it to *me.*"

"It's an emergency number," Catherine snapped. "What if something happened to you and I needed to reach him?"

"I could call him. Duh."

"Listen, young lady, I've had enough of your crap. I know you think you've got this whole world all figured out, but you better wake up. I'm your mom, you got it? As long as you're living in my house, you need to start showing me some damned respect."

Catherine rarely swore. When she did, Alice knew she was pissed. But she had no right to be. Alice firmly believed what she'd now told her mom twice. *If Dad wanted Catherine to have his number, he could have given it to her directly.* Her mother was overreacting like she always did. "You're insane."

"That's it. Go to your room."

"Gladly." Alice dramatically slung her backpack over one shoulder and went up the stairs, slamming her sneakers into the wood as hard as she could with each step.

"You can forget that concert tonight!"

Alice froze in her tracks. She spun around. "What?"

"You heard me. I'm not playing around anymore. You're grounded. Indefinitely. If you can figure out how to start showing me some respect, we can talk about you getting your freedom back."

Alice curled her hands into fists and let out a sound that was something between a growl and a scream. Catherine was out of control. Alice thought of a whole bunch of things she could have said right then, but all of them would have made the situation worse. More than that, saying them would mean she was acting just as out of control as Catherine was. She would not do that. She would not be like Catherine in any way. She bit her tongue, charged to her room, and slammed the door.

Catherine wasn't going to chase her up here. As long as she stayed in her room, Alice would be left alone. She dropped her bookbag by her desk and collapsed onto the bed. As she got control of her emotions, she stretched and straightened her back. Standing like she had been was uncomfortable.

Alice had been waiting three months for this concert. No matter what Catherine said, she wasn't going to miss it. But since she'd have to leave well before Catherine went to bed, simply sneaking out the front door (like she had on other nights) wouldn't be an option. She'd have to find another way.

Alice glanced around her room, thought about the layout of the house. There was only one option. She hadn't opened her window before and doing so took some effort. Humidity had gotten into the wood, nearly locking it in place. A cold breeze rushed in and Alice shivered.

She popped loose the screen, awkwardly working it in through the opening. She tucked the screen under her bed so Catherine wouldn't see it if she broke precedent and came to her room to talk to her.

She returned to the window and leaned out. There was a short overhang that wasn't too steep within reach. That would work.

Liam Parker

LIAM BLEW PAST THE receptionist and found Ava at a young designer's drafting table. He caught enough of what she was saying to know she was critiquing his work. The receptionist called for Liam to stop and apologized as Ava looked up from the sketches.

Ava removed her glasses. Liam could tell she was assessing his new look, but instead of commenting on it, she said, "Liam. What are you doing here?" Ava had moved to the United States with her family when she was a child, but he could still hear remnants of a French accent in her voice.

"We need to talk." He'd been moving fast since he'd gotten off the elevator. He sounded winded, although that had more to do with emotion than exertion.

"I'm sorry," the receptionist said again. "I couldn't stop him. Do you want me to call security?"

"No, it's fine," Ava said. She approached Liam. "Come with me." She led him to her office and closed the door. "What is this about? What are you doing here looking like that?"

"I'm here about Rick Hawthorne." He searched her face for a tell, even something small. A flinch, a narrowing of the eyes, a subtle nod— any gesture might be enough to let him know she recognized the name. It was half the reason he'd blown past the receptionist in the first place. He wanted to catch Ava off guard. The other half was because without using the alias he had no name at all he could give. Even here, using his real name was too dangerous. That wasn't paranoia, that was common sense.

But Ava's only reaction was to ask, "Who?"

"Jacob."

"What about him?"

"You didn't know his real name was Richard Hawthorne?"

Ava stared inscrutably at Liam for several seconds, then moved to one of the velvet chairs meant for guests. "Perhaps you should sit down and tell me what's going on."

Liam didn't feel like sitting, but he sat because Ava asked him to. He told her the important parts of his story, ending with the discovery that the name on the ID Jacob had given him was his own.

Ava sighed. "This is concerning."

"So you didn't send him to help me? You didn't have anything to do with this?"

"Liam, I like you. But no. Even if I'd known what was going on, I wouldn't have gotten involved. This, right here"—she gestured in such a way as to indicate not only her office but the entire suite—"is my baby. I would not do anything that could put it, or my life in general, in jeopardy."

Liam thought about something that should have struck him as odd right from the beginning. The people who attended Ava's poker games were well off, if not outright rich, at least as far as he knew. All except Elise. So what was she doing there? "How did Elise get in here to play?"

"Jacob recommended her." Her lips twisted with disgust and she corrected herself. "Rick recommended her."

"How did *he* get in?"

"Emmanuel. He'd been my dealer since day one, and I'd known

him for years before that. He was going to be out of town for a while, he said. Family emergency. Told me he knew someone who could fill in. I was in a pinch. I could either suspend the games until he came back or I could trust his referral. And why wouldn't I trust him?"

Although Ava did not look as disgusted by this second realization, Liam was certain it must have hit her harder than the first. To be betrayed by a friend was always worse than being betrayed by a stranger.

"I need to find Rick," Liam said. He knew something about Elise. Maybe a lot. And now there was this whole bizarre ID thing Liam needed to understand. And Ava's. What were they doing there? He could feel there was some sort of connective tissue that bound these things together. But maybe that was wishful thinking. Either way, this was where his investigation had led, and Rick was the person he needed to talk to next.

Ava got up and walked around her desk. She removed a lone key from her purse and unlocked the bottom-right desk drawer. She took out a collection of hanging file folders, then pried off a panel on the bottom of the drawer. Underneath was a thin stack of papers. "There are certain things you don't keep on the computer," she said.

She flipped through the papers until she found the one she wanted. "After I hired Jacob—*Rick*—I did my due diligence. I tried to, anyway. Couldn't find much. I got a copy of his credit and that looked okay." Ava took a pen and a piece of paper out of another drawer and started copying something onto it.

"It's probably a real name, just not his," Liam said.

"Yeah, well, anyway, I needed more than that. I trusted Emmanuel, but I needed to know where to find this Rick if it ever came to it, so I had someone follow him home his first night." Ava handed Liam the piece of paper. On it was an address.

Christopher Bell

RICK HAD USED HIS real name when renting his apartment and opening his CTA account. He liked to keep his legal activities as far away from his illegal ones as possible. Until Chris Bell had showed up at his door, that had seemed like a good idea.

Chris, of course, didn't know this. What he knew was that somebody named Richard Hawthorne had stolen his wallet, broken into his safety deposit box, and, for some strange reason, shown up at his office.

It was so unfathomable that the more he thought about it the less sure he was the receptionist had said "Richard Hawthorne." He could go downstairs and ask the security guard for the name himself, just to make sure he wasn't crazy. But he suspected there might be another option, one that would drive out the uncertainty in a way hearing the name again couldn't.

Chris brought up a browser and performed a search very similar to the one Liam had earlier. He hadn't looked Rick up when Arkin got his address from the CTA system. The thought hadn't even crossed his mind. Why would it? As far as he was concerned, a name and address was all he needed. And after things went awry at the apartment, what was the point in looking him up then? It wasn't as if Rick was likely to walk into his office one afternoon and announce himself.

But one profile after another—Facebook, Twitter, Instagram—all told him that was exactly what Rick had done.

So strange.

He'd come asking about a girl who'd run a con on Chris years earlier. Why? What was their connection? He didn't look like the man who had been with her that night, but that was years ago, so maybe he was. Either way, it didn't make sense. So, again, why?

Chris wished he hadn't brushed Rick off just to get away from him. He should have heard the man out, found out what he wanted, then dragged him to the parking lot and . . . what? Pinned him down and started breaking fingers until Rick told him where the ring was? That was ridiculous. He didn't know what he would have done after he listened to what Rick had to say. But he should have started there and perhaps instinct would have told him what to do next.

He fumed, pounded his desk. A coworker walking by asked if everything was all right. "Leave me alone," he snapped, and slammed his door shut.

Rick had walked right into Chris's office and he'd let him go. He'd missed his best opportunity to get the ring back. Maybe his last.

Maybe, maybe not.

Chris still had the alert set up to notify him if Rick used his credit card. Hoping for a miracle, he logged into the email account to see if he had received any notifications. It was empty.

Richard Hawthorne

RICK FELT LIKE HE was on a stakeout. He'd heard this was the kind of thing cops sometimes did—sitting in a car, watching a house, waiting for something to happen. It was incredibly boring. He couldn't understand why anybody would choose to do this more than once. Of course, a cop would be prepared to handle more than his most basic needs. He'd have a sandwich and snacks, a thermos of coffee, and maybe someone to talk to. While Rick had none of that, at least he had enough gas to keep the heater running and an empty water bottle to pee into.

The sun went down. The shadows of trees that lined the street grew long, melding into those of the houses until they became a single sheet of darkness punctuated by streetlights.

Rick almost fell asleep twice. In between, he fidgeted with the vents because it was something to do. Eventually, he hooked his phone up to the stereo, turned the volume almost all the way down, and fired up a Spotify playlist. It started with a modern remix of an Elvis song.

"*A little less conversation, a little more action,*" sang the King of Rock 'n' Roll. Right now, Rick would have settled for either one.

When his head lolled forward and he instinctively jerked it back for the third time, jolting himself out of sleep, he saw what he had been waiting for.

A window on the second floor slid open. A figure crawled out of it onto a narrow overhang. It had to be Alice. He had assumed she had permission to attend the concert and thus had expected to see her walk right out the front door.

Alice remained on all fours, crawling backwards to the edge of the roof, then slowly lowering herself over. She hung there for several seconds, no doubt judging a fall that looked higher than it was, and dropped the last few feet to the ground.

While she was doing all this, a car rolled past and Rick leaned over into the passenger seat to make sure he wasn't seen. The car was moving slow. Although, with its lights in his rearview mirror, he hadn't gotten a good look at it when it had come up from behind, he didn't think it was a coincidence that a car was coming down this quiet street at this time. When he rocked back up, he was certain it wasn't.

The car was a white Volvo, exactly like the one Alice's friend had been driving. It stopped in front of Alice's house, she got in, and the car sped off.

Rick followed from a safe distance. He knew they were going to the Bowards Arena, so when they caught a light right before it turned red, he wasn't worried he'd never find them again. But since he didn't know where they would park or where they were seated, he also couldn't let them get too far ahead.

When they got to the arena, he slipped on the same baseball cap he'd worn into the bank. The girls hung around outside near the ticket booth. They appeared to be texting their friends, trying to coordinate a place to meet. Like he had in the mall, Rick faked a phone call to look busy.

Concertgoers swarmed past. The delay made him nervous. He worried if he stood out here too long, Alice might notice him. Eventually, Rick's nerves got the best of him and he headed for the nearest entrance.

It was a safe bet that this was where they would come in as well, Rick told himself. With a concession stand on the other side of the glass, he could continue to watch them from the line.

After Rick had learned Alice was going to the concert, he'd bought one of the few remaining tickets. It was a floor seat and expensive. The ticket had been delivered in digital form. A woman working the door scanned it and the scanner flashed green. She held out a hand, letting Rick know his next stop was the metal detector. He passed through without a hitch.

The line at the concession stand moved faster than he thought it would. He ordered nachos and took a seat on a bench. This was worse than sitting in the car.

When Alice's friends arrived, the group hugged and chatted for a few minutes before making their way inside. Rick watched them figure out which direction they needed to go and dropped his head when they walked past, using the cap's bill to hide his face. He threw his remaining nachos into the trash can and wiped his hands on his jeans, glad to once again be on the move.

This will all be over soon, he thought. It couldn't happen fast enough.

He followed the teenagers through a gate where an usher checked their tickets. This gate, however, was not Rick's. The usher told him to go to D3. Rick apologized for the mistake and stepped out of line, keeping an eye on the teenagers as long as he could without arousing suspicion.

He went to Gate D3 and, once beyond the final ticket check, began working his way through the crowd back to where he'd last seen Alice. With only a small portion of the arena to search, finding them wasn't too hard. He ascended the stairs, going straight past them and then several rows higher. He found an empty seat at the end of an aisle.

Rick watched Alice and her friends closely. They joked, laughed, took pictures together. He didn't like being here. He didn't like what Liam had turned him into. But he took some comfort in the knowledge that what would happen next—all of it—was Liam's fault.

Liam Parker

A TAXI DROPPED LIAM off in front a squat brick building. A knee-high iron gate surrounded a patch of grass in front of it. To the side, a short flight of steps led down to a stone patio. Ava had said Rick lived in the basement unit. He asked the cab to wait for him, then took the steps down to the patio. The door to the unit was ajar, the window beside it smashed in. The second and only other window was also open.

Apparently, Liam wasn't the only one interested in finding Rick. He wondered if someone had beaten him to it. Still, he hadn't come all this way for nothing. He glanced at the dead fern in the corner and gently pushed the door open farther. "Hello? Anyone here?"

Silence.

He stepped inside. The heater was working, but it wasn't much warmer in here than it was outside. He zipped up his army jacket. The place was trashed. Every cabinet in the kitchen was open. Every drawer had been pulled out. The couch and TV stand were turned over. Broken dishes, takeout cartons, junk mail, and trash littered the floor. Someone was looking for something. Maybe that something had to do with why Elise was killed.

Liam doubted he'd find anything the intruder hadn't. But without Rick here to question, he might as well look. A stench—something like rotten meat—crept into his nose. It was enough to turn his stomach and he made a point of breathing through his mouth.

He made quick work of searching the living room and kitchen, and checked out all the same drawers the intruder had. He looked under the toppled furniture and sifted through the takeout cartons, careful not to touch any of the food.

When he came up empty, he went to the bedroom. The door, already opened far enough for him to squeeze through, wouldn't open any farther. A dresser had been pushed up against it. Rick must have been here when the intruder arrived, Liam concluded. He'd run into the bedroom and pushed the dresser against the door to try to keep him out. Liam looked at the open window. He must have crawled through there to try to get away.

Liam guessed Rick had escaped because the bedroom was also trashed. On the floor in front of the dresser he saw a dozen or so diamond rings. He turned on the light, kneeled to get a closer look. They all appeared to be the same.

He wondered why Rick had them and why the intruder hadn't taken them. But those questions, like so many others, were ones only Rick could answer. Since they weren't what he was looking for, he moved on.

Liam looked under the bed, inside the empty dresser drawers, through the stacks of clothes on the floor. At some point, he heard footsteps and he froze. He worried someone—Rick, the intruder, a cop—was coming. Thankfully the footsteps passed by the unit and faded away.

If it had been Rick, he'd realized after the initial alarm, that would have been okay. Liam had come looking for him, after all. But with what had happened here, he was also the least likely of the three to show up.

Liam needed to finish his search and get out of here. Scratch that.

He just needed to get out of here. He didn't know what he was looking for and his search so far had been fruitless.

But as he crossed the bedroom, he saw the corner of a notepad sticking out from underneath a bedside table. Liam had seen that notepad before, or one like it. Rick had been carrying it around in his back pocket at Ava's. He'd noticed the edge of it protruding from his pocket once in a while much like it was sticking out from underneath the dresser now.

It was probably nothing, but why not be sure? He grabbed the notepad and left. He could examine its contents from the safety of his hotel room. Then, as he was mounting the last step that would take him from patio to sidewalk, his phone rang.

It took Liam by surprise. There were only two people who had his number—Anita and Alice—and he had no reason to expect a call from either. He pulled out his phone and checked the caller ID. He recognized the ten digits as David's. His number was one of the few he knew by heart.

Liam wondered how David had gotten the number and whether he should answer. He hadn't wanted to involve his friend in all this, but it seemed like perhaps his friend had involved himself. David wouldn't have gone to the trouble to track him down if it wasn't important.

Liam answered.

"Thank God I got ahold of you," David said.

"What's going on? How did you get this number?"

"Alice gave it to me. Don't be mad at her. I've got information on your case. I need to see you immediately."

"What are you talking about? What information?" Liam asked, on the way back to the taxi.

"It's better I tell you in person. But it's good news, I promise. It will clear your name. Can you meet me at The Crown in thirty minutes?"

"I'll be there."

Richard Hawthorne

RICK OCCASIONALLY LOOKED UP at the stage, but he spent most of his time with his eyes on the teenagers four rows down. Three girls and one boy. Alice was on the end. After the opening band finished their set, the lights came up and roadies went to work breaking down equipment, preparing the stage for the headliner.

Alice and the friend with the white Volvo broke off from the pack. They headed down the cement steps and out through the gate they came in through. Rick did the same, hoping the usher wouldn't remember him.

He followed them to the bathroom where they went in together, came out together, and returned to their gate together. Rick was annoyed. He needed Alice alone, even if for just one minute. He went back to his own gate, made his way across the arena to his seat four rows up from Alice, and continued to wait.

Felix Winkler

FELIX PACKED UP HIS leather briefcase and slipped into an overcoat that was too big for him. It had been a long day. The plumbing had backed up in the public bathroom on Heartland's first floor for the second time in less than a month. A nurse had quit without notice, leaving his already shorthanded staff spread even thinner. And good old Roland Burris, who had no relationship to the former senator but often joked he was in fact the senator himself in disguise, went into cardiac arrest and had to be taken to Northwestern, where he was in ICU.

Days like this were hard. To unwind, he would go home, have a glass of brandy, and listen to Bach alone in his living room.

Felix turned off the lights to his office, locked the door, and spun around to find himself face-to-face with Nurse Cox. His head jerked back before he realized who it was. "Jesus, you scared me." Then he added, "I'm sorry, I shouldn't have—"

"It's okay," Cox said, looking down at her white shoes. Nurse Cox was soft spoken and agreeable, which made her one of Felix's favorite employees. She was a religious woman, and had asked him not to take the Lord's name in vain the first time he'd done it. Felix had tried to respect that request.

"What can I do for you?" he asked.

She held out her right hand. "Someone found this on the floor.

They brought it up to the nurses' station. We weren't sure what to do with it, so I brought it to you."

Felix took the ID. He recognized Rick immediately and didn't bother to look at any more of it. Sometimes Nurse Cox came to him with stuff like this. It was a problem that wasn't a problem. "Call Rick. Let him know he lost his ID."

"Are you sure?"

"Why wouldn't you?"

"But, the name . . ."

Felix looked at the ID again, and then he understood why Nurse Cox had come to him. The name on the ID was Christopher Bell. That was disconcerting. There weren't a lot of good reasons, if any, for Rick to have an ID with someone else's name on it.

"Never mind. I'll take it from here. Thanks for bringing this to me."

Nurse Cox did an odd little bow like she often did and scurried off. Felix put his briefcase down without taking his eyes off the ID, trying to decide what to do. He studied the license as if somewhere on it he would find an answer. Going to the police was the obvious choice, though not one he relished. Rick was the only family Ms. Hawthorne had. Felix didn't care for Rick, but he liked Ms. Hawthorne. It was why he had downgraded her to a shared room instead of simply kicking her out two weeks ago. If Rick was arrested, there'd be nobody left to pay for her care. That would leave Ms. Hawthorne in a tough spot. Felix could keep her around for a while, especially if he didn't move her back to her private room. But once her account started accruing debt again, even he could only keep her around for so long.

Felix decided he was jumping to conclusions. Rick had a fake ID, and that looked bad, but how bad was it really? What if this was all a misunderstanding? Maybe he would have to go to the police eventually, but he wanted to get more information first.

He took the elevator to the third floor and followed the hall to Ms. Hawthorne's room. If she was lucid, a quick conversation with her might be all it would take to clear this up.

He knocked on the door. Ms. Hawthorne was all smiles when she opened it, but Felix knew that meant nothing. She was happy to see people whether she recognized them or not.

"Ms. Hawthorne?"

"Yes?"

Felix looked past the old woman and could see her roommate in the distance. "Could you come with me? I need to talk to you for a minute."

She followed him into the hall. "What is it?"

Felix tried to come up with a good way to explain the reason for his visit. In the end, he simply handed her the ID and waited for a reaction.

Liam Parker

ONCE THE TAXI WAS moving, Liam pulled the notepad out of his pocket and flipped it open. On page after page, he found notes about his life, including his children's names; their ages; his favorite song; his favorite color; the names of his elementary, middle, and high schools; the names of his ex-wife, his first pet, and childhood friends; the name of the restaurant where he and his ex-wife met; the year they divorced.

It went on and on.

Liam recognized some of the notes as things he had told Rick. The rest Rick might have been able to dig up online.

By the time he finished going through the notepad, the other thing he noticed was that there was no information on the other players— Eric Ricci, the Grunter, Emily Stewart. Just him.

Why was Rick keeping notes about his life? And what did Elise have to do with it?

Hands shaking, he closed the notepad and slid it back into his jacket pocket. This was not where he had expected the murder investigation to take him. Once he had a chance to sift through these newest surprises, he would. But solving the murder had to be his number one priority.

If David was right, though, he might not have to worry about that much longer. But what could he have? How could he have uncovered something so important that Liam had missed? The camera in Elise's building was on the fritz, so there was no video footage. Elise's lies only led to more lies, more secrets. David had never been to Ava's or met Rick. The only witness Liam knew about was Elise's neighbor, and that certainly hadn't gotten him anywhere. So what could David have that would clear his name?

Two blocks from The Crown, Liam said to the driver, "You know what? You can let me off here. This will be fine." He wanted to get a look at the place before he got too close. Just in case . . . In case what? It was the paranoia getting to him. It had to be. If there was anybody Liam could trust, it was David. He knew that. Still, he got out of the cab two blocks early and made the remainder of the trip on foot.

David hadn't seen him since he'd dyed his hair or bought new clothes. He wouldn't recognize Liam like this, not right away. It would give him plenty of time to assess the situation.

As Liam got closer to The Crown, he examined every pedestrian who wasn't on the move. There was a homeless woman sitting on a bench in front of the restaurant, a group of people waiting at a bus stop on the corner, a couple loitering in front of a Starbucks on the other side of the street.

Liam also looked at the cars parked along the curb. Darkness had set in. He couldn't see into them from a distance, so he made a point to check each car as he passed it.

A bus came. All but two of those waiting for it got on.

Liam froze in his tracks. At other bus stops, that wouldn't be unusual. Many served more than one line. This one served only Line 82. There'd be no reason to pass up one bus for another, especially in this cold.

Liam was suddenly sure he wasn't being paranoid—he was being set up. David hadn't uncovered any evidence. He was working with the police to bring Liam in.

He turned around and started walking back the way he'd come.

Stop thinking like that. David wouldn't do that to you.

No, he wouldn't. Liam had to be making a mistake. If David had evidence that could exonerate him, Liam needed to see it. Then again, if David had evidence that could exonerate him, why hadn't he taken it to the police?

Liam ducked into the next shop. Collectables and Collections. It sold rare stamps, old comic books, ceramic figurines. A sign by the register said "Best price for your rarities."

The shopkeeper, a woman in a peplum dress with white hair pulled back in a ponytail, was leaning over a glass case looking at something another shopper had brought in. She glanced at Liam and said, "Let me know if I can help you."

"Thank you," Liam said, "I'm just browsing." He pulled out his cellphone and dialed David's number.

"You close?" David asked.

"I'm not going to be able to make it," Liam said, watching The Crown through the shop's windows.

"What? Why not? This is important."

"Can't you just tell me what it's about?"

"It's not something I can explain. You have to see it."

"Take it to the police, then. Ask for Detective Wyatt. If it's something that will clear my name, you should give it to him."

"Liam—"

"I have to go." Liam hung up and continued to watch the restaurant. As he feared, David stepped outside and the two men loitering by the bus stop approached him. So did the couple with Starbucks cups. Then a car door opened and Bash got out. He glanced over his shoulder, seemed to look right at Liam, and joined the others.

For a second, Liam was sure he'd been made. He thanked his lucky stars he had listened to his instinct. Bash's car was parked perhaps twenty feet from where he'd turned around. If he'd gone much farther, he might not have been able to slip away.

He knew he couldn't stay here and wait for the group to disperse. The shopkeeper was already looking at him funny. No wonder—even if she hadn't heard him mention the police, his behavior had to seem strange. But he couldn't go back out on the street either.

"Do you have a back way out of here?" he asked the shopkeeper.

She stammered through a series of "ums" like she was unsure what to say. As she did, the pudgy man in the sweater vest on the other side of the counter turned to look at Liam.

"Never mind." Liam charged through the shop, found a backdoor just beyond the one that separated Collectables and Collections private and public spaces. It dumped him into a dark alley. Turning right would lead him toward The Crown, so he turned left. He moved fast, past dumpsters and stacks of discarded boxes, hoping he wouldn't encounter an undercover officer at the end of the alley.

Richard Hawthorne

FRESH SYNC PERFORMED "HERE and Now," "I'm Back," and "Forever You." Strobes flashed in time with the music, while smoke machines puffed and massive digital displays projected an endless and nauseating stream of video.

They're like pack animals, Rick thought with disdain as he watched the teenagers four rows down dance with a carefree jubilation he had never known.

He wondered if he'd missed an opportunity to separate Alice from her friends. But when would that have been? At the McDonald's? At the mall? When she and Ms. Volvo had gone to the bathroom?

Rick was starting to think that wasn't going to happen when—God bless her—Alice tapped the shoulder of her friend, said something to her and, after all four briefly huddled, descended the cement stairs alone.

Rick kept his distance. Alice went to the concession stand closest to her gate and Rick meandered up behind her, pretending not to notice her. He cleared his throat a few times, hoping she would say something first. When she didn't turn around to look, he said, "Excuse me, Miss?"

When she did turn around, her expression suggested she didn't recognize him.

"Didn't I run into you at the mall earlier today?" He waited. *There it is*, he thought when her face changed.

"You were the guy at Urban Outfitters."

"Guilty as charged."

Alice nodded, seemingly pleased with herself for remembering who Rick was. "All right, well, nice to see you."

She was about to turn away. Rick could tell Alice wasn't interested in having a conversation with him. That wouldn't do. He had a question to ask, but because he felt like he first needed a segue, he said, "Good band, huh?"

"Yeah," she said, pausing briefly.

"My friend, Joe, couldn't make it, so I've got an extra backstage pass. You interested?"

The line in front of Alice moved forward. Her gaze cut to her gate and back.

"May I take your order?" shouted a man in a white bowling shirt with Bowards Arena emblazoned on the breast pocket.

Rick glanced over Alice's shoulder and saw the arena employee was talking to her. "Once in a lifetime opportunity," he said with a smile.

"I'm sorry. My friends are up there. I can't."

Rick didn't think this was about her friends. If he was younger, perhaps better looking, she'd have gone with him. It would have made everything so much easier.

Alice stepped back, spun on her heel, and approached the concession stand. She ordered sodas and popcorn. Four Cokes—one diet. The arena employee handed them to her in a disposable cup carrier.

Rick ordered a bottle of water, dropped a five on the counter. With Alice moving back toward her gate, he didn't wait for change. He came up behind her and grabbed her arm. "Your mother is Catherine Parker," he whispered. "She lives at 2421 West Brook Lane. You have a brother named Thomas; you call him Tommy. You're a student at Aubury High."

Alice's expression remained unchanged but her complexion faded and, unlike when he'd first grabbed her arm, she became still.

"They're both okay for now, but that could change."

She jerked her elbow once. Rick's grip tightened.

"What do you—"

"Lower your voice."

Alice took several ragged breaths. Her eyes darted left and right even though her head didn't move. The corridor was largely empty. Most attendees were inside, enjoying the show. "What do you want?" she asked, her voice shaking.

"Right now, I want you to walk," Rick said. He jerked her arm forward to put her feet in motion, shoved the water into his coat pocket, and wrapped his other arm around her waist so they might look like a couple to anyone passing by.

He led her through a steel door with a glowing "Exit" sign above it. "Drop the drinks," he said as they entered the stairwell, and she did. He likewise got rid of his water. They went down a flight, where another exit sign hung above another steel door and Rick led Alice through that one too.

It dumped them out in front of the arena parking lot. Rick looked around to get his bearings, then pointed. "This way."

As they crossed the parking lot, Alice started to whimper.

"It's going to be fine," Rick told her. "Do what I ask you to do and this will all be over soon."

He opened the passenger door of his rented Ford. "Get in."

Alice looked at the car seat, then at Rick. She shook her head, let out a weak and whiny "No."

Rick shoved her a step closer—"Get in"—and wrestled her into the seat. Looking down at Alice, he said, panting, "Why are you making this hard? This isn't about you. This isn't about your mom or your brother. But I'll make it about all of you if you keep this up. One phone call and they'll be dead before you get home, you hear me?" He didn't actually have anybody he could call who would kill Catherine or Tommy, nor did he think he could give that order even if he had someone to follow it. It was all just part of the show, like the earbuds he'd worn when posing as a UPS employee. Rick was merely playing his part.

He pulled out of the lot and drove west across the city. Alice had a death grip on the door handle. She never took her eyes off Rick. Finally, she asked, "Why?"

The word came out so soft, Rick hardly heard it. "What?"

"Why?" Alice asked, louder. "Why are you doing this?"

Rick ground his teeth together. He could tell her. Perhaps he *should* tell her. She deserved to know. But he decided it would be better coming from somebody else. "Ask your father."

Liam Parker

LIAM WAS IN OVER his head. His questions had led only to more questions. David had turned against him. How long could he keep running around the city with a fake ID chasing down leads before he got caught? Maybe it wouldn't be such a bad idea to let Ryan Reyes look for the killer. Maybe he should take that flight to Belarus. He fished around the inside pocket of his army jacket and found the crumpled ticket. He still had several hours until the plane left, more than enough time to get to the airport.

Liam wasn't sure how to square the plane ticket Rick had given him with the notepad he'd found in Rick's apartment or the pictures of himself online with Rick's name. But a ticket was a ticket—what did it matter right now? Ryan would be far better suited to investigate those things than he would. As long as Liam got out of the country, the rest would eventually be okay. He could set up bank accounts in countries around the world, funnel money through them until it was untraceable. He could live comfortably in Belarus while he waited for Ryan to unravel these mysteries.

He should have done this from the beginning. It was stupid to think he could solve a case the police couldn't. It was stupid to let Anita help him. He'd put them both in enough danger.

The alley dumped Liam onto a busy road. There were no cops there waiting for him. He headed north, moving away from The Crown at a healthy clip. He flagged taxis until one stopped and told the driver, "Take me to the airport."

The farther he got from downtown, the safer he felt. This was definitely the right decision.

Richard Hawthorne

RICK PARKED A BLOCK from Liam's building. For the first time since Alice had gotten in the car, she took her red and watery eyes off him. "What are we doing here?"

"You're going to get me into Liam's condo."

Alice shook her head. "No, I—"

Rick gently took hold of her hands. They were shaking. Although he expected her to pull away, she didn't. "Hey, I know this is scary," he said, in as soothing a tone as he could manage. "I just need you to walk me past the concierge and unlock the door to Liam's apartment. That's it. You do that, and you're done. You're safe. Catherine is safe. Everyone lives happily ever after, got it?"

"You'll let me go?"

"Once I'm done, you'll never see me again, okay?"

"My dad isn't home. If you're looking for him—"

"I'm not."

Rick could see the front of the towering glass building where Liam lived, and when Alice turned toward the windshield, he knew that was what she was looking at too. She was weighing her options, he figured. He imagined the thought process: *What does this madman want? What's he going to do once he gets inside? Am I betraying my father by going through with this? But what choice do I have? This madman will kill my mother. He'll kill my brother. Maybe I can warn the concierge when we get*

into the lobby. No, better not. He's not working alone. He said he has
someone he can call. If I try to warn anyone, my family might not make it.

She looked back at Rick and nodded. She wiped her eyes.

Although Rick believed she'd ruled out the option of warning the concierge, he didn't know that for certain, so he said, "You know what will happen if you try to signal for help."

She nodded again.

"Let's go."

He got out of the car. Alice didn't move.

Rick went around to the passenger side and opened her door. "Don't make this harder than it has to be."

Alice looked at him with as much hatred as he had ever seen. But she got out. Rick wrapped an arm around her waist like he had at the arena and guided her toward the building.

Liam Parker

THE TAXI DROPPED LIAM off at the airport. He made his way to the security checkpoint. The line weaved back and forth, following the roped path until it ended, and from there another fifty feet or so. Liam had completed the TSA Pre-Check months ago to avoid lines like this, but since it would be a bad idea to do anything in the airport under his real name, he resigned himself to a long wait.

He wasn't going to feel safe until he was on the plane. Standing still like this, just waiting in line, was the worst. A sheet of stainless steel tacked to the wall reflected a man in a pair of sunglasses. Liam had gotten so used to wearing them he'd forgotten he had them on. They would draw attention when he reached the checkpoint, so he took them off.

It won't be long now, he told himself. *Relax.*

When he got close to the checkpoint, he decided he should call Anita. No—he'd text. She needed to know what he was doing and where to find her gun, but there were too many people here who could listen in on his conversation.

He pulled out his phone and felt a pang of sadness in his chest when he realized he wouldn't be able to call his children as long as he was in hiding, nor would he have any chance of keeping them in Illinois. Even if he hired a lawyer, there was no judge in the world who would rule in his favor as long as he was on the run.

Liam pushed away the heartbreak that came from knowing he would lose his kids for a long time, if not forever. It was too much for him to handle. He had to take this one step at a time. He'd lose custody if he went to jail and he'd lose custody if he ran. He needed to focus on the things he could control.

He typed: *Thank you for your help. I have to go away for a while. I will be hiring Ryan Reyes to continue our investigation. I have your gun in the safe in room 132 at the Best Western. The code is 5342.*

While Liam felt like he was letting Anita down, this was better for them both. He'd already put her at too much risk. But that didn't stop him from adding *"I'm sorry"* at the end of the message and sighing when he pressed SEND.

If she texted him back, he wouldn't respond.

Liam looked around for a trash can. With the text sent, he didn't need the phone any longer. But, facing only one more switchback in the security line and surrounded by travelers, he'd have to wait until he reached the other side of the checkpoint to get rid of it.

A TSA agent waved him forward. "Ticket and ID, please."

He handed over both as confidently as he could. The agent looked at the picture on the license, then at him. She compared the names, scanned the barcode on the ticket with a digital reader. It beeped, flashed red. She frowned and tried again. Another beep. Another red flash.

"Could you step over here?" she said, as a second TSA agent approached Liam.

Richard Hawthorne

ALICE AND RICK ENTERED Liam's building. Rick kept his head down and his baseball cap low until he was sure the concierge working the desk was not the same one who'd denied the delivery.

Getting through the lobby went better than Rick had expected. The concierge waved and said, "How you doing, Miss Alice?"

"Just going up to see my dad," Alice said, trying to force a smile.

The concierge looked concerned once he saw Alice's face—he could probably tell she was upset—but he wasn't concerned enough to say anything. Likely he thought it was a personal matter. Walking as they were, with Rick's arm around her waist, he probably believed they were a couple. Alice might not have thought Rick was boyfriend material by looking at him, but that didn't mean the rest of the world agreed.

"You're doing good," Rick said as they approached the small bank of elevators.

Alice puttered to a stop in front of the elevators and stood there, arms crossed over her chest. She didn't press a button, didn't turn to look at Rick or see if the concierge was still watching them.

Rick suspected it was some sort of protest. A way of saying she would help him because she had to, but wouldn't do any more than was necessary. He didn't care. As long as she did what he needed her to, she could have as many of those little protests as she wanted.

He pushed the elevator button. The car came quickly. Once they'd reached Liam's door, Rick gave Alice her next instruction. "Unlock it."

She pulled a keyring out of her pocket, found the right key, inserted it into the lock, and turned, all with a slowness Rick assumed was deliberate.

He pushed her inside and listened for an alarm. When there was none, he guided Alice through the condo, keeping her in front of him so he could see her at all times. He found a small sunroom that had been converted into an office and told Alice to lie down on her stomach. He removed a rope from his jacket. It was part of the show, Rick told himself again as he tied her hands to her feet, making it impossible for her to get up.

"Stay there." Rick noted the irony only after he'd already moved the three feet from Alice to the computer. The first trick would be getting past the login screen. That would be far simpler than most people imagined. Rick inserted a USB stick with software downloaded from the Internet, then restarted the computer, forcing it to launch from the stick instead of the hard drive. The software that loaded let him reset the password to nothing and, with one more restart, he was in.

While Rick waited for the machine to finish booting up, he heard Alice crying. He could tell she was trying to do it silently, but still she whimpered and sniffled, her chest shuddering, her breathing uneven. He imagined how he would feel if Alice was his daughter and cursed Liam again for putting him in this situation.

Finally, the computer was ready to go. Time to get to work.

Liam Parker

FOUR TSA AGENTS ESCORTED Liam into a small room. He thought about running, but he was surrounded. "I'm sure it's a mistake," he said, hoping that was right. Had Rick given him a forged ticket as well as a forged ID? "The barcode probably got messed up carrying the ticket around in my pocket like I was."

"Probably," said the large TSA agent leading the way. He spoke without looking back and walked with his thumbs clipped under his belt.

Unlike the public parts of the airport, which had a sleek, modern feel, this room was made of linoleum flooring and painted cinderblock. The only windows ran along the side facing the terminal. There were a few plastic chairs for people to sit in and a security camera mounted to the ceiling.

Liam was directed to a chair that faced away from the window. "Stay right here," the agent instructed. "We'll get this straightened out in no time."

Liam sat, leaned forward. The longer he waited, the more his panic grew. He'd been hoping they'd take him directly to the Delta counter to get the matter resolved. At least there he'd be able to see what was happening.

The room brought back memories of his cell. He should have tried to make a break for it. He'd probably have gotten arrested, but he was

214

going to get arrested anyway, wasn't he? They were going to find out the ticket was fake, the ID was fake, and that would be that.

Don't panic. You don't know how this is going to play out. Maybe the ticket really was damaged. Just wait and see what happens. Besides, what choice do you have?

Damaged. Yeah, right.

Liam looked at the camera, then the door. While there was probably somebody watching him, there were no TSA agents within sight. Was he sitting here like a sucker when all he had to do to escape was walk out of the room?

He got up, made his way over to the door as casually as he could, and tried the knob. The door wouldn't budge. So much for that.

Richard Hawthorne

LIAM KEPT A TWO-DRAWER filing cabinet behind his desk. Rick leafed through it. The documents were well organized, making the search a breeze. He found statements from Bank West and Fidelity, which appeared to reference personal accounts. He turned to the computer, cracked open and awaiting his command. He scoured digital folders, checked Liam's browsing history, and compiled a list of seven financial institutions that he believed held the entirety of Liam's wealth.

Now it was simply a matter of logging into them and setting up a series of wire transfers. This, more than anything, was why he had to get into Liam's condo. With the two-factor authentication most financial institutions had these days, it was nearly impossible to log in without being on an authorized computer.

Rick brought up the Bank West website, hoping Liam had saved his login information into the browser so that it would autofill the required fields. He had saved the username, which was partially obscured by a series of dots. But when he clicked to the next screen, the field for the password was blank.

All the while, Alice continued to whimper. She couldn't see what Rick was doing and didn't ask.

Rick went back to the digital folders in search of a file containing Liam's logins, but came up short. Fortunately, people were predictable, and despite all the warnings out there not to use the same password on multiple accounts, many did. All Rick needed was one good login from anywhere and odds were Liam's digital world would open for him.

Bank West was the only financial institution he knew Liam used before arriving at the condo, and he had tried to get that login through phishing emails—"You have an important notice from Bank West. Click here to read it."—but Liam hadn't taken the bait.

Rick plugged in a second USB stick. Before Chris Bell had shown up at his apartment, he had installed a brute force program on it and loaded it with all the information he'd collected on Liam. He fired the program up and put it to work. It began attacking Facebook and Twitter, using Liam's email address and a sort of educated guessing system to generate passwords.

"It'll just be a little longer," he told Alice.

When the program returned a valid Facebook password, he tried it on the Bank West website. It didn't work. Then he tried it on Gmail, and it did. He requested a new password from Bank West, clicked the link they sent to Gmail, and logged in.

Liam had three accounts at that bank. Transferring the money out of them was a piece of cake.

Next.

He opened the Greenwire Trust website. From the look of it, the company appeared to specialize in alternative energy investments. Rick tried the Facebook login again. It didn't work there, either. He hadn't expected it would. But he hit a snag when he went to the password reset: Greenwire insisted on sending a code to the registered cellphone. That was going to be a problem, and he had five more financial institutions to break into if he wanted to empty out all of Liam's accounts. Rick needed another way.

He looked over at Alice and had an idea.

He called Liam's cellphone, but it rolled over straight to voicemail. The phone must be off. Rick got up, crossed the room, and knelt in front of Alice so she could see his face. "Do you have any way to reach your father?"

She whined, mumbled something Rick couldn't understand.

"What?"

She repeated herself, speaking in an exaggerated way. "*Nooo.*"

"You wouldn't lie to me, would you?"

Alice shook her head as best she could.

"Let's make sure of that, shall we?" Rick searched Alice for her cellphone, then browsed to a contact labeled "Dad." It had two numbers. One he had called and the second looked familiar. Was it his imagination—a random series of digits to which he was wrongly applying significance? He didn't think so.

Rick looked through his own call log and found the number. This was the call that had come in when he was at the nursing home. He remembered seeing it on his way out of Heartland. He wondered what Liam had wanted, then decided he didn't care.

Liam Parker

LIAM WAS BACK IN the chair, waiting for the TSA agents to return, expecting them to come with police in tow. A tremor worked at his hands. He clasped them together and held them in his lap. This was not how things were supposed to go down.

Liam's cell phone vibrated against his thigh. He pulled it out of his pocket and didn't hesitate to answer. At this point, what did it matter?

"Listen to me," said the caller.

Liam knew who it was. "Rick." For a second, he forgot about the TSA agents and the locked door and the camera overhead. He stopped shaking. Even the room he was in faded into mere background noise, no more significant than the hum of warm air being pushed through the vents. "What's going on? Why did you give me an ID with your name on it? How do you know Elise?"

Rick didn't answer. Instead, he began listing off the names of the financial institutions Liam used. "Greenwire. Fidelity. MicroTrust. Bank of America. . . ."

"Wait," Liam said, talking over him. "What does—"

"I want the username and password for each."

It only took a second for Liam to figure out what this phone call was about. Rick was planning to empty his accounts and, if Liam had heard him right, he had found all of them. Including those used by ConnectPlus. It would leave Liam and his firm penniless. "You can't do that."

"Say hello." Rick's voice sounded strangely far away, and the words were so out of place that Liam was unable to make sense of them—until he heard Alice's voice.

"Dad! Dad, he's got a knife!"

Then Rick was back. "Give me the logins."

Oh, God. Rick had his daughter. Suddenly, the money no longer seemed important. Liam didn't know every login off the top of his head. But he told Rick where he could find them. They were buried deep on Liam's computer, in a folder called "Family Photos." The file was encrypted, and for that file Liam was able to give him the password.

He expected Rick to say something about releasing his daughter after accessing the file. But after thirty seconds or so, he simply hung up.

Liam didn't know what that meant, but it terrified him. He tried calling back several times. Each call went straight to voicemail.

Rick had been planning this for a while, Liam realized. He'd been writing down things Liam had said in that notepad as far back as Liam could remember. They hadn't seemed important at the time. Liam did not construct his most important passwords using common memory tricks. But they were exactly the kinds of things you'd want to know if you were going to hack into someone's online accounts.

Was Elise involved? Had Rick killed her? Was he going to kill Alice too?

If Liam tried to tell the TSA agents or the police about his phone call, he doubted they'd believe him. Perhaps eventually someone would listen—maybe even Bash—but it wouldn't be until after he was taken to jail. That would be okay if Liam was only concerned about the money. It might not be soon enough for his daughter.

When Liam had run from Bash at his office, he'd told himself he was doing it to find the killer. But, on some level, he knew he was just running. He never had a real chance of figuring out who had killed Elise. That was who Liam was—a runner. He wouldn't have started ConnectPlus without David; he wouldn't have had the courage. Despite what he told himself, he had known Catherine was unhappy in their marriage. It was part of the reason he stayed at the office later and later. He was always running.

Liam couldn't run anymore, though. He couldn't get on the next international flight, even if that were an option. He had to save Alice. But how was he going to get out of here? And, more important, where was she?

Richard Hawthorne

RICK WORKED HIS WAY through each of Liam's accounts. When he was done, he pressed *67 on his phone to hide his number and placed one more call. It rang several times before Chris Bell answered.

"Who is this?" Chris demanded.

"You're looking for Richard Hawthorne, right?" Chris didn't say anything, so Rick continued. "You'll find him at the Best Western on State Street." He gave Chris the room number and hung up.

Rick didn't know if Liam was still at the hotel—Liam had been doing some digging and Rick didn't think he could have uncovered his real name from the room. Actually, Rick wasn't sure how he'd managed to do that no matter where he might have gone, but it had only emphasized the importance of sowing chaos where he could until he was out of harm's way. Sending Chris after Liam—something he planned to do at this point, anyway—was his only play.

There was one last decision to make before he left: What should he do about Alice?

Liam Parker

IT DIDN'T TAKE LONG for Liam to figure out that Alice and Rick were at his condo. That was why Rick hadn't said anything after Liam had told him where to locate the file with the passwords. No "This better be the truth or else." He didn't need to. He'd found the file while Liam was on the phone, opened it, and hung up.

Liam had to get out of here.

He let the tremor in his hands spread throughout his body, then exaggerated it. He slid off the chair and collapsed onto the floor in spasms. He hoped it looked like he was having a seizure.

It took almost a minute before a pair of TSA agents came to check on him. Liam was starting to wonder if there was anybody behind that camera. One of the agents stayed by the door. The other kneeled down beside Liam and grabbed his arm. "Hey, buddy, are you all right?"

Liam didn't answer. He just kept shaking.

The agent cursed. "Go get help."

Liam heard footsteps as the second agent scurried away and the metallic click as the door automatically locked. This was it. Now or never.

Be brave.

Liam slammed his fist into the soft flesh between the agent's legs (something he would have never thought himself capable of before) and yanked the badge off his belt as he went down.

Liam was on his feet in a flash. He held the badge up to the scanner beside the door. The lock released with the same metallic click he'd heard seconds ago. He ran without looking back. He had to assume TSA agents, and probably police officers, were after him. Even if they weren't within sight, they were watching him on the security cameras throughout the airport. Blending into the crowd was not an option. He wouldn't be safe until he was in a cab.

Christopher Bell

EMMA AND CHRIS WERE sitting on the sofa watching a Jennifer Aniston rom-com on Netflix. A fire was burning in the fireplace, the lights turned low. It was a quiet evening, until the phone rang.

Emma gave him a look that said, *Don't answer it.* He couldn't help himself. A ringing phone at this hour could mean a tip on the Asian markets.

Chris answered without looking at the Caller ID. Emma's eyes narrowed to angry slits and, hoping to appease her to some degree, he feigned annoyance. "Who is this?"

"You're looking for Richard Hawthorne, right?"

Chris's pulse quickened. His anger level shot up to a ten upon hearing Rick's name. He tried to figure out who the caller was. Arkin's voice was raspy, with a hint of a Southern drawl; it wasn't him. Chris wondered briefly if it might be somebody on the police force, but quickly ruled that out, too.

Emma, just to be spiteful, turned up the volume on the TV.

"You'll find him at the Best Western on State Street," the caller continued as Chris pressed a finger to his other ear so he could hear. Then the caller gave Chris the room number and hung up.

Chris let the phone fall away. He had no trouble processing the stacks of business documents he read every day and analyzing them for clues on future stock performance, but this was something he couldn't quite get his mind around. Why would somebody—a stranger—call him and tell him where he could find Rick? Who besides Emma and Arkin would even know Chris was looking for him?

"Anything important?" Emma asked. Her question was insincere, filled with sarcasm.

"Did you talk to somebody about Rick? Do you understand what kind of trouble I could get in if anybody finds out what I have done?"

"Of course I didn't. What the hell is going on?"

"Someone just called and told me where I could find him."

Emma paused the movie. "Are you serious?"

Chris nodded, and thought about it a little more. He decided he only had two options. He could either follow up on the anonymous tip or let it slip away, fretting about who it was from. And what did it matter who it was from if it turned out to be true? Worst case, it wouldn't lead him anywhere but right back to where he was now.

He hopped up, moved to the closet to put on his shoes. "I have to go."

"Who was it?"

"I don't know."

"What do you mean you don't know? They didn't say?"

Chris shrugged on a jacket. "No, they didn't."

"That's—"

"Strange. I know. But if we want to find Rick before the police this might be our last chance."

Arkin was more than happy to accompany Chris Bell to the Best Western. For a price. Chris, who didn't want to make the trip alone, agreed to pay it.

They parked in a lot in front of the hotel.

"This place looks sort of trashy," Chris said. It certainly wasn't somewhere he would stay.

Arkin shrugged. "It's not that bad."

The men followed the signs to Rick's room and knocked, each of them standing to one side of the door so they couldn't be seen through the peephole. Chris listened carefully for any sounds of movement. There were none.

"Are you sure he's staying here?" Arkin said.

"Let's find out."

They returned to the front desk. A receptionist in a suit and tie asked how he could help.

"We need to leave a message for one of your guests."

"Certainly. Who?"

"Rick Hawthorne. He hasn't checked out yet, has he?"

The receptionist looked something up on his computer. "Nope. Not yet. What message would you like to leave?"

So, whoever the caller was, he'd been telling the truth. Chris glanced at Arkin, then said, "You know what, I don't want to bother him. We'll catch up with him at the office tomorrow."

"Suit yourself," the receptionist said with a smile.

Chris turned, exited the lobby. Arkin followed his lead. Neither of them spoke until they were back in the car.

"What do you want to do?" Arkin said.

Chris turned on the engine. He cranked up the heat and slid his seat back to make himself comfortable. There was only one thing they could do. "Wait."

Liam Parker

LIAM BOLTED PAST THE baggage carousels. Cops fell in behind him, coming out of this door or that, appearing from places he wouldn't have anticipated. Twice they almost grabbed him. But luck had been on his side, and, so far, he was still a free man.

Then a kid dragging a suitcase as big as he was walked directly into Liam's path, and it was too late for Liam to stop. He tumbled over the bag, rolled, scrambled back to his feet. The kid screamed and his mother shouted. Liam couldn't make out what she was saying. He thought it was something about slowing down, paying attention, looking where he was going.

He passed through a pair of sliding glass doors, saw a line of taxis idling along the curb, and hopped in the closest one.

"What's the rush?" the driver asked, turning to face him.

"Take me to 1712 Walker Avenue," Liam said, out of breath.

The driver shrugged and pulled away from the airport. Liam looked over his shoulder and saw a flock of officers, bigger than he'd expected, coming out of the same sliding glass doors he had. He instinctively slid down in his seat, even though he knew there was no way they could see him.

Once the driver pulled onto the interstate, Liam relaxed a little and sighed with relief. A momentary reprieve as the stress of one situation gave way to the stress of the next. Even as the air was exiting his lungs, all his muscles tensed back up as his attention shifted entirely to saving his daughter.

Over the next twenty minutes, the driver made idle chitchat and Liam did his best to play along, claiming he was here to see family and in a hurry because his flight was delayed. He didn't want to raise any more red flags than he already had. The last thing he needed was the driver watching him in the rearview mirror, wondering what sort of passenger had gotten into his cab.

As they closed in on State Street, Liam realized they were going to go right past the Best Western he'd been staying in. It would only take an extra minute to run in and get Anita's gun. Liam didn't expect he would be any more comfortable handling the weapon now than he had been earlier. He could fake it though, and it seemed like a good idea to take the Beretta with him. Who knew what he'd be up against when he came face-to-face with Rick?

Liam asked the driver to stop by the hotel, claiming he wanted to check in. When the taxi driver pulled into the Best Western parking lot, Liam got out and hurried to his room.

It took two tries to open the safe. He slid the gun into his inside jacket pocket and ran back down the hall and through the lobby. On his way out, the receptionist said, "You're Mr. Hawthorne, aren't you?"

The name didn't register at first. When it did, it didn't even register as Liam's alias. *Hawthorne. Richard.* Liam stopped. "What'd you say?" Then he remembered. "Are you looking for me?"

"You're Mr. Hawthorne?"

"Yes."

"Your co-workers already left."

"What?"

"If you're looking for them, I just wanted to let you know they're gone. They said they'll see you in the office tomorrow."

Liam didn't like the way that sounded. He looked suspiciously at the receptionist as he backed away, wondering if he might be involved in all this. Rick had put Liam up in this hotel. Maybe they were working together. It was crazy, paranoid thinking; he knew that, but he couldn't help himself.

Liam shook off the idea and ran. It didn't matter. None of it mattered. He had to save his daughter.

Christopher Bell

ARKIN TAPPED CHRIS'S SHOULDER and pointed to a taxi pulling into the Best Western parking lot. "Look. Could that be him?"

Chris squinted, saw the man get out of the cab. The man didn't turn around, but he was wearing the same green army jacket Rick had been wearing earlier in the day. "It's him."

"What do you want to do?" Arkin said.

Chris originally planned to repeat the knock-and-wait strategy they'd implemented earlier. But he had also expected when Rick returned to his room he would stay for a while. The waiting taxi suggested otherwise. If Liam got back in that taxi, they might lose him in traffic. Since they weren't the bad guys here, there was no need for them to be subtle. "Let's go get him."

They got out of Chris's car at the same time, their doors shutting in unison as if the move had been choreographed. As they crossed the parking lot, Chris studied the hotel. He thought about where Rick's room was. He saw a side entrance that would get them there faster. "That way."

The men went through the door and caught a glimpse of Rick at the end of the hall. Then he was gone. He had disappeared into the lobby and was no doubt headed back to the cab. Just like Chris and Arkin had gotten out of the car in unison, they broke into a run in unison.

Chris pulled ahead. He was using every ounce of energy he had to push his legs faster and then faster still. Rick had outmaneuvered him when he stole Chris's wallet. He wasn't getting away a second time. They rounded the same corner that led to the lobby and Chris saw the thief stepping through the sliding glass door.

"Hey! What—" the receptionist shouted, but his voice was swallowed up by the wind as Chris passed through that same door.

Rick was twenty feet from the taxi when Chris catapulted himself into the air and landed on top of the thief. "Where is it?" he shouted.

Liam Parker

LIAM SQUIRMED, CONFUSED AND trying to escape as the two men fought to contain him. His whole left side was screaming out in pain after colliding with the cement. He recognized one of the men as Chris Bell. Questions sped through his mind too fast to ask. All he could do was try to push the hands away.

Liam got to his belly, then his knees. Somehow, by pushing and shoving, slipping this way then that, he managed enough wiggle room to slide out of his jacket and get free, then ran to the cab.

He was almost there when a shot rang out, muting the world around him and leaving his ears ringing. He reflexively ducked, curling inward to make himself smaller, but kept running. The taxi was right there.

Was.

The driver slammed on the gas and sped into traffic, seemingly without looking.

Liam slowed to a stop, watching in horror as his only means of escape drove off. Behind him, someone said, "What the hell are you doing?"

Then someone else said, "Do you want it back or not? Turn around!"

Liam reluctantly obeyed. He saw Chris going through the pockets of the army jacket. The second man, arms extended, had both hands wrapped around the handle of a gun and the barrel aimed at Liam.

Anita's gun.

Chris threw the jacket on the ground. "Where is it?" he shouted.

"What?"

"You know damn well what."

Liam didn't think it would do him much good to say he didn't. These men believed he was Rick and at least one of them was willing to shoot him. But standing here like this, saying nothing, wasn't going to do him any good, either. And neither option would get him any closer to saving Alice. Only one thing would do that.

Liam bolted toward the street, betting that the man with the gun wouldn't shoot into traffic and hoping his aim wasn't very good if he did. It was crazy, but what choice did he have?

The gamble paid off. He glanced over his shoulder to see the men pursuing him, but at least nobody was shooting. Liam weaved through the traffic, thinking it might help put some distance between them. Perhaps it did, though not much. Chris and his friend were quick to find their own path between the cars.

Liam was burning time. Every second he spent running from Chris might be the second he needed to save his daughter. He had to lose these men fast. He thought about ducking into an alley, but decided that would probably be the worst choice he could make. In an alley, he would be isolated, just like he had been in the alley behind Collectables and Collections. If the man with Anita's gun was serious about shooting him, he'd have no qualms pulling the trigger there. Liam needed a crowd. Someplace like—he looked as far down the street as he could see—that. Mariano's.

Mariano's was an upscale supermarket chain, and Liam knew it well. He carried the Mariano's discount card and shopped at locations around the city. This one he had only been to once. He had forgotten it was here.

The supermarket spanned two floors and had an underground parking garage. On the first floor was a variety of food stations that sold made-to-order pasta, burgers, pizza, salad, and sandwiches. You could get a gelato from a woman in a paper hat, a coffee from a barista, and a drink from a bartender. Two dozen tables were cramped together in rows near the front of the store. All of them were occupied.

Liam made it inside and went for the escalator. He hoped, with the crowd, the small lead he had would be enough for his pursuers to lose sight of him. It wasn't.

Chris and his friend came through the door, scanning faces. Chris pointed straight at Liam and they started moving again.

Liam couldn't see the gun, but he was sure the men still had it. He pushed past the shoppers in front of him, quickly scaling the escalator. He didn't have to look to know Chris and his friend were doing the same.

The second floor looked more-or-less like an ordinary grocery store, with aisles of food and cashiers near the elevators. The escalator ended beside rows of shopping carts and directly in front of the fruits and vegetables.

Liam ran down the closest aisle looking for cover, past shelves stacked high with pet food. In the middle of the store, the aisle ended and another began, creating an additional route for shoppers to navigate the space and cutting down on unnecessary traffic in the aisles.

At that intersection, Liam turned the corner and pressed his body as flat as he could against a Cheerios display without knocking the boxes over. On the end cap in front of him hung all kinds of gift cards. He held his breath, looked around for something within arm's reach that would work as a mirror, but saw nothing.

He pulled his TracFone out of his pocket, confirmed it had a front-facing camera, and fiddled with the phone until he saw an image of himself on the screen. He held the phone horizontally and moved his hand barely an inch at a time. When the camera cleared the end cap, he could see the entire aisle behind him.

Just in time too, since a second later Chris and his friend barreled past it. They turned their heads, doing a quick examination of the aisle as they moved to the next one.

Liam doubled back the way he'd come, using the camera again at the end of the aisle to peek around the corner. A woman with a small child and an overflowing hand basket gave him a funny look. He smiled, trying to appear relaxed. "It's not what you think," he said. Of course, he had no idea what she thought, couldn't even imagine, and Liam's assurances clearly didn't assuage her concern. She pulled her daughter close and moved around him.

Liam put his eyes back on his phone. Last time he'd looked at the screen, he could still see Chris and his friend making their way, aisle by aisle, to the far end of the store. Now, they seemed to be gone.

This was his chance. He had to get back downstairs and outside. It would take Chris and his friend several minutes to figure out they'd been duped. Liam ran for the escalator, and he was almost there when out of the corner of his eye he saw Chris's friend coming at him full speed.

The escalator was more crowded going down than it had been going up. He pushed his way through the shoppers and glanced back when he got to the bottom. Chris was nowhere to be seen, but his friend was closing the distance between them fast.

If Liam went out onto the street, he'd be right back where he started. He needed a place to hide. It had to be somewhere that would lead the men to think he'd left the store even though he hadn't. The stockroom?

Maybe. He could fold himself up in a cardboard box. They'd search the area and determine he'd gone out through the loading dock.

But there were problems with that plan. The biggest was that he didn't see a door to the stockroom that wasn't behind a manned food counter. What he saw, instead, was an empty elevator, arrow pointing down, doors starting to close.

Liam made a break for it. As he slid between the doors, they bounced back. With Chris's friend nearing the bottom of the escalator, Liam furiously pressed the close button.

Finally, the doors obeyed. Chris's friend was only seconds from reaching Liam when they shut.

When the doors opened again, Liam was inside the parking garage. Most spaces were full, but there were no shoppers within sight. There was a stairwell that no doubt led to the street and a ramp at the end of the lot that did the same.

Liam had to think fast. He desperately wanted to get back to the street, hail a cab, save his daughter. But the stairs weren't an option. They might connect to the store, as well; Chris's friend could be coming down them right at that very moment. And he might not make it to the end of the lot without being seen.

His best move would be to hide in the dumpster.

Stick with the plan, he told himself. But the street was right there. There were taxis going up and down this road all the time. It was stupid and irresistible and he ran.

I can do this.

He repeated the four words over and over in his head, pushing himself faster.

I can do this. I can do this. I can do this.

He was almost at the bottom of the ramp, hadn't heard any doors open. There'd been no ding of the elevator. He was going to make it.

Then he heard more than felt a thump on the back of his head. It was like a low thud that echoed around his skull before pain blossomed along the same paths, following it like thunder follows lightning.

Liam felt the world slip away. The shadows of the parking lot were swallowed up by a nothingness that was black and all-consuming.

Liam Parker

UNCONSCIOUSNESS GAVE WAY TO a dull ache. It rose slowly through the darkness, began to pulse, then throb. Liam groaned and put a hand to his head. He tried to remember what had happened and where he was, but all that would come back to him was running. Up a ramp. To the street . . . to save his daughter.

Alice.

His eyes shot open as the phone call at the airport and the chase that followed flooded back. The world was as dark as it had been when they were closed. Where was he?

Liam was rolled up in the fetal position shivering when he awoke. Wherever he was, it was cold. He tried to get up, banged his feet against something after they'd moved only a few inches. Then, as he lifted himself off the ground, he banged his head.

With growing panic, he reached out and touched the wall in front of him. It felt like fiberglass. He walked his hands up it, along the ceiling, and down the other side, mapping the space he was in. It was barely big enough for him to sit up in. And there was something else— it seemed to be moving. Rocking. Or perhaps that was only the pounding headache playing tricks on his equilibrium.

Wherever he was, he had to get out of here. He had to save Alice. She was out there and in danger and, dammit, he was the only one who could help her.

Then Liam saw a sliver of gray light, something like the outline of a door only much smaller. He reached out, found a handle. Relief washed over him as his fingers wrapped around the steel.

But the handle wouldn't turn.

He pressed down harder, leaning into it, hoping he could break the lock. He couldn't. His strength gave out. His muscles told him the effort was useless. He screamed, pounded the door, kicked the walls.

When that didn't work, Liam felt his pockets for his phone—he could call Anita, or, better, the concierge in his building—but it wasn't there. His pockets were empty. No phone, no keys, no wallet. He searched the ground around him by touch, hoping it all had slipped out of his pocket. He found nothing. Chris and his friend must have taken everything after he was knocked unconscious.

Finally forced to admit there was no getting out of here and no sending Alice help, he gave up. What would it matter at this point, anyway? Liam didn't know how long he'd been out, but it had been long enough for somebody to move him here. No matter where *here* was, a quick calculation put that at thirty minutes, minimum. Plenty of time for Rick to kill Alice and get away, if that was what he had planned.

Liam collapsed against the fiberglass wall behind him, pulled his knees to his chest, and cried. He stayed like that for an eternity, remembering Alice as a baby, a child, a teenager. He imagined what her life would have been like as an adult. He pictured her graduating from high school and then college. In his mind, he was there, in the front row, beaming as Alice walked across the stage to accept her diploma. Then she was even older, with a child and family of her own, working a job she loved, maybe following in Liam's footsteps, becoming her own boss, and still—always and forever—too little in his eyes to be doing any of it.

Liam pounded his shivering fist against his forehead, which made the pain worse. He had to get these thoughts out of his head. It felt selfish—taking his mind off his daughter to think about himself—but he didn't know Alice was dead, did he? And what good would it do him thinking that way in here?

Here. Again, he was forced to use that mysterious pronoun.

Where was he?

The rocking was not a trick on his equilibrium. Liam was sure of that now. He was moving. Not the way he would be if he was in a car or a truck, though. This was something else. This was . . . a boat.

Why was he on a boat? What did Chris and his friend have planned?

Sooner or later, he was going to find out. They were going to come get him. Then what? When Chris and his friend had confronted Liam at the hotel, they'd demanded he hand over "it." But they weren't asking Liam for "it." They were asking Rick. What would they do when Liam couldn't give it to them? Kill him? Dump his body overboard?

Liam assumed it was still night. He imagined something not much bigger than a sailboat out on Lake Michigan, alone in the dark, and was forced to admit that, yes, maybe they would.

Was this the reason Rick had given Liam a fake ID with his name on it?

It could be.

Think it through.

What did he know?

Rick had sought him out after Liam had been charged with Elise's murder. He had put Liam up in a hotel and given him a fraudulent plane ticket. Rick must have known the plane ticket would lead to Liam's arrest if he tried to use it, although perhaps he never thought Liam would get to the airport to find out. Maybe he had only given it to Liam to keep him in line, thinking that, ticket in hand, Liam had no reason to risk leaving the hotel until late tonight. And maybe, if all that was true, Chris hadn't shown up at the hotel when he did by chance.

Liam could feel pieces falling into place.

Rick had put Liam in a hotel to make sure his apartment was empty and to give him a place to hide. He wanted Liam out of jail for a little while so that when he transferred the money out of Liam's accounts from Liam's computer and in Liam's apartment, it would look to the police like Liam had done it.

But Liam wasn't the only one Rick had robbed, was he? He had also robbed Chris. And whatever Rick had taken was worth enough to Chris to kill for.

Had Chris been the one to break into Rick's apartment? Had he gone looking for what Rick had stolen?

If so, perhaps that was what tied this all together.

Clearly, Chris didn't know what Rick looked like. Thus, the fake ID and social media accounts in Rick's name. Rick wanted Chris to believe Liam was the man he was looking for and probably figured the best way to do that was with a picture on Facebook. (Rick couldn't have expected Liam to go to Chris's office. But, in retrospect, that had only helped Rick's cause. It gave Chris a chance to see Liam up close and match his face to the name Liam had given to security.)

Then what? After Rick had robbed Liam, had he tipped off Chris to Liam's location? Maybe he was hoping Chris would kill him. If he did, Rick would have gotten away scot-free.

As long as Rick killed Alice too.

Liam could feel his heartrate picking up. He was starting to panic again. He closed his eyes, took several deep breaths, urging himself to calm down. That theory was close, but it wasn't right. It depended too much on what Chris would do when he found Liam, and he doubted that was something Rick could control.

Then there was a clank of metal and the door opened.

Felix Winkler

"ST. MATHEW'S PASSION" CLOCKED in at almost three hours. Felix did not plan on moving from the sofa until he had heard the whole thing. As the music swirled around him, he waved his hands in the air, conducting an imaginary orchestra with an imaginary baton. He knew the Bach piece so well that, even though he did not speak German, he was able to mirror the opera singers by approximating the words.

Felix had sometimes wondered if he should look up the translation, ultimately deciding against it. His lack of understanding did not diminish his appreciation for the music. If anything, it enhanced it. He felt, by not understanding, he was able to listen with his heart instead of his mind.

The orchestra crescendoed and fell back. The opera singers dropped out and returned.

As Felix's whole being responded to the raw emotion infused into the music, his mind drifted. Dark waters soothed the stress of the day. Tomorrow, he would oversee the repairs to the first-floor restroom. Tomorrow, he would call Northwestern to find out if Roland Burris was still in ICU. Tomorrow, he would sort through resumes to find a replacement for the nurse who quit. But for the next hour and forty-eight minutes, he would think about only the music.

Normally, he would think about only the music.

Tonight, thoughts of Richard's fake ID kept rising above the dark waters that buried everything else. When Felix had shown it to Ms. Hawthorne, she'd noticed right away the name was wrong, and he had begun to hope that she would indeed be able to provide some information about it. But when she asked why he was showing her an ID with her brother's picture on it, that hope vanished. Even if there might have been an innocent explanation, she wasn't going to be able to tell him what it was during one of her episodes.

And then things got worse. Voice shaking, Ms. Hawthorne had accused Felix of playing a trick on her. She shouted at him to go, even as he tried to apologize and back away. She said it was mean to play a trick on a woman in her condition and that he should just leave, leave with his mean tricks and get out of there.

Felix put the ID in his briefcase and, when he got home, leaned his briefcase against the small table next to the door where he left his keys. He would call the police in the morning, he'd thought, mentally adding it to tomorrow's growing to do list. It was the decision he should have made from the beginning.

Felix tried not to get emotional about what this would mean for Ms. Hawthorne. While his predecessor wouldn't have cared, he couldn't help it. Try as he might to stay in the moment, he felt the music losing its spell over him. Reluctantly, he opened his eyes. The only light in the apartment came from a streetlamp placed directly outside his window. It filtered through and around the curtains, making him squint, and destroying the last of the magic the music held. All the stress of the day returned and was compounded by all he knew he had to do tomorrow.

There was no point in trying to get back into the music. The moment was gone. Felix pressed a button on the remote to turn off the stereo. Perhaps because he had nothing better to do, he took the ID out of his briefcase and studied it again. He'd only seen a fake ID one other time in his life. His son, who was now an adult and living in California, had one when he was nineteen. Felix had grounded him for a month. That ID, though, had clearly been fake. Felix never found out if his son had been successful in buying alcohol with it. If he had, it was because the cashier didn't care. This ID was on another level. If Felix didn't know the man in the picture, he would have thought it was legit.

What would he have done if that had been the case? he wondered. Nurses and visitors alike had turned in lost scarves, hats, and jackets. They had turned in single gloves, two decks of playing cards, and once a glass baking tray with unfinished brownies in it. All but the tray of brownies had gone into a large plastic bin Felix kept in his office. (The tray of brownies would've made a mess, so he kept it on his desk.) Most items, including the tray of brownies, were claimed within a couple of days. The few that went unclaimed for more than three months he either donated to Goodwill or threw away.

An ID, though, was not like the other items. It didn't belong in a large plastic bin. It was important. So what would he do? The question was entirely academic since he knew this was not simply a lost ID. Still, he thought through the answer, building a blueprint for him to follow should the issue ever arise.

Since Felix didn't know the names of every person on staff, he would start by checking the HR system. If that didn't work, he would search the residents database by last name. Then, if necessary, he would check the visitor logs for the last—how may days?—three days. He couldn't imagine a lost ID going undiscovered for that long, but it was best to be thorough.

But not every visitor's name went into the log. What would he do then if he still hadn't turned up a phone number? Would he have any choice other than to drop it into the plastic bin with all the other lost items? Even if he did, would he bother pursuing it?

The answers to all three questions were, respectively, *nothing*, *probably not*, and *no*. At some point, it simply wasn't his problem. But since this was entirely academic, and since his curiosity had gotten the better of him, he looked up the name Christopher Bell on his computer in the bedroom. Several listings came up. On a whim, he did another search, this time including the address. Since the ID was fake, he didn't expect a match. But there was one—it was one of those sites that harvested personal data—and it included a phone number.

Christopher Bell

AFTER ARKIN HAD THUMPED Rick on the back of his skull and dragged his body behind a dumpster, he'd searched Rick for a hotel key and returned with Chris to the Best Western to scour Rick's room. They hadn't found the ring. Arkin had asked Chris what he wanted to do, and Chris had said he didn't know.

Privately, Chris regretted bringing Arkin along. Arkin fed his worst instincts. He might have beaten Rick unrecognizable if he'd gotten the chance (and he still might), but he wouldn't have chased Rick through a crowded grocery store if he had been on his own. He wouldn't have fired a gun at the thief. (Arkin had said he missed Rick on purpose, but Chris had his doubts.) He wouldn't have broken into Rick's apartment or hotel room. Chris had his reputation to think about.

But when Arkin had said that if Chris wanted the ring back they couldn't leave Rick where he was, Chris didn't insist they put an end to the madness. He didn't tell Arkin they should turn him over to the police. What he said was, "I know somewhere we can take him."

That somewhere was the small yacht on which he'd considered proposing to Emma. Chris shifted in his seat and cracked his knuckles. He was sitting on one of two sofas in the cabin. Arkin sat on the other.

The boat, which Chris had named *Course Correction*, was docked at the Belmont Harbor. He had no interest in taking it out on the open water right now. As things stood, the heater was working as hard as it could to keep the cold to a minimum. He didn't think it would be a good idea to add wind to the equation.

Besides, there'd been nobody around when they arrived at the docks and Chris hadn't seen a soul since. It was too cold out here for anybody who wasn't looking to stash a body.

Neither Chris nor Arkin had spoken in a while. They were listening for signs of life. Rick was locked in an exterior closet, normally used for storing life jackets and inflatable rafts. Although Chris had said even in here they would hear him banging on the hull when he woke up, he wasn't sure that was true and had only said it because it was too cold to wait outside. He suspected Arkin knew that, which was why he was listening just as intently as Chris was.

That had been a while ago. Chris had thought Rick would have regained consciousness by now. Figuring he better check on him, he got up and was about to announce his intention when his phone rang.

Chris glanced at the Caller ID. He was expecting to see Emma's name on it. He had been gone for several hours and she was probably getting worried. But it wasn't her. The number wasn't associated with any of his contacts. He wasn't wild about answering a call from anyone, friend or stranger, under the circumstances. But considering how the last call from a stranger had gone, he decided he better.

A nerdy voice said, "I'm looking for Christopher Bell."

Chris had half expected it to be the same person who had called him earlier and given him Rick's location. He could tell right away that it wasn't. "I'm Chris."

"I have your ID. Well, not yours. This is clearly a forgery, but it has your name on it. I was going to call the police in the morning and let them know I found it. Then I started poking around the Internet and found your number and, I don't know, I guess I thought you should know."

Chris had a suspicion it was Rick's. "Where did you find it?"

"Oh, I guess I should have started with that, huh? My name is Felix Winkler. I'm the nursing home administrator over at Heartland. One of my nurses found it. She could tell it was a forgery right away because the picture on it was that of a resident's son."

"What's his name?"

Felix hesitated. "I'm not sure if I should—I mean, that might violate my resident's privacy and, well, isn't that up to the police?"

Arkin gestured as if to ask what the call was about and Chris waved him off. "Was his name Richard Hawthorne?"

Felix made a sound like he was about to say something, but didn't. Chris was pretty sure that was a yes. "Skinny guy. Spiky black hair."

Then Felix spoke, and what he said was not what Chris was expecting. "No. I mean, yes, that was his name. Richard Hawthorne. But that's not what he looks like. Richard has blond hair. Parted. Brushed to the side. He's very plain looking."

While Chris knew Rick had dyed his hair, the answer still bothered him. If he was just getting a call now about the fake ID, it must have been found at the nursing home recently. How long would an ID sit on the floor at a nursing home before somebody turned it in? Not long. "When was the last time you saw him?"

"Earlier today. He came by to drop off a check for his mother's care."

"Was he wearing an army jacket?"

"I've never seen him in anything like that."

"What time did you see him?"

"Sometime around three, I think. Why?"

Something was wrong. That was hours after Rick had stopped by his office. He had spiky black hair and an army jacket then. He had spiky black hair and an army jacket now. That could only mean one thing: whoever they had locked in the boat's small storage closet wasn't Richard Hawthorne.

As if on cue, he heard a series of thumps.

Liam Parker

CHRIS DRAGGED LIAM OUT of the storage closet and into the cabin. He pushed Liam onto one of the sofas. Liam was scared and confused, but also glad to be somewhere warm.

On the sofa across from him sat Chris's friend. He had Anita's gun in his lap, aimed at the ground.

Chris stayed on his feet. "Who are you?"

Liam wasn't sure which name to give them. He was certain these men believed he was Rick. That was probably what they expected him to say. Denying it could only lead to trouble. But they also wanted something he couldn't give them, and if he said he was Rick, things might get even worse. Before he could settle on the answer that would be best for him, Chris added, "Somebody called from the Heartland Nursing Home. They found an ID with my name on it. They say the person in the picture is Rick. His mother is a patient there, so I guess they know what he looks like pretty well, and it's not you. I've been through your wallet. You have an ID and credit cards for Liam Parker. Is that your real name?"

Liam was glad he wouldn't have to lie. Maybe these men had realized their mistake and were going to let him go. "Yes."

"How do you know Richard Hawthorne?"

Alice. "He's got my daughter. Or had my daughter. I don't know anymore. I need to see if she's okay."

Chris crossed his arms over his chest. "Why did you have an ID with

Richard's name on it?"

"He gave it to me. He acted like he wanted to help me. But he was just trying to get me out of my condo . . ." Liam trailed off. He realized the only way out of this was to tell Chris everything. The story wouldn't make sense otherwise.

He told them in brief about the night he found Elise's body, the arrest, the search for the killer, how he ended up at Ellison Trust, and Rick's help with the fake ID and hotel room. Chris listened silently. His friend scoffed here and there.

"I don't know why you're looking for Rick," Liam said when he was done. "But I need to find him too. I think he might know what happened to Elise. At least he'll know something—it just seems like he has to—and I know someone who might be able to help."

Chris and his friend exchanged a glance.

"He's full of shit," the friend said.

Chris pulled a cellphone out of his pocket and, after poking the screen several times, turned it around so his friend could see what he was looking at. Then he threw the phone to Liam. Liam recognized it as his burner and on the screen he saw an article about his escape.

"Call whoever you need to call to help your daughter," Chris said. "Then we'll deal with Rick."

Liam minimized the browser and was confronted with a message from Anita.

What are u doing? Call me.

Instead, he dialed the main number for his condo building. The concierge answered with a sleepy, "Hello?"

Liam knew everyone who worked the desk. He could tell from the voice that this was the man who had complimented Elise's dog. "It's Liam," he said, talking fast.

"Mr. Liam. What's up? What can I do for you?" He sounded surprised, but it didn't seem like he knew Liam was on the run.

"Have you seen Alice tonight?"

"Came through with a guy a couple hours ago. Didn't look too happy. She all right?"

"Are they still there?"

"The guy she was with left some time ago. As far as I saw, she didn't go with him."

Liam couldn't decide if that was good or bad. If the concierge was right, she wasn't a hostage anymore. But she would have called Liam and left a message if she was free, so she was either tied up or—

"Can you go up there and check on her?" Liam said, refusing to consider the alternative.

"Yeah, I guess so. What's going on?"

"I need someone to check on her."

"You want me to call you back?"

"I'll wait."

"All right. I won't be long." There was a click and then soft jazz cut in mid-song.

"I lied to you when you came by my office," Chris said, and Liam wondered if he could hear the hold music. "I met Elise once. It was years ago. Summertime. I was crossing through the park and saw her pacing around a fountain. When I asked what she was doing, she said she'd dropped her keys in the water and was trying to figure out how to get them out without getting too wet. So I played the hero and, as I'm sure she expected, asked her out. Anyway, when we went for dinner, she showed me a ring she said belonged to her grandmother. It was expensive, she said. A family heirloom, irreplaceable. I had my doubts. It didn't look expensive. But I played along. Then, halfway through the dinner she went to the bathroom. She was gone a while, and when she came back she was in tears. Said she'd lost the ring. It didn't feel right—losing a ring between her seat and the bathroom. Of course, when she went back to the bathroom once more to look for it, a guy came up to me and told me he'd found it, but he wasn't about to give it to me out of the kindness of his heart. He said he wanted money for it, and I'd better be quick about it because once my date came back from the bathroom, he was gone. I told him I didn't have any cash and he said lucky for me there was an ATM right around the corner. He just happened to know that, right? I went with him. We weren't two steps outside the door when I beat the crap out of him. And, lo and behold, who should come running out the door seconds later but Elise. 'What are you doing?' she shouted and tried to pull me off him and, right then, I knew for sure this was all one big scam. The whole fountain thing was a way to look for suckers. If you'd wade into the water for a girl's keys, you'd pay money to get her treasured family heirloom back, wouldn't you? Wonder how many times they used that."

Liam knew this must be the real story of how Elise had gotten the black eye. He didn't need Chris to tell him that when Elise came out of the restaurant he'd hit her too.

"Now I'm thinking that guy who helped her must've been Rick. I guess when he saw me on the street, he remembered me. Maybe he stole my wallet as some sort of payback. He should've stopped there. But he conned his way into my safety deposit box and took a ring that really *was* worth a lot of money." Chris's face softened. "Ironic, isn't it?"

That's what Chris must be after, Liam thought. *The ring.* No matter how much it was worth, it seemed to Liam like a petty thing to be concerned about. But he decided to keep his opinion to himself.

The phone line clicked, and Alice said, "Daddy?" She sounded like she was shaking, but at least she was alive.

"Honey, are you all right? Did he hurt you?"

"No, I'm okay. He tied me up and left me on the floor. He said he had somebody watching the building and if I tried to escape he'd kill me. I was so scared nobody would ever find me."

"It's all right. You're safe now. There's nobody outside the building."

Alice started sobbing, and Liam tried to comfort her as best he could. He wished he could be there in person. When she settled down some, he told her he would come see her as soon as possible and asked her to put the concierge back on the phone.

"Yes, Mr. Liam?" the concierge said.

"Call her mom please. Alice knows the number. If you can't reach her, take Alice home yourself, okay?"

While Liam was certain Rick was working alone and that he was long gone, Alice wasn't in any state to be left on her own and, frankly, Liam couldn't bear the thought of it. She was too upset. She needed somebody with her. And, most important, even though he knew she was as safe on her own now as she'd ever been, he didn't *feel* like she was safe. Perhaps that was his parental instinct working overtime—no surprise after what he'd been through. But until he could hold her in his arms and see for himself she was all right, somebody had to keep an eye on her.

"Sure thing," the concierge said.

Liam hung up. For the first time since finding out Alice had been taken, he was no longer scared or sad. He was angry. Rick had taken everything from him. He didn't need to log into his accounts to know

Rick had wiped them out. That would mean the end of his business. And his freedom, that was gone too, wasn't it? And Rick had been there, pulling levers in the background every step of the way, guiding his downfall.

He knew Elise. He'd worked with her. He'd set Liam up to take the fall when he robbed Chris. He'd abducted Alice. Then it clicked into place. He'd killed Elise.

That had to be right. Rick was at the center of all of this. He had to have killed her. But how did he get from Ava's to her place to do it before Liam arrived? And why? Why do it? Why do any of it? Was it just for the money?

Only one person could answer those questions and, dammit, Liam was going to find Rick and make him. He was going to get his money back and clear his name. It was time to make everything right.

Liam looked at Chris. "Let's go get Rick."

Liam Parker

LIAM'S BURNER COULDN'T SUPPORT Ava's app, so he downloaded it to Chris's Android via a private URL. He'd had to jailbreak his iPhone to install it; no such problems here. He logged in and requested a seat at tonight's game. He filled Chris and Arkin in on who Ava was as he worked. "I have a plan," he said. "She'll help us."

A few minutes later, he got a barcode and a six-digit PIN. "We're in business."

The three men piled into Chris's SUV and Liam directed Chris to Ava's building. They parked in the garage, used the barcode to unlock the elevator. Liam pressed the button for the ninth floor. He typed the PIN into the keypad beside Midwest Design's front door. The lock clicked softly.

He led Chris and Arkin through the lobby to the private room in back. "Stay here a minute," he told them.

"Hold on," Arkin said. "If you think we're letting you out of our sight—"

Chris placed a hand on his shoulder and squeezed. "It's fine," he said to Liam. "We'll be here."

Liam stepped through the door. Ava was sitting in her usual chair. Except for the bodyguards that flanked the door, she was alone. The light above the poker table was off.

One of the bodyguards patted Liam down. Ava was already on her way over by the time he was done. "So?" The last she'd heard about Rick was that Liam was going to visit his apartment. She was asking for an update.

"What's going on? Where is everyone?"

"Rick was supposed to work tonight. He didn't show up, so no game," she said, and Liam noticed, as he often did, the subtle inflections of the French she'd spoken as a child. She repeated the one-word question. "So?"

"He wasn't there."

"I'm not surprised."

Liam glanced at the bodyguards, then gestured to the door. "Can we talk privately?"

"Sure."

"I'm not alone," Liam said as he opened the door. "Turns out there's someone else looking for Rick." Even as he spoke, Chris and Arkin became visible through the widening crack in the door.

One of the bodyguards jumped to attention. "It's fine," Ava told him. She stepped out of the room, closing the door behind her. The four instinctively moved deeper into the dark space to be sure they wouldn't be overheard. They huddled close to a table covered with sketches of something that looked to be an atrium.

Liam told Ava about Alice's abduction and the thefts Rick had perpetrated against him and Chris. "That's not the worst of it, though. I think he killed Elise. I'm not sure how, but he seems to be at the center of all of this, and we need to find him."

"I don't know how I can help," Ava said. "I sent the two men in there to see Eduardo after we talked. Apparently Rick made a point of meeting him one night after he left here and paid him to get into my place as a dealer. Rick told him it would just be for a few weeks, said when he was done Eduardo could have the job back. Easy money. Nobody had to know. But Eduardo doesn't know how to get in touch with him. Rick was always the one to make contact."

Liam could hardly believe that Eduardo came right out and said all that, so he asked.

Ava shrugged, as if to say *No, he didn't*, and Liam could fill in the blanks.

"But Rick's been here for months," Liam said.

"He kept paying Eduardo to stay on longer."

"Do you know why?"

"Eduardo never found out. It sounds like you might have pieced some of that together though."

Liam wasn't so sure about that. He had a good idea of what had happened lately, but he didn't know what Elise and Rick were doing at Ava's to begin with. Maybe they were targeting her, working another con together, only that one went south. It would explain all the lies Elise had told. If she was working a con on Ava, she'd want to tell everyone the same story. Was that how Elise ended up dead? The con had gone south? Could be. Perhaps Rick got pissed because whatever he was up to was taking too long. Maybe that was even why Rick started writing stuff down about Liam in his notebook. Did he have other notebooks for other players?

The theory was falling apart again. It still didn't sound right. At the moment, however, it didn't matter. He'd come here with a plan and it was time he laid it out.

"My guess is Rick is on the run. I think there's a way we can get him back here."

Richard Hawthorne

RICK SPED DOWN THE interstate in the rented car he'd used to abduct Alice and crossed the border into Indiana. He wasn't sure whether Liam had made it to the airport and wasn't going to risk running into a Delta employee who'd encountered another Rick Hawthorne tonight taking a flight to Belarus. His would leave from the Weir Cook Municipal Airport.

As he drove, he imagined two competing scenarios. Both made him happy.

In one, Chris had gotten ahold of Liam and done God-knows-what. Maybe killed him. Whatever it was, Rick was sure it hurt.

In another, Liam had run to the airport (because, even though Rick had called him demanding access to his accounts, where else did he have to go?) and gotten arrested when he tried to pass through security with a fake ID and a bogus ticket.

Either way, justice served.

His phone rang. It was Ava. He was supposed to be working tonight and she was probably wondering where he was. He put the phone on silent. It continued to vibrate until the call ended, but at least it wasn't as annoying.

Ava called six more times over the next ten minutes. She wasn't just wondering where he was, she was pissed. Rick didn't care. His plan for the future was to find a nice girl in Belarus (or somewhere else without an extradition treaty), settle down, raise a family, maybe take some photos like those he'd seen in other people's wallets. He'd never step foot in Ava's again.

Then a text came in. Also Ava. He cared no more about it than he had the calls until he read it: *Where would you like us to bury Susan Hawthorne?*

Rick's mouth went dry. Ava had found out who he was. That wouldn't bother him if she hadn't also found out about his mother. While he had enough money to pay for her care for the rest of her life, there was nothing he could do to protect her once he was out of the country.

But would Ava kill her? Probably not. She was likely pulling the same con on him he had on Alice. But "probably" was too big of a risk to take with the only family he had.

Rick pulled over to the side of the road and tried to decide what to do. There was only one choice. He had to find out what Ava wanted and what she knew. Perhaps he could resolve this problem with a phone call. He dialed her number.

"Rick?" Ava said when she answered.

"How did you find out?"

"I want to see you now." She hung up.

So much for resolving the matter on the phone. Rick looked at the clock on the dashboard. It was almost one a.m. If he didn't keep going, he'd miss the flight.

For several seconds, he sat completely still, trying to figure out what Ava wanted. (It had to be about more than skipping out on the game.) She could have known his real name for a long time, he reasoned. If Chris and Liam could figure it out, certainly she could. And she might have known about his mother for just as long. Perhaps she'd been holding onto the information for a situation where she needed the upper hand. Ava was friendly to all the players, but with him she'd always kept her distance. Assuming the same personality he had used when dealing cards, he'd made numerous attempts to forge a friendship, hoping to transcend the strict employer-employee relationship Ava insisted upon. Such friendships could be helpful when working a con no matter who the target was. But all of his attempts had been unsuccessful. Was it because she always knew he was lying to her? If that was the case, why would she keep him around?

Rick pounded his fists against the steering wheel and screamed with frustration. He got out of the car, slammed the door, and paced the highway. The scam shouldn't have run this long. If Elise had done what she was supposed to, she'd still be alive and they'd both have gotten out of this thing rich and safe.

Cars whizzed past as little more than twin lights in the darkness.

Eventually Rick admitted to himself he wasn't going to figure anything out hanging around on the side of the road and thought about going to the nursing home. He could take his mom out of there, get them a hotel room. But that would scare her. And what if she was still having a bad day? Could he even get her out at this hour?

That wasn't an option. Besides, even if it was, what would he do after they got the hotel room? Set her up with a fake name as well? Take her with him to Belarus? That wasn't a life for his mom. He loved her too much to put her through that.

He paced some more before accepting his only choice was to go see what Ava wanted. It was a hiccup. Nothing more. He got back in the car, turned around at the next exit, called the airline to reschedule the flight, and requested access to Ava's using the same app Liam had.

The rest of the drive he made in silence. The only thought in his head was, *I'm so close. I can talk my way out of this.*

Richard Hawthorne

THE LOT WAS NEARLY deserted. Rick parked and crossed to the elevator, the sound of his footfalls echoing around him, making him feel even more alone.

I am so close. Whatever Ava wants, I can talk my way out of this. I am so close.

Rick thought he heard something and spun around. There was no one there. Every fiber of his being told him he was making a mistake coming here. Every step toward the elevator was an act of sheer will and a testament to his love for his mother.

He pressed the button.

I am so close.

The doors opened with a ding. When Rick saw who was standing on the other side of them, the will to run could no longer be suppressed. It was too late. Chris and Arkin grabbed him, dragged him onto the elevator. Liam punched the code in and pressed the button for the ninth floor.

Chris grabbed Rick's jaw, holding it still while he examined his face. "You didn't just steal the ring. You're the guy who helped Elise with that con all those years ago, aren't you?" Then he punched Rick in the stomach.

Rick tried to double-over, but Chris and Arkin held him tight.

"Where's the ring?" Chris demanded.

"Let's get him upstairs," Liam said.

Liam Parker

AVA HAD SEVERAL ROLLS of packing tape in a supply closet. Chris and Arkin sat Rick down in one of the chairs that surrounded the poker table, and Liam used liberal amounts of tape to bind him to it.

Rick begged to be let go. That wasn't going to happen.

"Do you think this is how Alice felt?" Liam said. "What about Elise? Do you think you are even half as scared as she was?"

Rick begged the men not to kill him. Then his eyes cut past them, and Liam glanced over his shoulder to see what he was looking at.

Ava was sitting in the same chair she always sat in, legs crossed, expression inscrutable. She was the only other person in the suite. At Liam's request, she'd sent her bodyguards home. He didn't want anybody here who wasn't involved.

"Please, Ava," Rick said. "I didn't do anything to you. Don't let them do this."

"You brought this on yourself," Ava said, without emotion.

Rick screamed for help, and Arkin punched him across the jaw hard enough to shut him up.

"Woo-hoo!" Arkin exclaimed. "Scream some more. I want to do that again."

Rick had gotten the message.

By the time Liam finished binding Rick to the chair, he was practically mummified. Liam stepped back and admired his handiwork. It felt good seeing Rick like that.

"Where's the ring?" Chris asked.

"What did we agree to?" Liam said to Chris. "First things first." He turned back to Rick. "Tell us about Elise."

"What are you talking about?"

"I want to know everything. Let's start with what you two were up to when you paid Eduardo to get you a job here. That's only fair because of where we are, isn't it?"

Rick's eyes grew wide and cut back to Ava. "I'm sorry, Ava. It was never about you. Please, don't let them—"

Arkin punched Rick again, and Liam reached around behind his back and pulled Anita's gun from the waistband of his jeans. He kept the barrel aimed at the ground. He didn't want to accidently shoot Rick and was pretty sure the sight of the weapon alone would be enough to scare him into cooperating.

"You're talking to us," Liam said. "What were you two up to?"

Rick looked at the gun.

Liam could tell he was terrified. "Well?"

Rick licked his lips, took several slow breaths. "It wasn't supposed to be complicated," he said. "We knew you came here regularly, so it seemed like the best place to set up a meet. Elise likes meet-cutes. We've used them before for small stuff. But for something like this, I didn't want to take a chance it might go wrong."

That statement alone was enough to let Liam know he had been the target all along. It was upsetting, undercut the last shred of hope he had his relationship with Elise had been real, but it also explained her lies better than anything else might. She'd said she worked in advertising because he worked in advertising. She said she grew up in Oak Park because he grew up in Oak Park. Every lie had been about shielding her identity and creating parallels between their lives over which they could bond. But there was a lot more to know and Liam wanted to hear all of it, so he pressed forward with the next question to occur to him. "What are meet-cutes?"

"Like the movies," Rick said. "Two people reach for the same flower in a flower shop. Their hands touch. Stuff like that." He was making an effort not to look at Chris and, based on the story Chris had told earlier, Liam knew why.

Chris turned red, likely with a combination of anger and embarrassment, but he kept himself in check.

"I thought it would be better to give you two some time to get to know each other," Rick continued. "I told her to let you make the first move."

Liam flashed back to things Rick had said when dealing cards. He'd called Elise pretty when she wasn't around. He'd said he'd heard she was single. They were subtly placed comments meant to get inside Liam's head. They had worked too. The more Rick talked about Elise, the more Liam noticed her. It was all obvious in retrospect.

"Once you did, all she had to do was get into your condo, hook a USB stick up to your computer, and install some software. Simple, right?"

Liam nodded. Elise had been in his condo plenty of times. From the way the conversation was going, though, it sounded like she had never installed the software. Why not? He'd seen her on his computer before, usually playing Solitaire or surfing the web while he was in the shower. But he didn't interrupt to ask. It seemed like the more Rick talked the more he wanted to, as if he somehow felt he was absolving himself by admitting to it all. And maybe that's exactly what he thought, because the next thing he said was, "I'm sorry for Alice. It shouldn't have gone that far. If Elise had tried to install the software sooner, everything would've been all right. It would've recorded your keystrokes, collecting all your login information for all your accounts, and allowed me to remote into your computer to transfer the money out without ever having to step foot inside your place."

"What do you mean *sooner?*" Liam barked.

"Elise came by my apartment. She said she didn't want to do it. She told me she'd started to care about you, and I told her if she didn't do it I'd make sure you found out who she really was. So that's what happened, right? You figured out she had installed the software and killed her over it."

Liam couldn't believe what he was hearing. There was so much information packed in that one statement it created a sort of emotional whiplash. Elise *had* cared about him. Beneath all the lies, there was something true in their relationship. Just as important—not only was Rick innocent of Elise's murder, but he thought Liam had done it.

"After you killed her, I couldn't let it go. We never planned to empty all your accounts. We were only going to take some of the money. A lot for us, a little for you. Then things changed. I wanted to punish you, and you deserved it. You'll still pay. Even though it's not the way I intended, the police will catch you sooner or later and you'll do thirty to life in some small cell as someone's bitch, I'm betting."

"I didn't kill Elise. I never saw her installing any software on my computer."

Rick looked confused. "But I got an alert saying the software had been activated. Only before I could learn anything, it stopped transmitting data. You must have found out about it."

"What reason would I have to lie to you now? It wasn't me."

Liam saw Rick's face transform as the truth sank in. Then he said softly, "I couldn't believe you had the audacity to attend the funeral. Now I guess it makes sense."

Liam remembered somebody standing at the edge of the cemetery. At the time, he'd thought it was the police, but it must have been Rick. Had he come to pay his respects too, only keeping his distance when he saw Liam at the gravesite? Then another thought occurred to him: Ryan Reyes had said Elise was seeing someone else—had he meant Rick?

Chris put his hands on his hips and paced back and forth. He was getting impatient. Arkin, however, appeared to be enjoying the show.

"Well, if she didn't install the software on your computer, she must've installed it on someone's," Rick continued.

Maybe that was the someone who killed her, Liam thought. "Do you know who it might have been?"

Rick shook his head.

"Why me?"

"Hell if I know."

"This was Elise's idea?"

"No, this was my idea." Liam could hear pride in Rick's voice. "But it didn't start that way. Someone came to Elise and said they wanted you in jail for a while. Elise was hard up for cash, so she took their money. But I told her I had a better idea, and what could they do about it anyway if we changed the plan?"

Liam couldn't believe what he was hearing. "Who are you talking about?"

"I don't know. I met them when Elise and I went to pick up the deposit. She thought it'd be a good idea to have someone with her. Man and a woman, that's all I can tell you. Well, that, and the man was tall, if that's worth anything to you. Really tall. Blond hair, balding a little on top."

Rick was describing David.

"Maybe they killed Elise."

"That's not possible," Liam said and took a step back as if the news itself had pushed him away.

Liam walked across the room, struggling to make sense of the information and moving closer to Ava without realizing it. "No, no, no," he mumbled to himself, shaking his head.

When he was within range, Ava reached out and gently grabbed his arm. "Liam."

He looked at her.

"Most people wouldn't think I run this poker game, would they?"

He got the message. As hard as it was to hear, there wasn't any point in denying what Rick had said. He was only telling Liam what he'd seen. David had tried to frame him and put him in jail. Liam repeated that fact to himself until it started to sink in.

But he wouldn't kill anyone, would he? Even for him that was a step too far. It had to be. Then again, only seconds ago Liam would have thought framing his friend would be a step too far for David, so who knew?

Chris took this as his opportunity to move in on Rick.

"Where's the ring?" Chris demanded, forcing Rick to look up to see his face.

Rick only did that for a second before his gaze shifted to the floor. "I don't have it."

"Where is it?"

"I sold it."

"To who?" Chris said through clenched teeth.

"A dealer." Then, with enthusiasm, he added, "But I can show you where. Tomorrow. When they open." In other words, *Please don't kill me.*

Chris nodded. He turned to Liam. "Do you need him anymore?"

Liam was so distracted he almost said no. He was sure Rick had told him everything he could. Anything else he wanted would have to come from David. But then he remembered the money.

Liam Parker

RICK HAD TRANSFERRED ALL of Liam's money to an account in Belarus.

Liam found the bank's information online using his TracFone. Thanks to the time difference, it was open at this hour. He dialed the number, was connected to a banker who spoke English, and held the phone up to Rick's ear.

Reading the account and routing numbers off a piece of paper, Rick set up a wire transfer to send all of it back to Liam's personal checking account at Bank of America. The banker protested—Liam could hear him resisting the request in broken English—but finally gave in. Liam expected as many questions from his bank, probably even some from the FTC. But since the money was his, he was sure it would all work itself out.

When the transfer was complete, Liam cut Rick free, then Chris and Arkin took him away. Chris had used some of the remaining packing tape to bind Rick's hands behind his back. Rick was terrified and sobbing, but as Liam watched him leave he felt nothing. He didn't care any more about what happened to Rick than Rick had cared what happened to him. What mattered to Liam was confronting David.

Ava stood up. "You know even if he admits to killing her, he'll never say it to the police."

"I know." Liam looked around, as if taking the place in one last time. "Rick is going to tell them about you when they get their hands on him."

"They won't believe him."

"They might. You're going to have to shut this place down for a while."

Ava offered up a smile unlike any Liam had ever seen from her. She looked strangely happy. "It's time. When I started, it was supposed to be fun. It's not anymore."

Liam understood. He began coming here to get away from his wife before the divorce. Then it became a distraction, a way of keeping himself busy so he could forget his children no longer lived with him. Then it became a habit. It would do him good to put this place behind him.

They hugged briefly. "Thank you," Liam said.

Ava patted him on the back. "Good luck."

Liam left, weaved his way through the suite for the last time. When he reached the elevators, he pulled out his cellphone and called Anita.

Liam Parker

LIAM BUZZED DAVID'S CONDO several times before David came to the intercom and let him up. When he reached the unit, the door was partially open—a clear sign David had been using for years that there was no need to knock.

Liam opened the door the rest of the way. He irrationally feared Bash would be waiting for him. All the lights were on. Elise's Pomeranian yapped from somewhere deep in the apartment. Dressed in wrinkled brown slacks and a white undershirt, David entered from the hall. He crossed his arms over his chest and leaned against the arched doorway. "What happened to you earlier today?"

"I need to talk to you."

"Why didn't you come to The Crown?"

"Why did you try to set me up?"

David rocked off the doorway. His arms fell to his sides. His gaze shifted left then right, as if he were trying to assess a new, hostile territory. "What are you talking about?"

"I know. I've had a talk with Rick."

David said nothing.

"Just tell me. What does it matter now anyway?"

David went over to the fridge and got a beer. "You want one?"

"No."

David popped the top off the Budweiser, took a sip, and returned to the living room. The two men stood in silence, watching each other as David drank the beer.

Liam could hardly believe where the journey had taken him. This man had once been his best friend. If he had denied knowing Rick—if he'd just asked "Who?"—would Liam have started to doubt Rick's story? He didn't know, and it didn't matter, because David hadn't denied it, hadn't asked who. That meant everything Rick had told him was true.

Finally, David spoke. "What the hell? You're right. What does it matter now? I mean—who are you going to tell? Even if you did, who'd believe you? But it's not exactly like you think."

More silence. Perhaps David was deciding what he wanted to say next. Liam waited.

"I didn't set you up. Catherine did."

His ex-wife. That must have been the woman Rick had referred to.

"She wanted you out of her life. She wanted to take the kids back to Mississippi and raise them without you around. But she needed a judge to rule on that and so she hired Elise to make sure a judge ruled in her favor."

"But . . . how would they ever have met? They wouldn't have exactly run in the same circles."

"Catherine met Elise when she came to St. Ann's looking to clean up."

The church Catherine volunteers at, Liam thought. It seemed obvious now that David had told him.

"She didn't stay on the wagon long. She got arrested trying to buy drugs immediately after an NA meeting outside the church. Catherine saw it. She told me the idea came to her a couple of days later. She suspected Elise would need money when she got out, and thought she might be the kind of person who would be willing to do what Catherine wanted."

"Which was?"

"She wanted Elise to get you drunk, then convince you to drive her through Lincoln Park."

Liam had a feeling he knew where this was going. Lincoln Park had a lot of bars and, because of that, a lot of cops.

"She told Elise to bump the wheel, start a fight. She wanted you to take your eyes off the road, swerve or have an accident, whatever it took to get a cop's attention. She was convinced that if you were charged with a DUI she could make you out to be an unfit parent. Elise wanted more money than Catherine was offering, though, so Catherine came to me."

David finished the beer in one long swig and placed the bottle on the coffee table without taking his eyes off Liam. More silence followed.

Eventually, Liam said, "David, tell me."

"You know, I'm surprised you're standing here in my living room right now after what you found out. That takes balls. Not exactly your strong suit, is it? And that was always the problem. There wouldn't be a business without me. You were a workhorse and a dreamer, but that's all you were. Do you remember how much you talked about starting your own firm? But it took me pushing you to make it happen. Then, once we did, you didn't want to do anything. You wouldn't take a single risk. I suggested we look at turning our firm into a full-fledged advertising agency and you said no. I said let's at least try a couple radio spots with our smaller clients, test the waters, and you said no. You'd found your sweet spot publishing ads online and that's all you wanted to do. It was intolerable. You wouldn't even agree to take out a loan so we could expand our sales team. There was so much money to be made if you just took a risk and you didn't care. I couldn't understand it then, and I don't understand it now. When Catherine came to me, I guess I saw an opportunity to get you out of my way too.

"Only for me, a DUI wasn't going to do it. So when Catherine and I met with Elise and Rick to hand over the money, I said it had to be drugs. Cocaine or heroin, preferably. Something serious enough to carry real jail time. I figured if anyone knew where to get their hands on something like that, she would. I thought it'd be a lot easier to pull off, too. Plant some drugs on you, tell a cop you're carrying. I needed to create enough controversy that you wouldn't have any choice but to step down for a while. Believe me, Liam, it would've been worth it. I would've made you so much money if I could've just gotten you out of my way."

"But that's not what happened."

"No, it's not."

"Did you kill Elise?"

The Night of the Murder

Elise Watson

ELISE WATCHED ERIC RICCI cash out his chips and then she did the same. Liam was still at Ava's. So was Rick. But they didn't need to know what she was up to. She bowed out, claiming a headache, and neither seemed suspicious.

She caught up with Eric in the parking lot, called his name to get his attention.

Eric turned around. He looked annoyed. He'd had a bad night and lost a lot of money.

"Where are you off to?" she said.

"Home."

She smiled in a flirty way. "You want some company?"

"Aren't you dating Liam?"

"He doesn't have to know. So?" She was sure he'd say yes. She'd been watching him watch her, and even though she hated herself for what she was about to do, she convinced herself it was necessary. Rick had threatened to make sure Liam found out about her past if she didn't do what she was supposed to. But as long as she could give him a new target, a way to justify all the trouble he went through to make this con work, she believed he'd leave her alone.

The whole thing was over quickly. Eric went to take a shower. Elise got out of bed, quietly dressed, and crept across the apartment to a small office, formerly a second bedroom. The entire apartment was a shrine to Eric's career. Framed posters for movies he'd been in and baseball cards with his face on them hung on the walls. Talk about narcissism. Elise wanted to get out of there as fast as possible.

When they had arrived, she had asked if she could use his laptop for a couple of minutes to check her email. "We've got this big thing for work and . . . well, I don't want to bore you with the details. It will only take a second." She tried to keep the story simple and hoped he wouldn't ask a lot of questions. He told her the password, urged her to hurry up, and kissed her neck. Her skin crawled, but she committed the password to memory and used it again to log in now.

She plugged the USB stick Rick gave her into the back of the laptop and the software began installing itself. A black box opened in the center of the screen and row after row of text appeared in it, too fast to read. Elise had no idea how long it would take and there was no progress bar to tell her how far she was from done. She paid close attention to the sound of the shower and from time to time glanced over her shoulder to see if she was alone. She worried she wasn't going to get away with this, but then the installation finished. The word "Complete" appeared at the bottom of the black box and the box closed on its own.

Before she could pull the USB stick out of the back of the laptop, she heard Eric ask, "What are you doing?"

Elise spun around. He was standing in front of her with a towel wrapped around his waist. All her senses heightened and she went on red alert. Halos formed around the overhead light. The flowery smell of the Herbal Essences shampoo Eric used turned her stomach. The shower was still on, the water hitting the tile like a hard rain. She didn't miss it. The cue she was listening for had failed her.

Elise stumbled over her words, desperately trying to come up with an answer. She fell back on the same lie she'd used before, only this time, Eric didn't buy it.

"You weren't checking your mail. What was that? What were you doing?"

Elise wanted to run, but Eric was blocking her path to the door, so she stayed completely still, watching him, ready to react to whatever he did next.

Eric moved in close. The smell of the shampoo grew stronger, almost making Elise gag. He pressed one hand down on the top of the laptop and closed it. The laptop automatically powered down. "I said, what were you doing?"

"It's not what you think," she said, and not just out of reflex. She was certain, no matter what he might imagine at this moment, it wasn't as bad as what Rick had planned.

Eric was barely a foot away when he said, "Get out."

Elise had expected this to go much worse and wasn't about to stick around to press her luck. She hurried to the door, then the elevator, afraid that if she looked back Eric would change his mind about letting her leave.

When she got to the street, she found the nearest bus stop and took the first bus that came. The digital display above the driver read "22 Clark." She was unfamiliar with the route, but she wanted to put as much distance between her and Eric as possible.

There were not a lot of passengers at this hour. Elise took an isolated seat at the back. She remembered the USB stick she'd plugged into Eric's computer and frantically checked her purse and pockets twice.

The purse was small. Her pockets were empty. This was not okay. She had to tell Liam the truth before Rick dropped him an anonymous email. Hopefully he'd understand. No, not her. Kate. Kate and that man she was with. They needed to tell Liam the truth. They were the ones who started all this.

Elise called Kate and said she needed to come over to her apartment, and bring the guy she came with.

"Yes, right now. It's urgent."

She hung up before she was forced to elaborate and called Liam. He didn't answer, which probably meant he was still at Ava's. Ava had a strict "no calls" policy when playing.

She switched buses, tried again. Still no answer. Back at her apartment, she started texting.

Present

Liam Parker

DID YOU KILL ELISE? Liam had asked.

David was as slow to answer that as he had been to answer every other question tonight. He ran both hands through his hair, down his face. He moved from the doorway to a chair. "Sit down."

Liam didn't.

"Elise was taking a long time to do what we wanted her to do. Catherine and I were starting to think she'd scammed us. Then, late one night Catherine gets a call. Elise says she needs us to come over to her apartment right away and gives Catherine her address. Of course, we went. We wanted to know what was taking so long.

"When we got there, Elise told us you were on your way over. She said either we could tell you what we were doing or she would. I told her she couldn't do that. It'd be bad for me, you, her, Catherine, the business—everybody. Nobody would win from telling you the truth. But she wouldn't budge. It got heated. After that, I don't remember much. Somehow, I ended up on top of her. I had her pinned to the floor. My hands were around her neck, and she was gone. Catherine was standing by the door. She looked horrified. She was saying 'What have you done?' over and over.

"I didn't know what to do. I tried to revive her but couldn't. Even if I wanted to pull the brakes on everything it was too late. Somebody was going to jail, then, for sure. Not for drugs anymore either."

Liam flushed with anger.

"I told Catherine to help me stage a suicide—it was us or you. So we cut her wrists and dumped her in the bathtub. Then I saw her phone sitting on the coffee table. It was unlocked and I could see the messages she sent you on the screen. I told Catherine to delete them while I cleaned up. I thought that would make it look to the police like you were trying to cover your tracks. Then it was mostly a matter of waiting and letting the wheels of justice do the work for us. The only close call came when we were leaving the apartment and a neighbor stepped out. Turns out anyone can be bought for the right price."

Liam had heard enough. This wasn't a fight he was going to run away from. He charged forward and, even as David was lifting himself out of the chair, punched him across the jaw.

David rolled with the blow, onto the floor, then leapt up and pushed Liam away. He glanced out the window. "Do it. I dare you."

Liam took him up on the offer.

Even though David was bigger, Liam ended up on top of him. David fended off most of the blows, but did little to fight back. Liam kept firing one punch after another. It wasn't until someone pulled him off that he understood David had wanted him to gain the upper hand.

Uniformed officers were everywhere. One pushed Liam to a wall and cuffed him. Bash entered Liam's field of vision. "Good to see you again, Mr. Parker."

David got to his feet slowly, moving as if he was in pain. He pressed the back of one hand to his lip to check for blood. "You should've known not to come here."

Liam saw an iPhone on the floor at the same time David did and David went over and picked it up. An app was open and recording their conversation. Liam tried to say it was his phone, that it proved his innocence, but no one was listening.

The police pushed him out the door, led him to the elevator, and from there to a cop car parked along the curb. He walked right past a shattered iPhone on the sidewalk.

David could have smashed it with a hammer, but he wanted Liam to know it was gone.

Christopher Bell

CHRIS KEPT THE REAL Richard Hawthorne locked up in his boat's storage closet until morning. Then he had Rick lead him to the jeweler who had bought the ring only to find out it was already sold. Gone forever.

When he got home, Emma was awake and waiting for him. He told her what had happened and then said, ever so casually, "You want to get married?" Chris was pouring a cup of coffee from the pot she'd made an hour earlier when he asked the question and seemed to be directing it as much to the mug in his hand as to her. He stirred in a spoonful of sugar and waited.

"What?" Emma looked confused.

"I've been thinking about it. The ring was valuable, but not irreplaceable. I didn't want it back because it was expensive."

Emma's eyebrow arched, doubtful.

"Okay, the money was part of it. But while I was out there waiting for the jewelry shop to open, I realized it wasn't the only part. Although I never gave the ring to you, it symbolized something. It was kind of like a promise to myself that one day I would ask you to marry me. I know that you're not going to sign a prenup, but so what? After everything that's happened over the last week, I don't worry about you leaving anymore." He sat down at the kitchen table and blew on the coffee to cool it off. "We're a team, right?"

Emma sat down across from him. She reached one hand across the table, palm up. When he took it in his, she smiled and said, "We're a team."

Liam Parker

LIAM SAT IN A small holding cell and waited. The last cop he saw said to make himself comfortable. They were going to process him out to county. It would take a while.

A couple of hours later, Bash appeared and unlocked the door. He was alone. Liam crossed the cell and, as he did, Bash held out his hand. "I'm sorry."

Liam shook it, but said nothing.

"Ms. Watson is waiting for you in the lobby."

For a second, Liam thought he meant Elise, even though he knew that was impossible. He followed Bash through hallways that reminded him of the jail he'd almost returned to. He thought about the days alone in his cell and the fight that broke out in the yard. That was something he would never have to live through again, thank God.

Bash buzzed them through a door. The focal point of the lobby was a massive, oblong desk with unformed officers behind it. Rows of chairs ran along the exterior walls, metal detectors by the entrance.

The room was filled with visitors of all types. They paced the floor, filled out forms, waited in chairs.

Liam scanned the faces until he found Anita, who had already spotted him and was headed in his direction. She hugged Liam, smiled. "You owe me a new phone."

Richard Hawthorne

RICK WAS ONCE AGAIN bound to a chair with packing tape. This time he was in the kitchen of his own apartment, still trashed and drafty now that the window had been broken. He tried for some time to get free, but it was useless. He was cold, hungry, and tired.

But that wasn't the worst of it. The worst was the flies, drawn in by the smell of rotting food. Rick did his best to shake them off when they landed on him. Shooing them away was, of course, futile.

Is this it? he wondered. *Has Chris left me here to die?*

At just after two o'clock, officers arrived, thanks to an anonymous tip, and a small part of Rick was glad to see them.

David Hayes

THE STAFF GATHERED IN the large breakroom. David had called another all-hands meeting. He started by saying he didn't want a bunch of rumors flying around. There would be more articles soon about Liam and his arrest, but as far as the company was concerned, this was all behind them. Then he asked if there were any questions and no one raised a hand, so after saying his door was always open to anyone who wanted to talk privately, he pointed them to the spread of cold sandwiches and sodas from Fred's Deli set up on the table in back and returned to his office.

Bash was standing by his door, waiting for him.

David stopped short when he saw the detective. "What's up?" he asked nervously. "Everything all right?"

Then officers appeared from nowhere, boxing him in.

"Mr. Hayes," said Bash, "you have the right to remain silent. Anything you say can and will be used against you in a court of law . . ."

Catherine Parker

CATHERINE HAD FOUND ALICE'S room empty when she went upstairs to apologize for the fight and knew her daughter had gone to the concert. She was furious. She stayed up until midnight planning to scold Alice when she got in. But by the time Alice came through the door, Catherine had given up and gone to sleep, even more mad and ready to unleash a rage unlike any Alice had ever seen in the morning.

Alice wasn't having it. They got into a shouting match. Alice said horrible things about Catherine and Catherine returned the barbs. Alice said she needed some time alone, that something terrible had happened.

But without letting her daughter tell her what had happened, Catherine said it served her right for going to the concert, and she was going to get her ass up and go to school no matter how she felt.

Alice grabbed some clothes off the floor in a huff, dressed, and stormed out the door.

Tommy watched the whole thing from his perch on the stairs.

Catherine then snapped at him, too. "Get ready for school."

"I *am* ready."

"Then let's go."

Catherine calmed down some once she was alone. She put the morning dishes in the dishwasher, then walked through the house picking up things the kids had left lying around. How socks ended up in the dining room and a shirt on the banister she'd never understand. Catherine felt bad for taking her anger out on Tommy. She would apologize to him when she picked him up from school.

With order restored to the house, she did the grocery shopping and settled in for some afternoon TV. She started with a *Friends* marathon on CBS and would switch over to *Seinfeld* later. She spent a lot of afternoons watching TV. It beat going to work. And soon, her life would get even better.

David had assured her once her ex was caught he'd be able to talk Liam into selling his share of the business and under the terms of their divorce she was obligated to receive a portion of that sale. The money would go far enough in Chicago, but in Mississippi, it would go even further.

When the doorbell rang, Catherine expected it to be Jehovah's Witnesses or a door-to-door salesman. (She was surprised they still existed but had seen several even in the last year or two.) She ignored it. It rang again, followed by several loud knocks.

She went to the door with the intention of shooing her unwanted visitor away, only to find Bash on the other side, flanked by uniformed officers.

"Well, this is unexpected," she said. "Liam isn't here, you know."

Bash entered the home without waiting to be asked. "We're not here about him."

When he tried to tell her she was under arrest, she began to scream and curse so loud she couldn't hear him. He shouted for the officers to restrain her, pushing her to the wall and wrestling her arms behind her back.

She didn't stop fighting until the cuffs locked into place.

Liam Parker

THE TESLA HAD SURVIVED the impound lot with little more than a scratch.

Liam took it to pick up the kids after school, but found only Tommy where he was supposed to be.

"Where's Mom?" Tommy asked as he climbed into the back seat.

"You're staying with me tonight," Liam said, opting for a simple explanation for now. Then he called Alice. He worried that she wouldn't answer, that something new had happened to her and it wasn't really over. But she did.

"I just needed a little time by myself," she said.

Liam understood. She'd probably need a lot more than that in the coming months to get over what Rick had done to her.

"Dad, are you . . . ?"

Liam wasn't sure exactly where the unfinished question would have led, but he got the gist. "It's all okay now."

"I'm glad."

He picked her up at a McDonald's and took both kids home. Elise's Pomeranian, Chloe, was already there; Bash had worked out getting the dog from David's condo. Happy as could be, she waddled out when Liam opened the door and sniffed first his shoes, then the kids, and looked up at all three of them, panting. Liam felt a small pang in his heart thinking about all the times she'd done that when he'd gone to see Elise.

"Say welcome to the newest addition to our family," Liam said.

Both kids dropped to the floor with oohs and ahhs, petting the dog, scratching her behind the ears.

"What's her name?" Tommy asked.

Liam smiled. "Chloe."

Alice picked up Chloe and kissed her on the nose. It looked to Liam as if having the dog in her arms made her feel a little better.

The doorman was right—the kids were going to love Chloe.

And Elise, if she was looking down, would love seeing Chloe in their care.

That night, Liam sat both kids down and told them they would be living with him from then on. There were a lot of questions. Most answers he gave were vague. Some details he clarified for Alice after Tommy had gone to bed.

One thing he didn't tell her about, though, was what had happened when he went to confront David and exactly how he had proven his innocence.

Liam had called Anita as he left Ava's. He gave her the rundown and asked if she could skip out of work. She said she could find a way. Then he asked her to reach out to Ryan Reyes. Liam knew that if David admitted to anything at all he wouldn't do it with anyone else around, certainly not a cop. He wanted her to find out if the PI had a way to record the conversation. Something better than the built-in voice recorder on most phones. (His TracFone didn't even have a basic one.) Liam wanted to make sure the audio wouldn't be lost if, say, David found out what he was up to and dropped Liam's phone out the window.

It took Anita a little while to get Ryan to come to the door, but he eventually did. Liam had expected to be outfitted with a mike taped to his chest. However, Ryan directed her to a publicly available app that would stream the audio to cloud storage in real-time as long as he had a decent cell signal.

Liam liked the simplicity of that solution. He also liked not having a wire on him. If David found a mike taped to Liam's chest, who knew what he'd do. If Rick was right, if David had killed Elise, that would be more than enough motivation to kill again. When he met Anita to get her cellphone, he returned the gun for the same reason. Liam would never fire it, and not only might finding the gun be enough for David to kill, it would also provide a means.

The quality of the recording was, unfortunately, not very good. Rustling fabric had distorted the conversation, often to the point of being inaudible. It was enough, though, to clear Liam's name, get a judge to issue arrest warrants, and send Bash in search of additional proof.

Over the next several months, Alice saw a psychiatrist once a week to work through the trauma of the abduction and Liam took the stand in trials against Catherine, David, and Rick.

At Catherine's trial, the DA entered into evidence cellphone records that tracked her to Elise's building the night of the murder and testimony from the neighbor who now admitted to seeing her. And when Liam testified, he was shown the letters Catherine had written Elise in jail and confirmed that, yes, some of Catherine's friends called her Kate.

At David's trial, Catherine, too, told her story in exchange for a lighter sentence.

And at Rick's, the DA presented the notepad Liam had found in Rick's apartment, security video showing Rick entering the condo with Alice, bank records detailing the transfers with a timestamp and Liam's

IP address, as well as testimony from the security guard, Alice, and, once again, Catherine. At sentencing, Rick attempted to use the cost of his mom's care to justify his actions. It didn't play as well as he'd hoped.

But when it was over, Liam made a trip to Heartland Nursing Home to meet the woman for himself. He wasn't sure why. Perhaps he was just curious.

Although a nurse told Liam it was increasingly rare, Susan Hawthorne was lucid that day. She was kind and believed her son made his living as a franchisee of several Subway restaurants. Then Liam asked around and found out that the fake ID with Chris's name on it was turned into Felix Winkler, and when he went to thank Felix, he relayed the justification Rick had told to the jury about needing the money for his mother's care.

"What will happen to her if nobody pays her bills?" Liam asked.

Felix sighed. "It's not your problem."

That was true, but Susan didn't deserve to suffer for the sins of her son, and since Liam could afford to pay for the care, he said he would. He owed it to Susan, or Felix, or maybe the nursing home in general. He wasn't sure. All he knew was that if the staff hadn't found that ID and if Felix hadn't called Chris when he did, things would have been much worse.

It took less than a year for the kids to entirely adjust to living with Liam and Alice to once again seem like herself.

Over that year, Liam met with Anita at The Griddle on numerous occasions for some unofficial therapy for them both. They talked mostly about Elise, reminiscing and, through sharing their separate memories, finding some peace. As time passed, the meetings became less frequent. Today, exactly one year since Elise had died, he realized he and Anita hadn't spoken for over two months. He called her up to see if she'd like to meet at The Griddle for one last chat.

And it was indeed their last one. Life had taken over and they were both too busy to do it again. But it was also a nice way to say goodbye once and for all.

GET AN EXCLUSIVE COPY OF
THE LAYOVER

Connor Callahan has been through a lot. More than anyone should. It has left him with an overdeveloped sense of justice. Perhaps that is why when he sees a man discreetly tag a stranger's suitcase with a black magic marker, he sets out to discover what is going on. It's a decision that will thrust Connor into a conflict far more dangerous than he could have imagined, and when it's over he will know one thing for sure: You're not always safer on the ground.

When you join my readers club, you will immediately get a free and exclusive copy of *The Layover*, not available elsewhere.

I usually e-mail once or twice a month with things I think you'll find interesting, such as behind-the-scenes stories, new releases, and fan discounts. Of course, you can unsubscribe at any time.

Join the readers club by signing up at
read.reagankeeter.com

MAKE A DIFFERENCE – LEAVE A REVIEW

One of the best ways to support authors you like is to leave a review. Honest reviews let other readers know whether this may be a story they, too, will enjoy.

It's also a great way to get feedback to the author. I care about what you think and take the time to read the reviews you write.

If you've enjoyed this book, it would mean a lot to me if you would take time to review it on your platform of choice. (The review can be as short as you like.)

Your opinion is much appreciated.

ABOUT THE AUTHOR

Reagan Keeter is the author of multiple Amazon bestsellers and a National Indie Excellence Awards finalist. He has worked as a writer and editor at Georgia newspapers. From Georgia State University, he earned his undergraduate degree in Journalism and from Southern Polytechnic State University his master's in Technical and Professional Communication. He lives with his wife and their two dogs in Atlanta, Georgia.

You can connect with him via:
His website: www.reagankeeter.com
Facebook: www.facebook.com/AuthorReaganKeeter
Twitter: @ReaganKeeter
Email: reagan@reagankeeter.com

I9781734394504
MYSTERY KEE
Keeter, Reagan.
The Redwood con /

Keeter, Reagan
The Redwood Con